MW01076102

**PATRI**

# KINGDOM LOST

PATRICIA WENTWORTH was born Dora Amy Elles in India in 1877 (not 1878 as has sometimes been stated). She was first educated privately in India, and later at Blackheath School for Girls. Her first husband was George Dillon, with whom she had her only child, a daughter. She also had two stepsons from her first marriage, one of whom died in the Somme during World War I.

Her first novel was published in 1910, but it wasn't until the 1920's that she embarked on her long career as a writer of mysteries. Her most famous creation was Miss Maud Silver, who appeared in 32 novels, though there were a further 33 full-length mysteries not featuring Miss Silver—the entire run of these is now reissued by Dean Street Press.

Patricia Wentworth died in 1961. She is recognized today as one of the pre-eminent exponents of the classic British golden age mystery novel.

# By Patricia Wentworth

# PATRICIA WENTWORTH

## KINGDOM LOST

With an introduction by
Curtis Evans

DEAN STREET PRESS

# Introduction

BRITISH AUTHOR Patricia Wentworth published her first novel, a gripping tale of desperate love during the French Revolution entitled *A Marriage under the Terror*, a little over a century ago, in 1910. The book won first prize in the Melrose Novel Competition and was a popular success in both the United States and the United Kingdom. Over the next five years Wentworth published five additional novels, the majority of them historical fiction, the best-known of which today is *The Devil's Wind* (1912), another sweeping period romance, this one set during the Sepoy Mutiny (1857-58) in India, a region with which the author, as we shall see, had extensive familiarity. Like *A Marriage under the Terror*, *The Devil's Wind* received much praise from reviewers for its sheer storytelling élan. One notice, for example, pronounced the novel "an achievement of some magnitude" on account of "the extraordinary vividness...the reality of the atmosphere...the scenes that shift and move with the swiftness of a moving picture...." (*The Bookman*, August 1912) With her knack for spinning a yarn, it perhaps should come as no surprise that Patricia Wentworth during the early years of the Golden Age of mystery fiction (roughly from 1920 into the 1940s) launched upon her own mystery-writing career, a course charted most successfully for nearly four decades by the prolific author, right up to the year of her death in 1961.

Considering that Patricia Wentworth belongs to the select company of Golden Age mystery writers with books which have remained in print in every decade for nearly a century now (the centenary of Agatha Christie's first mystery, *The Mysterious Affair at Styles*, is in 2020; the centenary of Wentworth's first mystery, *The Astonishing Adventure of Jane Smith*, follows merely three years later, in 2023), relatively little is known about the author herself. It appears, for example, that even the widely given year of Wentworth's birth, 1878, is incorrect. Yet it is sufficiently clear that Wentworth lived a varied and intriguing life that provided her ample inspiration for a writing career devoted to imaginative fiction.

It is usually stated that Patricia Wentworth was born Dora Amy Elles on 10 November 1878 in Mussoorie, India, during the heyday of the British Raj; however, her Indian birth and baptismal record states that she in fact was born on 15 October 1877 and was baptized on 26 November of that same year in Gwalior. Whatever doubts surround her actual birth year, however, unquestionably the future author came from a prominent Anglo-Indian military family. Her father, Edmond Roche Elles, a son of Malcolm Jamieson Elles, a Porto, Portugal wine merchant originally from Ardrossan, Scotland, entered the British Royal Artillery in 1867, a decade before Wentworth's birth, and first saw service in India during the Lushai Expedition of 1871-72. The next year Elles in India wed Clara Gertrude Rothney, daughter of Brigadier-General Octavius Edward Rothney, commander of the Gwalior District, and Maria (Dempster) Rothney, daughter of a surgeon in the Bengal Medical Service. Four children were born of the union of Edmond and Clara Elles, Wentworth being the only daughter.

Before his retirement from the army in 1908, Edmond Elles rose to the rank of lieutenant-general and was awarded the KCB (Knight Commander of the Order of Bath), as was the case with his elder brother, Wentworth's uncle, Lieutenant-General Sir William Kidston Elles, of the Bengal Command. Edmond Elles also served as Military Member to the Council of the Governor-General of India from 1901 to 1905. Two of Wentworth's brothers, Malcolm Rothney Elles and Edmond Claude Elles, served in the Indian Army as well, though both of them died young (Malcolm in 1906 drowned in the Ganges Canal while attempting to rescue his orderly, who had fallen into the water), while her youngest brother, Hugh Jamieson Elles, achieved great distinction in the British Army. During the First World War he catapulted, at the relatively youthful age of 37, to the rank of brigadier-general and the command of the British Tank Corps, at the Battle of Cambrai personally leading the advance of more than 350 tanks against the German line. Years later Hugh Elles also played a major role in British civil defense during the Second World War. In the event of a German invasion of Great Britain, something which seemed all too possible in 1940, he was tasked with leading the defense of southwestern England. Like Sir Edmond and Sir William, Hugh Elles attained the rank of lieutenant-general and was awarded the KCB.

Although she was born in India, Patricia Wentworth spent much of her childhood in England. In 1881 she with her mother and two younger brothers was at Tunbridge Wells, Kent, on what appears to have been a rather extended visit in her ancestral country; while a decade later the same family group resided at Blackheath, London at Lennox House, domicile of Wentworth's widowed maternal grandmother, Maria Rothney. (Her eldest brother, Malcolm, was in Bristol attending Clifton College.) During her years at Lennox House, Wentworth attended Blackheath High School for Girls, then only recently founded as "one of the first schools in the country to give girls a proper education" (*The London Encyclopaedia*, 3rd ed., p. 74). Lennox House was an ample Victorian villa with a great glassed-in conservatory running all along the back and a substantial garden--most happily, one presumes, for Wentworth, who resided there not only with her grandmother, mother and two brothers, but also five aunts (Maria Rothney's unmarried daughters, aged 26 to 42), one adult first cousin once removed and nine first cousins, adolescents like Wentworth herself, from no less than three different families (one Barrow, three Masons and five Dempsters); their parents, like Wentworth's father, presumably were living many miles away in various far-flung British dominions. Three servants--a cook, parlourmaid and housemaid--were tasked with serving this full score of individuals.

Sometime after graduating from Blackheath High School in the mid-1890s, Wentworth returned to India, where in a local British newspaper she is said to have published her first fiction. In 1901 the 23-year-old Wentworth married widower George Fredrick Horace Dillon, a 41-year-old lieutenant-colonel in the Indian Army with three sons from his prior marriage. Two years later Wentworth gave birth to her only child, a daughter named Clare Roche Dillon. (In some sources it is erroneously stated that Clare was the offspring of Wentworth's second marriage.) However in 1906, after just five years of marriage, George Dillon died suddenly on a sea voyage, leaving Wentworth with sole responsibility for her three teenaged stepsons and baby daughter. A very short span of years, 1904 to 1907, saw the deaths of Wentworth's husband, mother, grandmother and brothers Malcolm and Edmond, removing much of her support network. In 1908, however, her father, who was now sixty years old, retired from the army and returned to England, settling at Guildford, Surrey with an older unmarried sister named Dora (for whom his daughter presumably had been named). Wentworth joined this household as well, along with her daughter and her youngest stepson. Here in Surrey Wentworth, presumably with the goal of making herself financially independent for the first time in her life (she was now in her early thirties), wrote the novel that changed the course of her life, *A Marriage under the Terror*, for the first time we know of utilizing her famous *nom de plume*.

The burst of creative energy that resulted in Wentworth's publication of six novels in six years suddenly halted after the appearance of *Queen Anne Is Dead* in 1915. It seems not unlikely that the Great War impinged in various ways on her writing. One tragic episode was the death on the western front of one of her stepsons, George Charles Tracey Dillon. Mining in Colorado when war was declared, young Dillon worked his passage from Galveston, Texas to Bristol, England as a shipboard muleteer (mule-tender) and joined the Gloucestershire Regiment. In 1916 he died at the Somme at the age of 29 (about the age of Wentworth's two brothers when they had passed away in India).

A couple of years after the conflict's cessation in 1918, a happy event occurred in Wentworth's life when at Frimley, Surrey she wed George Oliver Turnbull, up to this time a lifelong bachelor who like the author's first husband was a lieutenant-colonel in the Indian Army. Like his bride now forty-two years old, George Turnbull as a younger man had distinguished himself for his athletic prowess, playing forward for eight years for the Scottish rugby team and while a student at the Royal Military Academy winning the medal awarded the best athlete of his term. It seems not unlikely that Turnbull played a role in his wife's turn toward writing mystery fiction, for he is said to have strongly supported Wentworth's career, even assisting her in preparing manuscripts for publication. In 1936 the couple in Camberley, Surrey built Heatherglade House, a large two-story structure on substantial grounds, where they resided until Wentworth's death a quarter of a century later. (George Turnbull survived his wife by nearly a decade, passing away in 1970 at the age of 92.) This highly successful middle-aged companionate marriage contrasts sharply with the more youthful yet rocky union of Agatha and Archie Christie, which was three years away from sundering when Wentworth published *The Astonishing Adventure of Jane Smith* (1923), the first of her sixty-five mystery novels.

Although Patricia Wentworth became best-known for her cozy tales of the criminal investigations of consulting detective Miss Maud Silver, one of the mystery genre's most prominent spinster sleuths, in truth the Miss Silver tales account for just under half of Wentworth's 65 mystery novels. Miss Silver did not make her debut until 1928 and she did not come to predominate in Wentworth's fictional criminous output until the 1940s. Between 1923 and 1945 Wentworth published 33 mystery novels without Miss Silver, a handsome and substantial legacy in and of itself to vintage crime fiction fans. Many of these books are standalone tales of mystery, but nine of them have series characters. Debuting in the novel *Fool Errant* in 1929, a year after Miss Silver first appeared in print, was the enigmatic, nautically-named *eminence grise* Benbow Collingwood Horatio Smith, owner of a most expressively opinionated parrot named Ananias (and quite a colorful character in his own right). Benbow Smith went on to appear in three additional Wentworth mysteries: *Danger Calling* (1931), *Walk with Care* (1933) and *Down Under* (1937). Working in tandem with Smith in the investigation of sinister affairs threatening the security of Great Britain in *Danger Calling* and *Walk with Care* is Frank Garrett, Head of Intelligence for the Foreign Office, who also appears solo in *Dead or Alive* (1936) and *Rolling Stone* (1940) and collaborates with additional series characters, Scotland Yard's Inspector Ernest Lamb and Sergeant Frank Abbott, in *Pursuit of a Parcel* (1942). Inspector Lamb and Sergeant Abbott headlined a further pair of mysteries, *The Blind Side* (1939) and *Who Pays the Piper?* (1940), before they became absorbed, beginning with *Miss Silver Deals with Death* (1943), into the burgeoning Miss Silver canon. Lamb would make his farewell appearance in 1955 in *The Listening Eye*, while Abbott would take his final bow in mystery fiction with Wentworth's last published novel, *The Girl in the Cellar* (1961), which went into print the year of the author's death at the age of 83.

The remaining two dozen Wentworth mysteries, from the fantastical *The Astonishing Adventure of Jane Smith* in 1923 to the intense legal drama *Silence in Court* in 1945, are, like the author's series novels, highly imaginative and entertaining tales of mystery and adventure, told by a writer gifted with a consummate flair for storytelling. As one confirmed Patricia Wentworth mystery fiction addict, American Golden Age mystery writer Todd Downing, admiringly declared in the 1930s, "There's something about Miss Wentworth's yarns that is contagious." This attractive new series of Patricia Wentworth reissues by Dean Street Press provides modern fans of vintage mystery a splendid opportunity to catch the Wentworth fever.

Curtis Evans

# Chapter One

THE CLIFF ROSE sheer from the blue, untroubled sea. Between sea and sky the sun made a shimmer of heat. The air was unstirred by the lightest breath.

Austin Muir looked down and saw the yacht below him. She looked small, like a toy; the sun dazzled on her, and dazzled on the water. It didn't do to look down. He frowned, and looked up instead. The top of the cliff cut across the hot blue sky in a sort of jagged scribble. And between cliff and sky something moved.

Austin threw back his head and stared. Something moved, peered down at him; a pebble tinkled against the zig-zag outcrop of rock and skipped past him. He hung there on the rocky face of the cliff and stared at the moving thing a good twenty feet above his head.

It was a hen.

He saw the craned neck, the beady eyes, hard, shiny and inquisitive, the half open beak. It was, most unbelievably, most indubitably, a hen. The rock to which he was holding cut his hand, and as he shifted his grip and took an upward step, he heard above him a squawk and a kind of flapping scramble. The hen was gone. But he had seen it.

He began to climb again. The hen was unbelievable; but he had just seen the hen. If he went back and told Barclay that he had seen a hen, Barclay would laugh himself purple in the face. Uninhabited islands don't grow hens. He would have to prove his hen or suppress it altogether. By the time he had reached the top of the cliff he had decided to suppress the hen.

The top of the cliff was not really the top at all—he knew that of course already; it was merely the edge of the crater. Seen from below from the yacht, the wall he had just climbed had appeared unclimbable; even if Barclay had not twisted his ankle he would never have got up it. Barclay would have to take off three or four stone before you could make a climber of him.

Well, the worst of the climbing was over now. The island was certainly volcanic—just the top of an old volcano stuck out of the bare blue water like Stromboli. The outer rim of the crater lay before him now; but inside the outer circle there was another wall, hiding the real cup of the crater.

Austin began to scramble down into the outer circle. He thought the island was a good deal like a Norman castle—first the wall, then this deep moat, and then the castle itself. Barclay's great-grandfather—was it two greats or three?—had certainly climbed the wall; the description in the old diary was quite a good one. But where did the hen come in?

Not for the first time, the suspicion that Barclay had not told him everything presented itself to Austin's mind. Barclay had never let him handle the diary. Why?—unless he was keeping something back. He had, of course, a perfect right to keep back anything he chose, the diary being his, to say nothing of the yacht. A man isn't bound to tell his secretary everything—Austin Muir had always felt that there might be something more to tell. Hang it all, a man doesn't go pelting off to look for an uninhabited island just to prove that his several times great-grandfather knew what he was talking about, and that the modern maps didn't. On the other hand, Barclay was such a rum fellow. Barclay might do a thing just because it wasn't the likely thing to do. Odd fellow Barclay.

He proceeded across the moat, thinking that it was hard luck on Barclay to have proved his ancestor right and then be done out of exploring the island he had found. It was like Barclay to keep the crew close to the ship and forbid them to land. He thought Barclay would have liked to forbid him to land too; he was as jealous over his island as if it was the sort of thing you could put under lock and key. He wondered again whether there was any secret about it.

So far, he had seen no water and no vegetation; they had sailed all round the island without seeing any; the unbroken, harsh volcanic cliff had confronted them. But the hen—a hen can't live on grit and do without water. He had an idea that they drank a lot. Hens—his mother had kept them; he could remember having to carry water, lots of it, in a battered tin can.

It was when he had come to the foot of the second wall that he saw the hen again. Perched on a tumbled heap of lava, it fixed him with a glassy, fascinated eye, then once more squawked and fled. As he climbed the second wall, he heard a prolonged and agitated cackle that died away in the distance.

There is a moment when sound trembles on the edge of silence. Austin could not have said just when this moment came. He heard the faint echoes fade. But just as silence came, something stirred it; the silence moved and was troubled; a new sound came to his ears.

He had come to the top of the wall. The ascent was an easy one. He passed through a gap, and the new sound met him—not as sound, but as a voice—words:

The islands feel th' enclasping flow,
And then their endless bounds they know.

Austin stood still in the most utter amazement he had ever known. The voice was a woman's voice, speaking clearly and sweetly Matthew Arnold's words. He had learnt them once, or he would scarcely have caught them now. The voice was clear and sweet, but it came from far away.

The sound ceased. He came through the mouth of the gap and looked down into a green hollow. The old crater was a garden. That was his first impression. The graceful feathered top of a cocoanut palm touched his foot. The place was a palm-grove. And somewhere in that green shade below him the voice took up another verse:

Oh, then a longing like despair
Is to their farthest caverns sent;
For surely once, they feel, we were
Parts of a single continent!
Now round us spreads the watery plain—
Oh, might our marges meet again!

The descent before him was precipitous. He looked to his left and saw steps cut in the face of the cliff. The voice went on, but as he reached the steps and began to descend, it became a low wordless murmur. He heard above it the sound of his own feet on the gritty path, the movement of the palm leaves as he brushed past them and descended into a shade as grateful as any he had known.

The trees grew as if planted in rows. He walked between them, rather past wonder, but conscious of a half angry sense of anticipation. A hen, palm-trees, and Matthew Arnold! The thing passed the bounds of the permissible; it was the sort of thing that didn't happen—a ridiculous thing.

Austin Muir had no affection for the ridiculous. He quickened his steps; but he was frowning as he came in sight of the clearing. The voice came from close at hand, speaking the last words of the poem with a certain musing beauty:

A God, a God that severance ruled!
And bade betwixt their shores to be
The unplumbed, salt, estranging sea.

Austin stood between the last two palm-trees and looked for the speaker.

Where the trees ended, the ground had been levelled. In the middle of the open space the sun shone on a wide, deep pool. On the farther side of the pool the rocks rose in a rough jumble; and ten feet up on an overhanging buttress sat a girl with bare brown legs and bare brown arms and a bare brown head; brown hands clasped her knee. She wore a brief, shift-like garment of old yellowish cotton. The brown head bore a mass of curling hair and a wreath of bright pink shells.

Austin stared. The face under the curls was brown too; but it was the brown of sunburn, not of pigment, and out of the brown there looked eyes as blue as seawater. He moved, and the eyes turned on him. Austin felt that half angry anticipation of his leap up into actual anger. He had the impression of some happening which he did not understand, something that antagonized and challenged. He saw the blue eyes sparkle and the vivid colour run to the roots of the brown hair. But behind these outward signs was that sense of clash, of anger. He took a step forward, and the girl sprang up, standing on the edge of the overhanging rock with a light, sure balance that amazed him. She leaned forward above the water, and her voice came to him, trembling with something that made the words sound strangely:

"Who—are—you?"

He came nearer before he answered, and as he moved, she sprang back and he was reminded of the recoil of some wild thing.

He said, "My name is Austin Muir," and she stood poised for another spring.

"Stay where you are!"

Voice, manner, accent spoke of culture, civilization, of a lettered, sheltered world, just as surely as her every look and movement betrayed the wild.

He said, "What are you afraid of?" and said it roughly because of that strange antagonism.

"How did you come here?" The blue eyes darkened as she spoke, her left hand touched the rocky wall.

Muir laughed.

"That was what I was going to ask you," he said; and then, "What on earth are you afraid of? I shan't hurt you."

He saw her quiver.

"Edward said—"

"Oh—so there's an Edward! Hadn't I better talk to him?"

She relaxed mournfully, drooped let her hand fall from the rock.

"You can't—he's dead. I'm all alone."

A little compunction came to him.

"I didn't know—" (Of all the ridiculous things to say!) He stopped short.

"Edward said someone would come some day. He said to be careful. Do you drink gin?"

"No, I don't."

"Or whisky?"

"Sometimes."

"Or rum?"

"Lord, no! I don't drink, if that's what you're driving at."

"Edward said I must be sure. How can I be sure?"

"I really don't know." (What a preposterous situation!)

She came a step nearer, brightening.

"Did you come in a ship?"

"In a yacht."

"That's a sort of ship, isn't it?—a little one?"

"Yes."

She brightened still more.

"Have you got a nice lady on your yacht?"

"No—I'm afraid we haven't."

"What a pity! Edward said—"

Austin felt inclined to say, "Damn Edward!" Instead, he mopped his brow. *A nice lady!* Good heavens! She might have been six years old. He tried to reconcile the nice lady with Matthew Arnold, failed, looked up, and found the bright blue eyes fixed on him with passionate interest.

"How red your face is! Edward said—"

"Look here," said Austin, "who are you, and what are you doing here? "Then, abruptly, "Is that water salt or fresh? I'd just about give the world for a drink."

"It's quite nice and fresh," said the girl; and with that he was on his knees scooping up the coldest water he had ever touched. He had the fleeting thought that it must come from very far below—some spring too deep to be warmed by all this dizzy heat.

He rose from his knees to repeat his question:

"Who on earth are you—and what are you doing here?"

The answer came at once in a most serious voice:

"I'm not doing anything—I'm just living. I'm Valentine Ryven."

"How did you get here?"

"On a ship, like you did—only of course I don't remember it."

"You don't remember it?"

"Because I was a baby. The ship was wrecked. It was called the *Avronia*. And nobody was saved except Edward and me."

Austin found himself frowning.

"Are you telling me that you've lived on this island ever since you were a baby?"

"Of course I have."

"For"—he sized her up—"eighteen or nineteen years?"

"Twenty years," said Valentine mournfully.

Austin had a spasm of unbelief. The island; the hen; Matthew Arnold; and the palm-trees—he was hanged if he was going to be hypnotized into believing in a perfectly preposterous story just because it was pushed at him in this preposterous setting.

"Are you trying to pull my leg?" he said, and was aware of the words falling back as from a blank wall.

Valentine looked at him inquiringly.

"I didn't understand that." She seemed interested. "I expect there will be a great many things that I don't understand."

He mopped his brow again.

"Do you mean you've really been here all your life?"

"Of course I do." She paused, and then suggested hospitably, "You may come a little nearer if you like. There's a stone there that's quite comfortable to sit on. You look so hot."

"I am hot," said Austin.

He made his way to the stone and saw the girl swing herself lightly down until she reached the water level. She sat clasping her knee and leaning forward. The pool was between them.

"Are you English? What is your name?"

"Scotch," said Austin. "And my name is Muir—Austin Muir."

"Edward said the Scotch were a very reliable people. Are you reliable?"

"I hope so."

"Edward said I must be very careful."

It is to Austin's credit that he restrained himself.

"Who on earth is Edward?"

"I told you. He was on the ship. He saved me when I was a baby, and he brought me up. He was a Fellow."

"A Fellow?"

"Of Trinity." She spoke with innocent pride. Then she drooped and looked into the water. "He always said people would come some day. He wanted to go back so much. He—"

The hands that were clasped about her knee tightened; he saw the knuckles show white against the brown. Her voice did not shake; it just left off. She became as motionless as the stone.

Embarrassment kept Austin silent. Presently he saw her pose relax.

"It was three months ago," she said.

He spoke then:

"Do you mean—you've been here alone for three months?"

"Yes—I counted very carefully. Edward always said that if anything happened to him, I must be very, very careful. He said if I wasn't careful, when the ship came, there wouldn't be any place for me in a modern civilization—and he said one of the most important things was not to lose count of time—so I counted very carefully."

"A modern civilization." The phrase called up a pedagogic shade. Austin began to believe the odd story, and then fell back into scepticism.

The hen—what about the hen? He fired the creature point blank at Valentine.

"Look here, you're having me on. What about the hen? Hens don't grow on uninhabited islands, you know."

He had said this to himself so often in the last half hour that it was an immense relief to say it out loud.

"A hen?"

"Yes, a hen."

She nodded.

"Semiramis, I expect. She *will* get over the wall."

Austin frowned portentously. She *was* having him on; he felt sure of it.

"Look here, why don't you tell me the truth? Don't you see that the hen puts the kibosh on this yarn of yours?"

He was prepared for anger, but not for glowing interest.

"Is that slang? Edward didn't know any—or at least hardly any. Do say it again!"

Austin did not say it again. He looked angry and said stubbornly, "Hens don't grow on uninhabited islands."

Valentine nodded again.

"No, they don't. And wouldn't it have been dreadful if we hadn't had the hens—and the cocoanuts? Edward often said—"

Austin interrupted her.

"What are you talking about?"

"About the cocoanuts and the hens. They were on the ship."

"Oh—they were on the ship. And how did they get here?"

"Edward brought them. First he brought me, and then he brought the hens. He tried to bring a goat, but it fell into the sea. And then he brought the cocoanuts. Wasn't it a mercy they *grew*?"

Austin stared. Was it possible?

"I thought you said the ship was wrecked."

"Yes, it was—it struck on the rocks." She pointed away to the right. "It's all straight cliff now, but there were rocks then, and a sort of beach. The ship stuck there for two years, so Edward had plenty of time to get things away. I don't remember about it—I don't remember anything before I was three. The big storm was when I was two and a half. The ship went then. Edward thought the island was going too, and when the storm was over, it had sunk twenty feet, and the beach was gone, and you couldn't see the rocks. If you've got a ship, you'd better be careful."

"He brought things away from the ship?" said Austin. "Papers—and things like that? You mean you can prove all this?"

She looked at him rather reprovingly.

"Of course. Didn't you believe what I was saying?"

"You can prove it?"

"I've got all my mother's papers. Edward said I must keep them *very* carefully."

Austin got up.

"Where are they?"

Valentine swung her foot and looked down into the water.

"Where are they?" he repeated.

He saw a little colour come into her face. Then her eyes lifted in a searching blue gaze. He was aware of being weighed in Edward's balance. He met the gaze half angrily.

Valentine unclasped her hands and sprang up.

"I want to see your ship! Take me first of all to see your ship!" she cried.

## Chapter Two

VALENTINE, SCRAMBLING WITH HIM over the rough ground towards the edge of the cliff, became imperceptibly less guarded and on the alert. Scrambling is perhaps the wrong word; she was extraordinarily sure and light on her bare brown feet. She had breath enough to talk with too, and she talked more and more freely.

Austin found himself believing every word of the strange, naïve tale. Twenty years ago, in the early spring of 1908, Edward Bowden, Fellow of Trinity, author of *England and the Renaissance, England and the Feudal System*, and half a dozen other standard works, had been taking a prolonged and rambling holiday necessitated by overwork. He had found himself ultimately on the *Avronia*, bound from New Zealand to San Francisco.

On the same boat was Mrs. Ryven, a young widow with a child six months old. She had lost her husband in New Zealand and was returning to England by way of America because her only brother had settled in California and she wished to spend some weeks with him. The ship encountered a terrific hurricane and was carried out of her course. At a moment when she appeared to be sinking the passengers took to the boats.

"Edward said he thought he would drown peacefully with the ship, so he didn't get into a boat though they wanted him to. And the boats all upset and everyone was drowned—only someone had asked him to hold me whilst they got my mother into a boat—he said she had fainted—so he did. And a great wave came and broke the boat to bits; and he doesn't know why he wasn't carried away—but he wasn't. And he crawled inside the companion and waited for us both to be drowned—and we weren't. Edward said when he found there was no one else left on the ship, but only him and me, he was very sorry we hadn't been drowned too. He said he didn't think we could be saved and it seemed to be taking such a long time. He said the wind kept carrying the ship along and banging it about, and he thought every minute it was going to go down—only it didn't. Everything was broken and flung down, and he had to crawl about and find something to feed me with, because I was hungry and screamed all the time. Edward hadn't ever had anything to do with a baby before. It was dreadful for him—wasn't it?"

Austin agreed. He was not imaginative; but a deserted ship, a hurricane, a baby, and an Oxford don struck him as making a pretty appalling combination.

"He found milk in tins, and afterwards he found there was a goat. And then we came to the island—I *think* it was three days after—Edward didn't like talking about it very much. The ship stuck on the island, on the little beach I told you about. It jammed there, tight. There wasn't anything on the island then—not anything to eat, except some sea-birds' eggs. I *am* glad we didn't have to live on sea-birds' eggs, because they taste like bad fish. There were lots of things on the ship. Edward got them all off. And he planted the cocoanuts, and they grew. He said he couldn't attempt to describe what he felt like when he saw the first little cocoanut-shoot."

"Where does the water come from?" asked Austin.

"It's a very deep spring. There's a hot one and a cold one. You can boil eggs in the hot one—Oh! Is that your ship?"

They had reached the edge of the cliff. The yacht lay beneath them, motionless on the unmoving water. Valentine gazed with all her eyes, standing so near the dizzy edge that Austin instinctively put out a hand to steady her. At his touch the wild thing showed again; her sideways leap literally brought his heart into his mouth. One moment she was there with his hand just brushing her arm; the next she was a couple of yards away on the brink, leaning seawards, her eyes darkly startled and her colour high.

"Look out!" he said, and in a flash she had gone farther still.

"Don't touch me! You mustn't!"

Austin found himself furious, partly because she had really frightened him.

"I don't want to touch you. I was afraid you'd fall."

She laughed then for the first time, a pretty laugh full of young scorn.

"Fall!" she said. "How silly!"

"It would be quite easy. You'd better be careful."

He saw her face change; whiten, her eyes cloud fearfully.

She said, "Edward fell," in a small whispering voice.

Austin said, "Oh—"

"There's a place we fish from. You have to climb down to it. He fell—into the sea."

"For heaven's sake come away from that edge!" said Austin, and saw her take a long breath.

"*I* shan't fall," she said.

She looked again at the yacht, bending forwards.

"I've never seen a ship. It looks so small! I thought they were bigger. Edward said—"

"This isn't a ship—it's a yacht. She belongs to a man called Barclay. I'm his secretary."

He looked down as he spoke, and could see Barclay's deck chair with Barclay's bulk spreading in it. It came to him that Barclay would certainly chaff his head off when he came back with his story. He had decided to suppress the hen; but he couldn't very well suppress Miss Valentine Ryven.

"Is he nice? Tell me about him."

"He weighs fifteen stone, and he's worth a lot of money. I wouldn't mind having half of it."

"Why doesn't he give you some?" said Valentine.

"He does—he gives me two hundred a year to write his letters and put up with his manners."

"What a nice lot! Isn't it?"

He laughed angrily.

"Didn't Edward tell you about money?"

"Of course he did. I can do pounds, shillings and pence, and francs, and marks, and dollars. Two hundred pounds is"—she screwed up her eyes and agonized in calculation—"is five thousand francs!" Her eyes opened triumphantly. "There!" she said. Then, a little more doubtfully, "That's right, isn't it?"

With an overpowering shock, it came home to Austin that there stood a benighted young savage for whom the Great War had never been. She lived in an Edwardian world where twenty-five francs went to the pound and the map of Europe was what it had been in Queen Victoria's days. Doubtless Edward had wasted much valuable time in drawing obsolete frontiers in the sand—a highly appropriate medium.

He opened his mouth and gaped, taking in the implications slowly. Nineteen hundred and eight—nineteen hundred and eight—the Wrights made their first flight in 1908. She wouldn't know what an aeroplane was. She wouldn't know about wireless. The war—wireless—aeroplanes—a hundred and twenty-five francs to the pound—the blessings of Bolshevism—cross-word puzzles—and jazz. He gaped, and recalled her phrase—no, not hers—Edward's phrase, parroted: "There wouldn't be any place for me in a modern civilization."

He shut his mouth with a jerk, then opened it and said with abrupt irrelevance:

"I'll go down to the yacht and tell Barclay."

## Chapter Three

"Well—well—*well!*" said Barclay. He gave his funny deep chuckle and rolled forward in his chair.

They were sitting round the table in the saloon, he and Austin and the girl. On the table stood a dispatch-box in a leather cover. The initials M.R. were stamped on the battered lid, which was open. There were letters in the box—letters and papers. In front of Barclay lay a book in a very old binding.

When Barclay chuckled, Valentine looked at him, and having looked, kept her eyes fixed upon him with the serious, interested gaze of a child. This was the third man that she had seen; and they were so different. Hens were not as different as this. She could tell Semiramis from Jessica, and Jessica from Evangeline; but they were the same size and shape and colour. It had not occurred to her that people would be so different from one another. She knew of course that there were black, brown, yellow, and white races. She had not thought that one white man would be so unlike another; she had thought of men as so many variants of Edward, differing from Edward in the same slight degree that Evangeline and Jessica differed from Semiramis.

Edward was thin, not much taller than herself, spare of frame, grey-haired, and colourless. Austin Muir was much larger, much redder, with brown hair and rather bright, cold eyes like steel. Barclay—Barclay interested her tremendously; there was such a lot of him, and he was so ugly. There was a picture of a walrus in one of the books that had come from the ship. Barclay was just like the walrus, only fatter, and he had black hair and his chin and half his cheeks looked blue, and the top half of his cheeks were red, and when he laughed, the red and the blue seemed to get mixed up and a purple colour ran right up on to his forehead as far as the roots of his sleek black hair.

He laughed now, with that chuckle in his laughter.

"Well," he said. "Well. Here we are, my dear! And what do you think of us? Good-looking couple, aren't we, Austin and I? Handsome young fellows—eh, Miss Robinson Crusoe? Don't you think you're in luck? Come now, my dear, what do you think of us—eh?"

She continued to gaze at him seriously. She was aware of Austin chafing on her right.

He said, "Hang it all, Barclay!" and Barclay laughed again.

"By gum, it's romantic! Tell you what, Austin, I don't mind doubling your salary on the strength of it! There, my dear—you've done him a good turn already! What's the betting you'll bring him luck? Now look here! Perhaps you don't know what a romantic occasion this is—in fact you don't—you can't! *I'm* the only one that knows. So you sit right up and take notice of me!"

He opened the worn leather book in front of him and began to flick over the pages. They were covered with fine brown writing, close, cramped, and illegible.

"Now, my dear—this island of yours, which isn't on any map, was discovered in 1651 by my several times great-great-grandfather, old Nick Barclay, who went to sea as a gentleman adventurer with Captain Joshua Talbot. Well, they lost their ship and took to the boats, and he and Talbot were cast on this island of yours and lived on it for three weeks, at the end of which time, as they'd nothing to eat, they put desperately to sea and were picked up a week later more dead than alive."

He struck the table with his hand. "And from that day to this, nobody—nobody, my dear—has believed in his island. Here's his diary, and here's what he says at the end: *'So they all, having with one mind and as it were one pen, writ me down a liar, I am most thoroughly resolved to say no more of the matter, but to leave it to posterity.'* See—posterity! That's me! When I read that, I said to myself, 'Well, that's me,' and I made up my mind I'd find that island if it was anywhere above water."

He began to turn the leaves of the book again, running backwards.

"Now, look here! Austin, you're witness to this. I've never let you handle the book, and you don't know what's in it—I'm going to prove that the old boy did discover the island, and I'm going to prove it right away. See those shells she's got in her hair? Where in thunder d'you think she's got 'em from? It don't look a very suitable island for shell gathering—does it? Now, my dear, don't you go saying anything— because I don't want you to speak; I want you to listen to what old Nick wrote down in the tail end of the year 1651."

He fixed on a page, turned it to get the light from a port-hole, and read in a triumphant, rolling voice: *"The island hath a wealth of water, both hot springs and cold. There is a hot spring in a cavern into which we did descend with some terror because the noise made by the water was like the growling of wild beasts. At the one end of the cavern the said spring doth rise up into a basin of rock, but at the other end the sea washes in upon a beach of sand, very fair and clean, bringing with it, on some current doubtless, a drift of shells, very curious and pretty, such as would be priced by women for their adornment, being of a rosy colour and very delicate."*

He shut the book with a snap.

"There! What about it now—eh? We're posterity, we three here—aren't we? What does posterity say—eh, Miss Valentine Ryven? Did old Nick discover the island, or didn't he?"

Valentine clapped her hands together.

"Yes, he did—he did! He found the cave where I got my shells! And Edward said—"

"There then!" said Barclay. "That's that! And I hope the old boy knows, because he seems to have taken it a good bit to heart being called a liar. Serious-minded you know." He chuckled again and pushed the book away. "Well, that clears the ground. I just wanted to get that done with. And now—about those papers of yours. What have you got?"

Valentine stood up and took a paper out of the open dispatch-box.

"Edward said this was very important. It's my birth certificate."

She gave it to him, and he unfolded the paper and read: "Maurice Ryven—Marion his wife—Valentine Helena Ryven. Hm—" He frowned and tapped on the table. "Helena Ryven—Helena. Hm—that's queer! Well, my dear, anything else?"

"Edward said—"

"Never you mind what Edward said! You trot out what you've got!"

He reached out, but, with one of those swift movements, Valentine had a handful of papers clutched to her breast and was standing back against the cabin wall, her blue eyes fixed and angry.

"Edward said not to let—people—touch."

Barclay laughed till the purple rose to his hair.

"You may look, but you mustn't touch—eh? That's it, is it? Oh, gosh! It's too hot to laugh like this! Come along, my dear! We won't lay a finger on your papers. But you don't want to kill me with curiosity, do you? Or if you want to kill me, you don't want to kill Austin? He's too young to die, and he wants to know what's in those papers every bit as badly as I do."

"I don't want to know anything you don't want to tell us," said Austin stiffly.

"Don't you believe him! He's not such a prig as he sounds."

"Look here, Barclay—"

"Dry up!" said Barclay with a rasp in his voice.

Valentine looked from one to the other warily. Then she came up to the table and put down the papers that she was holding.

"I'll show you—some of them," she said.

"That's right," said Barclay. "You just play I'm the family lawyer and get along with it."

Valentine spread out the papers, picked out a letter, unfolded it, and stood there hesitating.

"This one—Edward said she must be my father's sister-in-law—her name is Helena Ryven. My father went to New Zealand and married my mother. And then he died, and my mother was coming home—to England, you know—and this letter is from my Aunt Helena to say she is so glad we are coming. It begins 'My dearest Marion.' You can read it if you like."

Barclay took the letter.

She watched him as he read it. She herself knew it by heart. It said, "My dearest Marion"; and it said, "Your dear little baby"—that was her, Valentine; and it said, "warmest, warmest welcomes for dear Maurice's wife and child." She wondered if Barclay had got to that; and then she wondered whether he had got to the other bit where Aunt Helena said, "you mustn't feel that you're a stranger coming to a strange land. We have always been a united family, and you must feel that you are coming to your own place in that family."

Barclay was frowning. She wondered why. It felt so strange, this place. She felt as if she were looking at Barclay from a long way off; she felt as if she were a long way off from everyone in the world; she felt farther away than when she was all alone on the island. She was very pale as she put out her hand and took the letter again.

"You see—I've got—people," she said. "They want me."

Barclay looked at her, not unkindly.

"Well, my dear, they wanted you twenty years ago," he said.

Valentine cried out in a panic:

"Do you think they're dead? They couldn't all be dead!"

"Oh, they're not dead," said Barclay. "But twenty years is a long time, you know."

"You're *sure* they're not dead?"

"Well, Mrs. Ryven was above ground all right three months ago. I've got a sister who thinks a lot of her—works on committees with her and—"

"Oh!" said Valentine, "oh! Oh, you *know* her!"

"Well, I wouldn't say that—I don't sit on committees myself, you see. My sister knows her."

"Oh!" said Valentine again. She dived into the dispatch-box and produced a photograph. "Edward thought this might be her. Is it? Is it?"

It was a snapshot of a tall, handsome woman in the full, long, spreading skirt and trimmed bodice of twenty years ago. Barclay looked at it and made a face.

"It might be. I only saw her once. She don't dress like that now—not on your life, by gum, she don't! Skirts to the knee and shingled hair. By gum, it's a bit of change—isn't it? They all look seventeen till you see 'em close to—and then you get a nervous shock. Why, the only time I saw her, she and her son came into my sister's room together, and I'm blessed if he didn't look the older of the two till the lights went on."

"Her son!—Oh—she had a little boy—it's in one of the letters—a little boy older than me! His name is Eustace. He's my cousin."

"Well, he's not a little boy now, my dear—so don't you go building on something sweet in knickerbockers."

"He's thirty," said Valentine. "He's ten years older than I am. It's very old. Does he look very old? Does he look as old as you?"

Barclay roared with laughter.

"I'd lie down and die if I ever got to feel anywhere near as old as that young man! It's the committee habit—and he's got it bad. He don't talk to you—he addresses you. You may take it from me that your Cousin Eustace isn't what you'd call a human sunbeam."

The colour rose to Valentine's cheeks.

"You don't like him."

"Well, I don't lie awake at night wondering when I'm going to see him again."

"Perhaps he doesn't like you," said Valentine with a darting glance.

*"Kamerad!"* said Barclay.

# Chapter Four

"Funny thing my saying that!" said Barclay meditatively.

"Funny thing your saying what?"

"What I said." Barclay's tone was very lazy. He had a long drink at his elbow and a cigar in the corner of his mouth; he sprawled at length in a deck chair.

Austin Muir, leaning on the rail, looked over his shoulder.

"What did you say?"

"Said perhaps she'd do you a good turn."

"What d'you mean?"

"You've got a nasty, sulky disposition, Austin—comes of being Scotch. Now if I wasn't the best-natured man in the world, I wouldn't give you the tip I'm going to give you."

Austin glowered at the sea.

"All the same I'm sorry for the poor girl—but of course twenty years on a desert island don't make you particular. When you haven't had anyone to talk to at all, a man who says something about once a day is quite chatty. And then a girl can always do the talking herself. She's got about twenty years of conversation saved up, and you'd be quite a good listener if you could manage to look a little less murderous."

Austin's scowl became intensified.

"What are you driving at?"

"I'm giving you a real good tip. I know a bit about the Ryvens, and I don't mind passing it on. If I'm right—and the letters beat me out—that girl's going to be a bit of a human bomb when she turns up."

"Why?"

"Well, anyone coming back after twenty years is bound to break the china. When it's an heiress—" He paused and whistled expressively.

Austin made no comment. He looked across the water to where the island showed, three miles away.

"Your cue!" said Barclay, with a chuckle. "Cough it up! Say 'An heiress?' and put a proper amount of ingenuous surprise into your manly voice."

Austin said nothing.

The heat was dropping slowly out of the day. The sun was low. The island looked far away and insubstantial, a painted rock on a huge blue waste of water; presently it would be gone.

Barclay's voice broke in—Barclay's gross, fat voice:

"We'll take it as said. 'An heiress?'—that's you. And now I come along again, guide, philosopher, and friend, and I say, 'Yes, my lad, an heiress, and a pretty warm one. And if you can't make the running with a girl that's never seen a man in her life barring the late Edward—who don't count, being a don and *in loco parentis*—well, my friend, if you can't make the running with a poor, benighted young female savage like that, Scotland don't stand where it did."

Austin turned round.

"Look here, Barclay!"

"I'm too fat to quarrel," said Barclay. "And if you assault me, the captain'll put you in irons for mutiny on the high seas. You take my advice and weigh in. You'll never get another chance like it—field all to yourself—girl as pretty as the front tow of a revue chorus—and a pot of money waiting for you at home. Go away and think it over! And don't be more of a damned fool than you can help!"

He watched Austin fling away, chuckled, and took a pull at his drink. A little breeze was springing up as the sun dropped. He too looked at the island and saw it fade.

He began to think about old Nick Barclay. If he hadn't been so fat, he could have explored the cavern. He wasn't quite sure that he wanted to explore it. His feeling about the island never quite got into words. He had thought about it since he was a boy. He had wanted to prove that old Nick was right. Well, that was done. Nobody could say Nick Barclay hadn't found the island now. That bit was done.

The island faded. In his own mind he saw the island as he had always seen it; he had a feeling that he liked it better like that. He didn't really want to explore the cavern.

"Anyhow I'm too fat!" said Barclay with a chuckle.

On the other side of the deck Valentine stood by the rail and looked out over the water. She neither leaned on the rail nor touched it. She was quite still, but it was not the stillness of rest. She stood poised and looked, not at the island, but north-east along the course that they were taking. The sunset was behind them, the sun just gone. Out of the east the dark came streaming like an impalpable tide; the horizon was already lost; the arch of the sky was a pale fainting turquoise which melted by imperceptible shades into grey.

Valentine never turned her head. She looked into the dusk and saw it alive with adventure. People—her own people—Aunt Helena—Eustace, who was her own cousin and quite old. And, behind them, the whole world full of people and things which she hadn't seen.

As Austin flung across the deck, she came back, half across the world, quivering.

"Come and talk to me! I want to ask about two thousand questions! Are you too busy to talk?"

The last of the light showed her his angry look. When Edward looked like that, she always went away. But when Austin Muir frowned and towered over her with his hands stuck deep in his pockets, she didn't want to run away at all; it gave her a feeling of pleasant superiority of which she was not herself fully conscious. She only knew that she wanted to make him talk to her; she wanted it enough to put a hand on his arm and hold his sleeve.

"Please talk to me, Austin."

"Go and talk to Barclay if you want company."

"But I don't want to talk to Barclay—I want to talk to you."

Austin looked down at the hand on his sleeve, a little brown hand with slim, strong fingers.

"I thought you didn't like being touched," he said in an accusing voice.

"I'm not being touched—I'm touching you. That's quite different. Why are you angry?"

"I'm not angry."

"Edward said people shouldn't tell lies unless they were obliged to—and not then unless they could tell them really well. You tell them *very* badly."

He gave a half angry laugh.

"All right—have it your own way! I'm in a foul temper—I'm not fit to speak to."

"You're in a temper with Barclay. But you needn't be in a temper with me. What has he done to make you angry?"

Austin twisted his arm away.

"He's a coarse brute."

"I like him," said Valentine. "You don't like him because he teases you. But I think it's simply lovely to have someone to tease you."

"I'll probably knock his head off some day," said Austin gloomily.

"Then you would be hanged," said Valentine with extreme solemnity.

Austin burst out laughing.

"You are a funny kid!"

"Now you're not angry any more."

"Aren't I?"

"Not too angry to talk to me. Let's sit on the rail and talk. I want to know all about everything."

"You can't sit on the rail—it's not safe." Then, as she laughed, "Look here, if there's any tommyrot of that sort, I'm off!"

Valentine sighed.

"I think you're very domineering. May I lean on the rail?"

"Yes."

"Thank you, dear Austin! How kind you are to me!"

Her face, turned up to him, was a dim oval framed in ruffled curls. It was no physical sense that told him that there was sparkling malice in her eyes.

Next moment she was leaning on the rail, her face to the breeze. Darkness had fallen; the water slipped by them in a black wash just flecked with foam; the sky above was deeply, darkly blue, with a powder of stars coming out upon it; the west had a line of dying fire. The island was lost.

"Tell me about people," said Valentine.

"What d'you want to know?" He spoke indulgently now.

"Every single thing—every single thing you can think of."

"That's a pretty tall order! You see, I don't know what you know."

"Well," said Valentine in a considering voice, "I've read the Bible and Shakespeare, and Edward said they were enough to give you a liberal education and plumb the depths of human nature. That's what Edward *said*."

"It sounds a bit high-brow," said Austin.

"What's high-brow?"

"Brainy serious intense frightfully intellectual, you know."

He saw the dark head nod.

"I don't like Shakespeare very much—such dreadful things seem to happen to the people. But I like the way they talk."

"But, good Lord, you were reading Matthew Arnold out loud when I found you! *He's* high-brow if you like."

"That," said Valentine, "that was because Edward made me promise faithfully that I would read aloud every day if anything happened to him; because he said, if I didn't, I should forget how to talk, and turn into a real desert-island savage. So I read all the books we had one after the other, and I had just got to Matthew Arnold. But I do like him all the same. He feels like things look just before the sun comes up out of the sea—you know, all still, and the colour hasn't come into them yet, and it's so beautiful that you want to cry." She spoke in a soft, breathless way.

"What other books did you have?"

"There were a lot of novels. Edward called them trash. And there was a book about wild animals, with pictures. So I know what lions and tigers and bears and elephants and walruses look like. But I don't know what a cat looks like, or a dog, or a horse, or a cow. Edward tried to draw them, but he said they didn't come out very like."

Austin really laughed this time.

"Neither Barclay nor I can draw for toffee!"

"I don't want any more drawn cats—I want real ones—and pigs, and donkeys, and hedgehogs, and birds. I want birds *dreadfully*. And I want people most of all. I haven't ever seen a lady. Think of that!"

"You mustn't say lady—you must say woman."

"Why?"

"It's not done."

"Edward said lady."

"Well—er—you know—Edward was, not to put too fine a point upon it, a bit prehistoric."

"People don't say lady now?"

"No, they don't."

"I see. What else don't they do?"

"Well—"

"What sort of clothes do they wear? I want to know that dreadfully. You see there was a book—I love it, but it makes me cry so I can't read it—only I do! It's called *Rupert of Hentzau*, and it has pictures in it by a man called Charles Dana Gibson—Edward said he was a famous artist. And the lady in it—" she stopped, tossed her head, and repeated with emphasis, "And the *woman* in it has got clothes like my aunt Helena in the photograph, all up here"—she put her hands to her throat—"and all down here"—a barefoot described a semi-circle—"and all in here"—her hands went to her waist—"very small and very tight. And my mother's dresses in the box you brought on to the ship for me, they're just the same. And Edward said that *women's* fashions were always changing. And, please, can you tell me whether I shall have to be all tight and covered up, and my hair stuck up on the top of my head?" Her voice had become very earnest.

"Girls don't cover 'emselves up much. They don't wear much more than you do."

"My things are all made out of the sheets that were on the *Avronia*. There were hundreds and hundreds and hundreds of sheets. Edward said they would last us both for clothes till we were quite old."

"Oh, Lord! Did Edward teach you to sew?"

"He *tried* to. He said he'd darned stockings. I really found out how to do it myself. He said I'd better keep my mother's clothes in case a ship came. Can you draw me a picture, so that I can make a dress?"

"No, I can't."

She sighed impatiently.

"Do you think Barclay could?"

"Look here—you oughtn't to call him Barclay like that."

"But you do."

"That doesn't matter. Girls don't call men by their surnames."

"Why don't they?"

"They don't—it's not done."

Valentine sighed again.

"He feels like Barclay and he looks like Barclay, and I don't know his Christian name."

"You ought to call him Mr. Barclay."

"Well, I won't," said Valentine sweetly. "What were you so angry with him about?"

"Never mind."

"Why do you stay with him if you don't like him?"

"I stay because I can't get away. I don't hate him badly enough to jump overboard. As soon as we get home though—I'd rather starve than go on with him."

"I wouldn't. Why would you starve? Haven't you got any money?"

"Not a bean—till I get another job."

"I wonder if I shall have any," said Valentine in an interested voice.

Austin moved a little; the movement took him farther away from her. After a moment of indecision, he spoke:

"Barclay says you'll have a great deal of money."

Miss Ryven received the news with calm.

"Oh, then I can give you half."

Her casual tone roused his temper.

"Don't talk rot! People can't give each other money like that."

"But I'd like to."

There are disadvantages in dealing with pristine ignorance.

"It doesn't in the least matter whether you'd like to or not. A man can't take money he hasn't earned. Besides, a man can't anyhow take money from a girl—it's the sort of thing that simply isn't done."

Valentine leaned over the rail. Deep in the black water a fitful phosphorescence gleamed.

"You do say that a lot!" she said.

## Chapter Five

THE YACHT PUT IN at Honolulu and stayed there for two bewildering days. Barclay sent Austin ashore on a double errand; he was to dispatch a long cable to Mrs. Ryven, and he was to buy Valentine some shoes and stockings to land in.

"You won't like 'em, kid—but you've got to have 'em."

Valentine gazed at his feet.

"Will they be like yours?" Her tone was not enthusiastic.

"You wait and see."

She twiddled her bare brown toes.

Austin returned an hour later with tennis shoes and thick white stockings.

"I don't like them," said Valentine. She regarded her feet with a sort of chilly interest. "I don't like them at all." She lifted up first one foot and then the other. "Barclay, they feel as if they weren't me! They feel as if they had gone a long way off."

"They look fine," said Barclay. "You come along with me and we'll go shopping. Austin can meet us for lunch. We don't want him—do we?"

Valentine didn't seem sure. She edged up to Mr. Muir and looked at him rather wistfully.

"Aren't you coming at all?"

"He'll meet us for lunch," said Barclay.

Valentine took no notice.

"Austin—my feet do feel so funny—they feel all stiff. I think I shall fall if you don't hold my hand."

Austin held her hand as she went down the gangway. It was something quite new to have her clinging to him. It pleased him.

He watched her drive away with Barclay.

Valentine had made herself a new dress to land in. The stuff had survived the island years. Marion Ryven thought it very pretty when she bought it in Auckland. It was a flowered muslin with a blue stripe and dotted pink roses, rather like a wall paper—a wall paper in a house that had stood a long time empty, for the white ground had gone yellow, and the blue stripes were discoloured. She had made the dress out of her mother's flowing skirt. It had no sleeves, and the stuff hung about her in limp, uneven folds.

Valentine smoothed the folds over her knees. The white cotton stockings were slipping down. She pulled them up. How could one run and walk in things that wouldn't stay where you put them? Then, as the car began to move, she forgot everything except the newness and the wonder into which they were passing.

Everything that she saw was new; everything that she saw was a thing that she had never seen before. New feelings and impressions came flooding in upon her like waves that followed one another so rapidly that they came tumbling down helter-skelter, throwing up such a confusion of spray and foam that there was no time to take her breath. People. Horses. A dog with yellow ears and wolfish eyes. Houses. A cat that sat in a window licking smooth banded paws. Trees, grass, and flowers. Bright vivid fruits that shone like jewels in the sun. Women and girls, and babies; little babies in their mothers' arms. A boy who tossed a ball into the air—or was it a brilliant orange fruit? The boy was black; he grinned and showed how white his teeth were. Carts. More cars like the one that was carrying them along. And all these things seemed to swim in a whirlpool of noise. Everything in the new world made a noise. It made her feel giddy.

Barclay looked at her curiously; he would have liked to know what was passing in her mind. If Valentine could have answered him, she would have said that nothing passed. All these new things came crowding into her mind and stayed there. She did not think about them yet; their mere impact made her giddy.

Barclay did not speak to her.

A block in the traffic held them up. As their car stopped moving, Valentine relaxed a little. The unknown had ceased to flow past her; it stood still. It was less bewildering when it stood still. She gazed across the street and saw a girl of about her own age standing on the raised step of a shop not a dozen yards away.

The girl was slim and tall. She had pale gold hair; it showed in little curls on either side of her faintly tinted face. Her lips were very red. She wore a straight white dress that ended just below the knee; it was made of heavy silk; it had a narrow gold belt that matched the golden hair. Except for the belt, she was all in white. Her shoes and stockings were quite different to the shoes and stockings that clogged Valentine's slim brown feet and legs. The girl turned her head, and Valentine saw her bare white neck, crossed by a row of pearls. Above the pearls the pale fine hair was cut quite short.

Valentine drew a long, long breath. The car began to move. The fair-haired girl passed out of sight.

Valentine looked down at the folds of the old limp muslin and saw how yellow it was; she saw the thick wrinkled stockings and clumsy shoes. Then she heard Barclay speaking.

"Gosh, kid! What d'you want to look like that for?"

Valentine looked up at him without speaking.

"You had a good look at that girl. What did you think of her?"

*"Lovely!"* said Valentine. The word took all her breath.

Barclay laughed.

"Would you like a rig-out like that? We're going shopping, you know."

Valentine could only look.

They stopped again, this time because they had arrived. Valentine saw a shop window full of beautiful and mysterious things. Barclay let her look for a moment and then marched her in. Some men might have found the situation an awkward one. Barclay carried it off in so easy a manner that it had no embarrassments.

He asked at once for Madame, and when she appeared he was frankness itself.

"Mademoiselle has been in a shipwreck."

*"Juste ciel!"* said Madame Marie.

"She therefore requires everything. Now the question is, what can you do about it?"

Madame Marie was plump and voluble. She appeared to think that if monsieur would permit, she could supply mademoiselle in such a manner as to satisfy monsieur.

Barclay mentioned a hundred pounds. He allowed Madame to translate it into dollars and sat down to wait with exemplary patience; he was, in fact, quite pleased and amused.

Valentine followed Madame into a small room that was completely lined with mirrors. A girl in a draggled muslin dress moved to meet her. The girl was bare-headed; she had ugly, clumsy things on her feet; her round brown arms were bare to the shoulder. For a moment she did not realize that she was looking at herself. Then, as she turned, she saw a whole procession of girls, all in the same flowered muslin, the same thick stockings and shoes. They went away into the far distance, heaps and heaps of them, each one smaller than the last, each one moving when she herself moved.

After a dizzy moment she felt a thrill of interest. She had never seen the back of her head before; she had never really seen herself like this. It was interesting. Then she remembered the fair-haired girl, and the colour ran hot into her cheeks. She whirled round and saw all those other Valentines whirling too, and found Madame Marie looking at her inquiringly.

"If mademoiselle would remove her dress—"

Valentine slipped it off. Her only other garment was the one she had worn on the island. It had a hole for her head and holes for her arms, and it hung to her knee. It was made of cotton sheeting that had turned a yellowish grey with age, and it was sewn together with the large clumsy stitches of a child.

"To lose everything in a shipwreck!" said Madame Marie. "*Mon Dieu!* What an experience! To lose all one's clothes—could there be anything more terrible? Rosa—*vite!* Julie!" She began to pour out orders in French.

Rosa and Julie ran to and fro and produced the most bewildering and mysterious things. Valentine, pale, silent, and spell-bound, allowed herself to be dressed, undressed, and re-dressed with the most perfect docility. Madame Marie took the measurement of her foot and sent out for shoes. She produced stockings that were so fine and thin that you could hardly see them. She clothed Valentine in layers of exquisite and diaphanous garments.

"*Enfin, mademoiselle*—now we can begin," she observed, and Rosa and Julie began to run to and fro again, bringing frocks, coats, hats.

"For the hat, the question asks itself, does mademoiselle shingle?"

Valentine turned upon her the eyes of a puzzled child.

"The hair, mademoiselle—how will you arrange it?"

"I don't know."

She looked away and saw the turn of her head reflected in all the mirrors. She was wearing a plain white frock of heavy silk. Her dark hair fell in curls on her shoulders. That was wrong. She had only one idea—she must be like the girl whom she had seen for a moment in the street. She could not turn her dark hair pale, but she could have it cut all close and fine at the back, with a little point in the middle and curls on either side of her face.

She put up her hand and looked back at Madame.

"I want it cut *here*, quite short—and *here*"—her hands went to her temples—"like this."

"*Le shingle!—parfaitement!* Ah—that is a fashion that is always going. But it does not go—it is too convenient, yes, and too becoming. It will certainly become mademoiselle."

Barclay was summoned, and was pleased to approve. He found himself drawn into consultation.

"I don't know a thing about women's clothes. This is all very pretty, but you dig her out something she can wear if it's snowing when we get to England!"

"Snow, monsieur! In July?"

"It's been done," said Barclay with a Briton's gloomy pride in his climate.

The bill that he presently paid was for a good deal more than a hundred pounds.

Valentine came out into the street in all the agonizing discomfort of her first high-heeled shoes. But she was walking on air. She had a white dress and a white hat, and lots and lots of lovely things besides. Barclay had given her all these beautiful things. Her eyes shone in a way that actually caused him some embarrassment; never before had he been looked at with quite that sort of worshipping gratitude. She did not speak; she looked at him, her blue eyes dark with all the things for which she had no words.

They went from shop to shop. In one an earnest, talkative little man cut her hair; in another Barclay bought her a trunk to hold her beautiful new things.

They met Austin Muir for lunch. It was the most thrilling moment of Valentine's day. She did not know that it was going to be, but it was. She saw his face change, and her heart began to beat in an odd, bewildered fashion.

"Well," said Barclay, "I've earned my lunch. If there's another man in this hemisphere that says he deserves a good lunch more than I do, I'll call him a liar. After a morning like this I'm going to have the best lunch the hotel can raise, if I put on another half stone for it."

Barclay enjoyed that lunch greatly. He was hungry, the food was good, and he was able to derive considerable pleasure from the spectacle of Mr. Muir being polite to Miss Ryven, and Miss Ryven being polite to Mr. Muir.

Valentine behaved beautifully. Edward's instructions had extended to table manners; but she was being very, very careful. She watched Barclay, and she watched the other women, whilst Austin Muir watched her. She ate very little, and never, never for one moment did she forget her beautiful new clothes.

They had their coffee on a wide, shady verandah. Valentine sat on the edge of her chair with her hands in her lap. Presently she said, "Austin—"

The spell-bound feeling was wearing off. The natural Valentine thirsted to know what Austin thought about her new clothes. The most exciting thing in the world ceases to be exciting unless there is someone to share it.

She said "Austin" in a low, earnest voice and looked at him between her eyelashes.

Mr. Muir had also been collecting himself. He said, "What is it?" without any excess of politeness.

Valentine edged her chair nearer his.

"Austin—do you like me?"

"Why?"

She flushed a little. It was a flush of annoyance.

"Austin—"

"Well?"

The natural Valentine emerged.

"Why—because of my new clothes, and my hair, and everything. Don't I look lovely?"

Mr. Muir opened his mouth to speak.

"Austin, if you're going to say anything horrid—"

"Why should I be going to say anything horrid?"

She edged a little nearer still.

"You might have been going to say that I mustn't talk about my clothes. Edward always said that a lady didn't, and that it didn't matter what she wore, because she would still be a lady. But I don't think I want to be a lady if I can't talk about my clothes. So it's no good saying things like 'It isn't done,' because I'm going to do it." She dropped her voice to a thrilling whisper. "Austin—I've had my *hair cut off*! Austin, I've had it *shingled*! Austin—do you like it? *Austin*—it's cut quite short at the back like yours."

"What a pity!"

"No, it isn't." A new sort of sparkle came into her eyes. "It's what's done. That ought to please you. Doesn't it?"

"Not specially."

"Austin, *do* say you like it!"

"I can't see it."

To his horror, she pulled off her hat, bobbed the shorn head at him, and said,

"You can see it now. Do you like it?"

All the other people on the verandah were looking at them.

"I say, put your hat on again!"

"I want to know if you like it—and my dress. Barclay thinks I look lovely—he said so."

Austin's frown deepened.

"You'd better take care not to believe everything Barclay says."

Barclay, very comfortable in a long chair, looked at them benevolently. He was not near enough to hear what they said, but he had caught his name.

"Which of my ears has got to burn?" he asked.

Valentine had not put on her hat again; it lay on her lap. She nodded across it at Austin.

"He heard what you said."

"He didn't."

"I think you're horrid to Barclay. I love him."

Mr. Muir scowled.

"You'd better tell him so."

"I shall when I want to," replied Miss Ryven.

## Chapter Six

Barclay received an answer to his cable before they left Honolulu. It was of an economical length and ran as follows:

*"Waterson family solicitor will meet on arrival Ryven."*

Valentine looked at the words with a troubled expression.

"Who is it from?"

"Well, I cabled to Mrs. Ryven."

"She doesn't say she is glad."

"Well, my dear—"

"Why doesn't she?"

"Did you expect her to be glad?" said Austin Muir.

Barclay turned on him.

"Look here, Austin, you're not on in this scene—see?" He tapped the paper. "Cables are very expensive things. I've known a man sit up half the night to boil a forty-word telegram down to twelve. People don't say things like 'I'm glad to see you' in a cable, my dear, unless they're just chucking money away."

Austin attacked Barclay on the subject afterwards.

"What's the good of letting her think Mrs. Ryven's going to be pleased to see her?"

"Well—I don't know," said Barclay. "Seems to me she'll find out soon enough."

"She ought to be told."

"What are you going to tell her? You don't know anything—you've nothing to go on. My view is that there's no sense in looking for trouble."

After they had left Honolulu behind them Valentine developed a violent thirst for information. There were a good many novels on board. She read them through and used them as the basis for innumerable questions, some of which Barclay found embarrassing. He dropped one book into the sea, much to Valentine's annoyance.

"I couldn't understand any of it," she said.

"Thank the Lord for that!" said Nicholas Barclay.

"But I want to understand *everything*!"

"Little girls don't want to understand that sort of thing."

If he meant to divert her by calling her a little girl, he failed. She kept to the point.

"What sort of thing?"

Barclay's skin was too leathery to reveal a blush, but he experienced some of the sensations which accompany the act of blushing.

He said, "Er—"

"What sort of things?" said Miss Valentine Ryven impatiently.

Barclay said "Er—" again.

Valentine looked at him severely.

"Wasn't it a nice book?"

"No, my dear, it wasn't."

"Then why did you have it?"

"Gosh!" said Barclay; he mopped his brow. "You stop giving me the third degree and hop along and get yourself another book."

"Perhaps that won't be a nice one either."

It ended in Barclay consigning about half his library to the Pacific Ocean.

In the intervals of reading novels Miss Ryven practised the art of wearing shoes and stockings. It was not an easy art. She could wear them, and she could walk in them; but she was robbed of two-thirds of her spring and grace. She practised daily, and Barclay gave her dancing lessons—like most fat men he danced extremely well—and Mr. Muir, who was not a great performer, was set to change gramophone records whilst Valentine, in Barclay's arms, learnt to avoid treading on Barclay's toes or tripping up over her own. He became daily less cheerful and avoided Valentine.

It was not really very easy to avoid Valentine, because Valentine did not want to be avoided. When she had finished her dancing lesson with Barclay she wanted Austin to play deck quoits or to come and make a third at one of the card games for which she was developing a passion.

They played poker and *vingt-et-un* for counters, Barclay delivering some really fearful homilies on the subject of girls playing for money.

"I like his nerve!" said Austin after one of these sermons. "He'd go the limit any day of the week!"

"What does that mean?"

"Well, it's like his nerve to lecture you about playing for money. His trouble is he can't get people who'll play as high as he'd like to."

"Does he play high with you?"

Austin laughed rather bitterly.

"You can't get blood from a stone! I haven't got a bean."

He found himself involved in an explanation of the word bean, with excursions into other synonyms for money.

The days and weeks slipped by.

The last day of the voyage found the weather still fair and warm. Austin had certainly not intended to watch the sunset with Miss Ryven. But things which we have not intended to do are apt to happen when an undercurrent of desire pulls against intention. He leaned on the rail and watched a yellow sun sink into a bank of haze.

"Do you remember when we left the island?" Valentine spoke with her head turned away from him. She watched the haze brighten into smoke of gold.

Austin remembered quite well.

"You never even looked at the island," he said.

"I didn't want to look at it."

"No—because you were glad to leave it behind. To-morrow you'll be glad to leave us behind."

Valentine went on looking across the water. The gold dazzled. The sky was blurred.

"Why do you say that?"

"Because it's true. You're like that—you want to get on to the next thing. I don't blame you." He paused. Perhaps he expected a protest. When no protest came, he went on, his voice dropping and hardening. "I only hope you'll like the next thing when you come to it—that's all."

Valentine turned round. In the clear twilight he could see that her eyes were bright and her lashes wet; there was colour in her cheeks.

"Why did you say that?" she cried.

"Because I hope you won't be disappointed." The words were rather flung at her.

"You mean something horrid—you mean you'd like me to be disappointed so that I'd think how nice you were and want to be back on the yacht! And you're not nice at all—you're *horrid*!"

Austin Muir folded his arms and leaned against a stanchion.

"You say that because you don't like being told the truth—women never do—they always want someone to butter them up and tell them lies so that their feelings shan't get hurt."

"I *don't* want to be buttered and told lies."

"Yes, you do."

"I don't!" Her cheeks burned. She stamped her foot.

"Well then, what about a little truth for a change? Personally, I think it's unmoral to tell lies. I told Barclay all along that you ought to know the truth; but he simply shirked it because it was unpleasant. That's Barclay all over."

Valentine's left hand clenched on the rail.

"What do you mean?"

Austin jerked his head back.

"What's the use of it anyhow? I call it rotten to let you go on believing a lot of fairy tales right up to the last minute. It's bound to end in your getting a most awful jolt."

Valentine began to feel frightened; she stopped feeling angry. That was one of the things that frightened her. The colour began to leave her cheeks. She said,

"Why don't you tell me what you mean?"

"I'm going to, because I think you ought to know. Look here, Valentine, do you really suppose that these relations of yours are going to be glad to see you?"

*"Oh!"* said Valentine. She might have cried out just like that if she had slipped and fallen.

"Well, is it likely they're going to be pleased?"

She recovered her breath.

"Aunt Helena said in her letter—"

"Twenty years ago! Have a little sense and think what it's going to mean to have you turning up like this. Barclay says there's a place—a house, you know, and land that belongs to it—a good bit of land. Well, they've lived there for twenty years. Barclay says there's money. Well, they've had the spending of it for twenty years. Then you turn up, and they've got to hand over the place and the money and everything. And you're fool enough to think they're going to be pleased."

He stopped, and there was a silence. He had not meant to say so much. His heart thumped against his side. He was angry; but he didn't know why he was angry.

"I don't want to take anything away," Valentine said in the smallest thread of a voice. "I don't—" The thread of voice broke.

"How can you help it?" said Austin scornfully.

"I won't take anything away."

"You'll have to."

"I won't. I only want them to be pleased—to like me. I thought they'd be pleased." She made one of her sudden movements and caught his arm. "Austin, you were being horrid! Say you were just being horrid! Say you didn't mean it! *Austin*—say it isn't true!"

She pressed upon him, shaking his arm to and fro.

He began to say, "It is true"; and then quite suddenly he found that he wasn't speaking at all, and that his other arm was round her. He felt her strain away and then lean forward against him. He heard himself say angry, broken things.

"You'll go away—you don't care a damn—why should you—I haven't got a bean—you'll go away—you'll never think of me again."

The hands that had been shaking his arm closed on it convulsively. She was trembling in his arms, shaking and sobbing as if she had been no more than a passionate, wounded child. He found himself kissing her, her hair, her neck. Her face was hidden.

"Val—don't cry! Why are you crying? You haven't got anything to cry for." He kissed her angrily, desperately. "Why should you cry? You don't care!"

She raised her head, panting, choking.

"I hate you—I hate you! I *do* care!"

"You don't. You'll go away and forget me."

"No, I won't!"

"You'll have to." He pushed her away from him. "I don't think it'll be very hard for you. But whether it's hard or easy, you'll have to do it."

"Why?" said Valentine on a shaken breath.

"Because you must. I've no money."

"But you said—Barclay said—I would have lots of money."

"And you think I'm the sort of swab who marries for money?"

"Not for money—for me."

"Not for you, or for anyone else. I'll marry when I'm making enough to keep a wife, and not before."

Valentine threw up her head.

"I don't want to marry you—I don't want to marry anyone! I *never* said I wanted to marry you. Oh, I *didn't*!"

"It's just as well," said Austin in his roughest voice.

He heard her catch her breath on a sob; her hands went to her breast. She said "Unkind!" in a voice that he had not heard before; there was wonder in it, as if she had not thought that he would strike her like that.

"What's the good of talking?"

"Why did you kiss me? You *did* kiss me. Why?"

"Because I lost my head."

"You oughtn't to kiss me if you're not fond of me. Why did you?"

"I tell you I lost my head. I shan't do it again. You won't be bothered with me any more after to-morrow."

Valentine's hands dropped.

"Won't you come and see me?"

"No."

"Or write?"

"What on earth's the use?"

She came a step nearer.

"Why are you being so horrid? I want to write to you and tell you all about everything. What's the good of anything if I haven't got anyone to write to about it? You said I could write to you."

"I didn't."

"Oh, you did! You said it only a week ago. You said that you were going to be in London, and that you were going to be secretary to your cousin who is in Parliament. And you said we would write to each other—you *did*, Austin!"

"I was a fool."

She came nearer still.

"Austin—aren't you a little bit fond of me?"

"I'm fool enough to be in love with you, if that's what you mean."

She clapped her hands.

"Really? *Truly?*"

He did not answer.

"Austin—"

"That's enough," said Austin in a choked voice.

"Austin—"

He turned and strode away, knocking over one of the deck chairs as he went.

Dinner was not a very lively meal. It was obvious that Valentine had been crying, and that Austin Muir was wrapped in gloom. Neither of them ate very much, and at the first possible moment Austin disappeared, to be seen no more that evening.

"Well, well," said Barclay. He sipped his coffee. Then, "Master Austin's in a fit of the sulks—eh?"

Valentine sat with her elbows on the table and said nothing. She had been happy; and suddenly all the happiness had gone, just as the light used to go on the island when the sun went down—it was light, and then it was dark. She had been happy; and now she didn't feel as if she were ever going to be happy again. She looked up at Barclay with eyes that hurt him.

"What's the matter, kid?"

"He's unkind."

"Austin? Well, my dear, I shouldn't let that keep you awake at night."

"It doesn't," said Valentine literally. "But it hurts—here." She touched her side. "Why does it hurt, Barclay?"

"It won't go on hurting, kid. Things don't. You think they're going to, but they don't. What's Austin been doing?"

"It's my money. He says he hasn't got any, and he says he won't marry me because I've got a lot. And I said I didn't want to marry him or anybody."

Barclay leaned towards her over the table.

"Now look here, kid! I'm going to talk to you like a Dutch uncle."

A fleeting gleam of interest crossed the mournful face.

"How does a Dutch uncle talk, Barclay?"

"Like I'm going to. You just sit up and take notice, and you'll know. Now, my dear, don't you be in a hurry over this marrying business. For one thing, you're a lot too young; and for another, you don't know enough. See? Take Master Austin. I haven't got anything against him except his temper. But you'll meet dozens of young fellows that would suit you better and be a heap easier to live with. Why, I'd be a heap easier to live with myself—and if I thought it was playing the game, I'd make the running and cut Master Austin out." He laughed good-naturedly, but he was watching her. "Eh, kid? What would you think of it if I did? Too old—eh—and too fat? That's about the size of it—isn't it?"

Valentine looked interested.

"You're much fatter than Austin. Are you very, very old?"

"Old enough to be your Dutch uncle anyway—and old enough not to make a fool of myself."

Barclay's voice was sufficiently rueful to attract her attention.

"Why did you say it like that?"

"Because I *am* a fool. Look here, kiddy, I'm going to play the game all right. But just supposing that things don't turn out right for you, and there isn't any fairy prince, and you ever come to feel that I'm not too old and too fat—well, I'd like you to know that as far as I'm concerned it would be a deal."

Valentine took her elbows off the table and sat up straight.

"What does all that mean?"

"Well, my dear, it means that if you ever want Nicholas Barclay, you can have him."

A bright and beautiful colour came into her face; her lips parted eagerly.

"Are you proposing to me?"

"Well—"

"Like in a book?"

"That's about the size of it," said Barclay.

"How lovely! I wish Austin was here! I wish he could hear you doing it! Barclay, will you say it all over again for Austin to hear?"

Barclay leaned back in his chair and laughed until his eyes almost disappeared.

"Well, I'm blessed!" he said.

"Won't you?"

"It's not done," said Barclay. "Gosh, kid! How old do you call yourself?"

Valentine looked offended.

"I'm twenty and a half. And I don't think you ought to laugh when you're proposing to me. None of the people in the books do."

He pushed back his chair and got up.

"See here, Val—No, you wouldn't understand."

She looked up at him seriously.

"Yes, I would. I'm very intelligent—Edward said so."

"Well, he hadn't tried proposing to you, my dear. Would you understand if I told you that I laughed because, if I hadn't laughed, I might have cried?"

"You're too old to cry," said Valentine decidedly.

"And too fat! Gosh! What a fool I am!" He came nearer. "Will you give me a kiss, Val?"

She sprang from her chair, and was out of reach even as he put out a tentative hand. There was fire in her eyes.

Barclay looked at her in amazement.

"What's the matter? Did you think I'd kiss you against your will?" His voice wasn't good-natured any more. "Gosh, kid, if I was that sort!"

"Edward said—"

"Look here, if you're going to tell me what Edward said, you'll start me saying things I oughtn't to."

Valentine tapped with her foot; her eyes still sparkled. She put her head a little on one side.

"Edward said—"

It is to Barclay's credit that he remained silent.

"Aren't you going to say anything?" inquired Miss Ryven.

He resumed his self-control.

"Not before the child," he said, and was pleased to observe that she flushed.

"Oh, but I wanted to hear what you were going to say!"

Barclay burst out laughing.

## Chapter Seven

"WELL, I DON'T KNOW how you can *knit*!" said Ida Cobb.

Mrs. Ryven went on knitting. She sat in the sofa corner, upright, but not stiffly upright. She knitted in the continental fashion, her hands low and almost motionless. The stocking between them moved rhythmically as the needles clicked; but Helena Ryven's hands hardly seemed to move at all. She had been very handsome twenty years ago, and she was very handsome now. Her thick dark hair was becomingly shingled and only lightly sprinkled with grey; her skin was as smooth as a girl's. Yet she looked her age; there was something set about her whole aspect—a suggestion of achievement, completion, which made youth and its striving uncertainties seem very far away.

Her sister, Mrs. Cobb, was of a different type—fairer, softer, with a lined plump face and greying hair precariously held in an old-fashioned coil by a great many hairpins. She had been standing by the window of her sister's drawing-room looking out into the steadily falling rain. The window commanded a magnificent view of the Downs, but to-day the view was visible only as rolling cloud and driving mist. The house stood high amongst beech woods, now a mass of drenched, straining foliage. Where the trees had been cut away to frame the view, the mist was swirling in like the spray of some wild sea.

Ida Cobb turned to the window and said, for the twentieth time, "What an afternoon! What frightful weather!"

"You won't make it any better by talking about it," said Helena Ryven.

Mrs. Cobb made an impatient sound.

"Well, how you can *knit*!" she said again.

"I promised the stockings to little Maggie Brown, and I see no good reason for disappointing her."

"Goodness, Helena! *Reason!* I should think you'd fifty thousand reasons for disappointing anyone. *Honestly*, I don't feel I can bear it when you just sit there and knit."

Helena Ryven smiled with her lips. Her very handsome eyes remained grave.

"What would you like me to do, Ida?" she inquired with a faintly sarcastic inflection.

Mrs. Cobb threw up her hands.

"*Do!* Well, I should think it a great deal more natural if you had hysterics."

"That would be so helpful—wouldn't it?"

Mrs. Cobb came forward with an exasperated rustle of a blue taffeta dress. She was the only woman of her age in England who still wore a silk petticoat. She sat down on the sofa with a flounce.

"Well, if it was *me*, I couldn't sit and knit. Helena, for goodness mercy's sake, put that stocking down, or I shall scream!"

Mrs. Ryven continued to knit. Barclay had wronged her good sense when he accused her of wearing skirts to the knee; the hem of her brown washing silk was at least three inches below it.

"Scream if you want to, my dear," she said.

Instead of screaming, Mrs. Cobb looked at her watch.

"Half-past five," she said. "How soon do you think they'll be here?"

"Any time after a quarter to six."

"Then Timothy ought to be here. Hadn't I better telephone and see if he's started? Honestly, Helena, I'm not *going* to face it without Timothy. You may say what you like, but a man is a stand-by. What's the use of having a brother if he can't come and support you in family emergencies?"

"I don't feel in any need of support, thank you, Ida."

"You don't—but I do."

"My dear, considering that Timothy is twenty years younger than either of us—"

"He's a *man*," said Ida Cobb. "And when everything's going to bits I like to have a man to hold on to. And you may say anything you like, but Eustace *ought* to be here."

"Eustace had a committee meeting."

Mrs. Cobb clapped her hands together.

"What's the good of his going to committee meetings when everything is crumbling, literally crumbling, under his feet? Helena!" She leaned forward and touched her sister's knee. "Helena! What will Eustace do?"

Mrs. Ryven shifted her position very slightly; the movement took her out of Ida's reach. She said in a colourless tone,

"Eustace is not entirely dependent on the estate."

"Eustace isn't; but all these schemes of his are. You know as well as I do—"

Mrs. Cobb stopped short. Helena would not like what she was going to say. She invariably felt impelled to say the things that Helena did not like. But she could not surmount a certain flutter of apprehension.

"Well, Ida, what is it that I know as well as you do?"

"Reggie says—someone told him the other day—he says—"

"I don't think I'm particularly interested in what Reggie says, Ida."

Reggie's mother experienced an access of valour.

"Reggie goes about a great deal and hears everything," she declared. "And only this morning he said that if this girl did turn out to be Maurice's daughter—" She hesitated on the brink, then plunged. "He said it might be the means of keeping Eustace out of the bankruptcy court."

Mrs. Ryven laid little Maggie Brown's stocking on her knee and folded her large white hands upon it.

"Thank you, Ida," she said.

Mrs. Cobb tossed her head. A wisp of hair tickled the back of her neck, and she put up an impatient hand.

"Well, Helena, you know as well as I do that it won't be his fault if he doesn't land there—pulling down all those houses. And Reggie says of course most of his income must *come* from the London property."

"Slum property, Ida."

Mrs. Cobb dug a hairpin ferociously into her coil.

"Eustace calls anything a slum which he wouldn't like to live in himself. I hear he's putting bathrooms into his new tenements, and giving them laundries and hot water—as if people like that wanted to wash!"

Mrs. Ryven had fought this battle before. She replied with aggressive calm and just that tincture of superiority which could be depended upon to annoy Ida:

"People who can't wash soon lose the desire to do so. If you had six children and a drunken husband to care for in a room about ten foot square, and every drop of water had to be heated on the same small grate where you were trying to cook, how long do you suppose that *you* would stay clean?"

Mrs. Cobb drew herself up.

"*Really*, Helena! What a thing to say! Anyhow, if this girl *is* Maurice's daughter, Eustace won't be able to go on building bathrooms—so we needn't quarrel about *that*."

"It takes two to make a quarrel, Ida." The tinge of superiority was a little more marked.

It was perhaps as well that at this moment the door should open. Timothy Brand came in.

His half-sisters did not quarrel before Timothy. Mrs. Ryven took up her knitting again. Mrs. Cobb, who had not seen Timothy for some weeks, got up and kissed him. Helena merely nodded.

"Well?" he said. "What's happened? Lil said you didn't tell her anything on the telephone—only that I was to come up at once. Have you heard from Waterson?" His cheerful round face wore an air of concern.

Mrs. Cobb burst into plaintive speech:

"Oh, yes, dear boy! It's dreadful—he telephoned."

"I think, Ida—if you will allow me to speak."

Timothy looked at her with apprehension.

"What is it, Helena?"

"Only what I've anticipated ever since the cable from Honolulu."

"Waterson thinks—"

"He thinks that there is no doubt at all that she is Maurice's daughter." Helena Ryven's tone was unruffled; no one could possibly have guessed that a cold, sick anger lay at her heart.

"He met her?"

"He went on board the yacht. He told me he had been through all the papers. She has every proof—her birth certificate—letters from me—letters from Maurice to Marion." She paused, perhaps because her voice had for an instant threatened to betray her. If this were so, she was able to impose her usual control upon it as she continued, "He was telephoning from an hotel—he could not go into details. He is bringing her here."

"Oh, I say!"

Ida Cobb nodded.

"That's just what I said. If you have her here, it's just the same as acknowledging her—isn't it, Timothy?"

"Did Waterson advise it?"

Helena Ryven said, "Yes." She made the word sound momentous.

Timothy ran a hand through his thick fair hair and wondered whether Helena got off her platform when she was asleep—she certainly never did during her waking hours. Then his kind heart smote him. He sat on the arm of the big chair next the sofa and leaned forward.

"I say—that means—"

"Yes," said Helena again.

Mrs. Cobb put out an impulsive hand.

"Mr. Waterson's an old donkey! Reggie says he's frightfully out of date. Personally, I consider that family solicitors are a mistake. They know a great deal too much about you, and they're so horribly afraid of publicity."

These sentiments, though not ascribed to Reggie, were so obviously from his address that Timothy grinned.

"Hullo, Ida! How many secrets of your shady past does old Waterson know?"

Mrs. Cobb beamed upon him.

"Naughty boy! Be quiet! No, no—we must be serious. Tim, tell Helena that she's making a mistake. Of course she won't listen to me. But you must see that if she has this girl here, she's simply giving the whole show away."

"If Waterson advises it—" said Timothy slowly. "I say, where's Eustace? He's really the person to be consulted. Where is he, Helena?"

"We didn't expect the yacht till to-morrow. Eustace has his usual Wednesday committee meeting in town."

"He's been going on with the work?" said Timothy quickly.

"Naturally. Why?"

"Gray—"

"He had an extremely impertinent letter from Colonel Gray, which he put in the fire."

Timothy hesitated.

"If the girl is really Maurice's daughter, Gray is her trustee."

"So he informed us."

"Eustace might find himself in an awkward position."

"Colonel Gray appeared to take a good deal of pleasure in pointing that out."

Mrs. Cobb broke in:

"That's what Reggie said. He said Eustace would find himself in Queer Street if he went on spending money when perhaps it wasn't his to spend."

Timothy frowned at her, but without effect.

"I do think Waterson ought not to bring her here," she concluded irrelevantly.

Mrs. Ryven threw up her head and looked coldly at her sister.

"I think Mr. Waterson knows very well what he is doing. If he thought we had a case, he would certainly say so. He does *not* think that we have a case. He said, in so many words, that the girl is Maurice's daughter." She laid her knitting on the arm of the sofa and rose to her feet. "And if she is Maurice's daughter, it is not a case of my having her here or not having her here. The house is hers."

She walked quite slowly to the window and looked out. The rain swept everything; the beauty of the place was obscured. But twenty years of possession had stamped every detail of it upon Helena Ryven's mind. She saw the change of the seasons turn the bare tracery of the giant beeches to a mist of faint, frail green that deepened to summer's wealth of foliage and flamed in gold and copper at the touch of the autumn frosts. She saw the ordered garden lying out of sight behind tall walls of rosy brick—fruit trees of her planting, her rose garden. No, not hers. For twenty years she had had in her mind the day when Eustace would bring home a wife; she had schooled herself to meet it. Now fate had cast her for a part for which she had not schooled herself. She stood in the wings and waited for her call. Neither anger nor that cold shrinking should prevent her taking that call finely. If it was difficult, the triumph would be all the greater, and the applause.

Helena turned back into the room, and heard the distant sound of an approaching car.

## Chapter Eight

THE SOUND WAS a very faint one, for the drive lay on the other side of the house; if Mrs. Ryven had not been almost painfully on the alert, she would not have caught it.

It was with a great effort that she came calmly back to her seat. As she put out her hand for her knitting, the door opened.

"Eustace!" said Mrs. Cobb in tones of the liveliest surprise.

Eustace Ryven came in and shut the door. A very slight frown crossed his face at the sight of the assembled family. Then he came over to the hearth and stood with his back to the carved mantelpiece, looking down at his mother.

She said, "How did you get away?" and he answered at once in the same low, confidential tone,

"There was no committee meeting."

"No committee meeting?"

"No. Gray came up."

"What did he want?"

"I expect you know. He'd had a call from Waterson. Waterson says the girl is certainly Valentine Ryven."

Mrs. Cobb and Timothy might not have been present. The conversation was between Eustace and his mother; his manner very definitely excluded the other two.

"Yes," said Mrs. Ryven. She felt a passion of resentment, a passion of protective love, and a passion of pride. The pride was for Eustace, for the unmoved dignity of his bearing in the face of this blow.

Eustace moved a little.

"I take it that Waterson has communicated with you."

"Yes—he's bringing her here."

The last word slipped into a silence. Eustace took a full half minute before he said, "You thought that best?"

*"Inevitable."*

She rose and stood beside him. She was a tall woman, but her head only reached his shoulder. The two were alike. Eustace had the same fine build and carriage, the same handsome features; but his eyes were blue instead of dark, and his whole colouring paler. He would have been a noticeable figure anywhere. It was a bitter pill to Ida Cobb that, even to her maternal eyes, Reggie came off a very poor second.

"You think there's no possibility of a mistake?" said Eustace.

"Mr. Waterson seems quite sure she's Valentine. I don't see how there can be any mistake. There was no other child on the ship, and she has all the papers—Maurice's marriage certificate, her own birth certificate—everything."

"I see."

There was a pause. And then once again the door was thrown open. It was Bolton. He announced Mr. Waterson and withdrew.

This time no one had heard a warning sound. Helena Ryven, taken unawares, felt a sickening pang. She came forward with her hand out, her eyes on the kind thin face. He looked concerned; he was sorry for them. Her pride rose. It was all over. But no one should pity them, not even this kind old man, who had known her since her wedding day. No one should pity Eustace.

She spoke conventionally.

"You've had a wretchedly wet journey. Do come to the fire."

Ida of course must needs come forward too.

"But, Mr. Waterson, what have you done with her? Where is she?"

"How do you do, Mrs. Cobb? No, thank you—no, thank you—I'd rather keep away from the fire. Well, Eustace, I'm glad to see you. Very glad you were able to get down—very glad indeed."

"But where is she?" Ida Cobb repeated.

"In the study. How do you do, Brand? Yes, I just asked Bolton to let me take her into the study. I thought, you know, that I'd better see you and run through the papers before you meet her."

Mrs. Ryven turned to her sister.

"If she's alone—I don't think she ought to be alone—Ida—"

Mrs. Cobb very distinctly jibbed. How like Helena to try and get her out of the room just when things were getting interesting!

"Oh, I don't think that would do," she said.

"You, Timothy, then. I don't think she ought to be alone—it looks—"

"Oh, I say!" said Timothy.

Mr. Waterson smiled.

"You needn't be alarmed."

Ida Cobb broke in again:

"Oh, do tell us what she's like! Is she at all civilized? I mean of course a South Sea island—a *desert* island—I mean of course—they don't really wear clothes, do they?"

"Don't talk nonsense, Ida!" Mrs. Ryven spoke with some asperity.

"Yes, but *has* she any clothes?"

"Charming clothes," said Mr. Waterson. "Go along and talk to her, Brand."

Timothy went with reluctance. He had no desire at all to assist at a family council; but he blenched a good deal at making the acquaintance of a young female savage. On the other hand, Helena was right—you couldn't leave the poor girl alone in a strange house. A strange house? A strange world. If it was rough on them, it was rough on the girl too. Beastly for her to feel she wasn't wanted.

Timothy opened the study door and went in.

Valentine had been up since six o'clock. For nearly twelve hours she had been coming nearer and nearer to this moment—England—her own people—her father's house—Aunt Helena—Eustace.

She had said good-bye to Barclay with a child's careless affection, and to Austin Muir with clinging hands, wet eyes, and scarlet cheeks.

"You *will* write to me, Austin. You *will* come and see me. Oh, promise, promise, *promise*! Oh, you have promised—haven't you? I won't go unless you do—I *won't*! Oh, *make* him promise!"

All this under the eyes of Mr. Waterson, Barclay, and the crew of the yacht, her hands fast on the lapel of his coat. Small wonder that Austin in a rapid undertone promised anything that would end the scene.

"Yes, yes—I'll write. Yes, yes—of course."

The emotion of saying good-bye ebbed as she drove with the kind old man who had come to meet her. She borrowed his handkerchief to dry her eyes, and found so many new and exciting things to look at that she did not want to cry any more. Austin would write to her. There wasn't anything to cry about. He would come and see her. And to-day—to-day, she was going to see Aunt Helena.

For the first half hour she asked innumerable questions, then fell into a deep silence, sitting straight up in the car and looking through silvery veils of wind-driven rain at the roads, the woods, the villages, the open spaces green with bending bracken. This was England—the rain; the greenness; the grey skies; the sweet, wet scent of the pines. This was England. This was her own country. Presently she would come to her people, her own home.

As they turned in at the Holt gate, Mr. Waterson spoke to her with pleasant courtesy.

"I hope you're not tired."

She said "No," the word hardly audible, and he looked at her curiously. She was so white that her eyes looked almost black in contrast. Her lashes were quite, quite black. They framed the wide, dark, brilliant eyes. Someone much more dense than Mr. Waterson would have been aware that it was excitement that had drained the colour from her cheeks.

They stood in the porch, with the rain behind them and the heavy oak door opening. Valentine stared at the butler, old Bolton, who had been thirty years at Holt. Who was this? She had a moment of uncertainty; and then, just as she was going to put out her hand, Mr. Waterson stepped between. In some mysterious way she understood that she was not to shake hands with Bolton. Mr. Waterson was explaining that she would have to wait a little, and asking her if she would mind; and she said "No." And all at once she began to feel, not exactly frightened, but as if she might feel frightened soon if Aunt Helena didn't come.

They crossed the big, square hall, dark with panelling, and came into a little room lined with books. There was a fire; there was a writing-table; there was a window that framed a purple beech, a square of emerald grass and a bed of scarlet flowers. She saw the window first. It seemed to hang like a picture against the dark, book-covered wall.

Valentine found herself alone in this room. She stood in the middle of it, looking at everything with the same strained, curious gaze. This was different from the hotel at Honolulu; it was so shut in, so dark, so full of things. She touched the thick carpet on the floor with her foot. It was soft, like sand. There were curtains at the windows, heavy red curtains. It was a new sort of place, and through all her excitement it felt strange to her. It felt strange and cold.

Timothy Brand opened the door. He saw a girl standing in the middle of the room with her hands holding one another tightly. She was dressed in white—white shoes and stockings, a white felt hat, and a long white fluffy coat. All this whiteness looked chilly. There was something curiously rigid about her pose.

He only saw her like that for a moment. When the door opened, Valentine's heart gave such a thump that her hands involuntarily clutched one another. It had come. The moment had come.

She saw a rather heavily built young man with rough fair hair, light nondescript-coloured eyes, and a sunburnt face. He wasn't at all beautiful. Just in the moment it took him to come into the room, she had decided that he was not nearly so good looking as Austin, and she was conscious of disappointment. He wasn't as tall as Austin. And Austin had a straight nose. And Austin had golden-brown hair and colour in his cheeks.

Timothy came forward with a feeling that someone ought to give him the V.C. And then all of a sudden Valentine ran to meet him.

"Are you Eustace?"

This was very daunting. But at any rate she spoke ordinary, human English.

"Er—no."

She stopped and sprang back. He had never seen a girl move like that before. It was the sort of thing that kittens did.

"You're not Eustace?"

"Er—no—not *Eustace*."

What a bally idiot he was making of himself! The dark blue eyes looked at him reproachfully. It was apparently very inconsiderate of him not to be Eustace.

"What are you?"—as if he were a table, or a chair, or a black beetle.

"Well—I'm Timothy."

"Are you?"

The open gaze was one of puzzled dismay—"Who the deuce is Timothy?" in fact.

Timothy made a bold plunge.

"I say, I'm being most awfully rude. Won't you sit down? Helena won't be a moment."

"Aunt Helena?" A rapt tone came into her voice.

"Yes—she won't be long."

"Oh—I thought you were Eustace."

She looked at him reproachfully again and ignored the proffered chair.

"I'm Timothy Brand—I'm Helena's brother."

He was unprepared for the sudden movement which brought her quite close to him.

"Oh—are you my uncle?"

Timothy simply did not feel able to live up to being an uncle.

He said, "Oh, good Lord, no!" and then was afraid that he had been rude because he saw her face change. She looked, yes, she looked rebuffed, and she said "Oh" again in a soft, disappointed way.

"Why aren't you my uncle? If you're Aunt Helena's brother, and she's my aunt—"

"I say, do come and sit down by the fire!"

"No—I don't want to. I want to know why you're not my uncle."

"Well—" said Timothy. "I say, we're a most awfully complicated family—and I'm most frightfully bad at explaining things—"

"What do I call you?" Valentine interrupted him. Her eyes were fixed reproachfully upon him. He felt he wasn't behaving quite nicely in not being her uncle.

"Oh, you call me Timothy."

Valentine sighed.

"It's a very ugly name."

"You'll get used to it. I say, do sit down—because I don't think I can explain about the family with us just standing in the middle of the room looking at each other."

She sat down then on the edge of a chair.

"It's this way." He sat himself down beside her. "My name's Brand—and Helena's name was Brand before she married Edmund Ryven—and Edmund Ryven was your father's younger brother."

"Are you married?"

Timothy laughed.

"Do I look married?"

"I don't know. Are you?"

"Rather not!" He ran a hand through his hair. "Look here, I'm making an awful mess of this—I told you I should. My father—his name was James Brand—my father was married twice. Helena and Ida are the first family—they're a good bit older than I am."

"Who is Ida?"

"Ida is Mrs. Cobb. And her husband is in business. And she's got a son called Reggie and a daughter called Marjory. You'll see Ida in a minute, because she's come down to assist in the family powwow. She's a good sort—you'll like her. I say, I have got frightfully mixed! I hope you're keeping your head. Well, I'm the second family. And then my father died, and my mother married a man called Egerton, and Lil—"

"Who is Lil?"

"I'm explaining rottenly—I'm no earthly good at it. Lil's my half-sister—like Helena and Ida, only on the other side, you know. She's five years younger than I am and she lives with me."

"Here, do you mean?"

"No—at Waterlow, about three miles away. I'm one of the poor wretches who are trying to make agriculture pay."

Valentine did not know anything at all about agriculture. She held up one brown hand and touched the fingers in turn.

"Helena—Ida—you—and Lil. Is that right? And Helena is Aunt Helena, but you're not my uncle?"

"You've got it."

A pleased look crossed her face.

"Edward said I was very quick at getting things." Then, with a complete change of manner, "They're talking for such a long time. Why doesn't Aunt Helena come?" She leant forward as she spoke. "Timothy—"

Timothy had stopped feeling shy a long time ago. He had never felt shy with children; and this was a child.

"What is it?" he said with a friendly look.

"Timothy—I feel all frightened."

"Why?"

He found her hand in his, and found it cold.

"I don't know—I feel all frightened. I thought she would come at once. Isn't she—isn't she pleased because I've come?"

"Who?"

He felt his hand squeezed—not the whole of it, but a little bit of the palm.

"Aunt Helena."

"Of course she is," said Timothy in rather a loud voice.

She went on pinching his hand.

"She said—in her letter she said—"

"What letter?"

"It was to my mother. She said how pleased she was—about me."

Helena Ryven was holding that letter in her hand as Valentine spoke. She had read it through, but she did not lay it down. Her own letter—twenty years after. It read strangely—it read very strangely now. All that grief for Maurice, all that warmth of welcome to his young unknown widow and her child, read like something in a book long out of date. The letter had been written at the height of that grief and sympathy. It had been written by a younger, softer, kinder Helena Ryven. Perhaps the thing that Mrs. Ryven never forgave Valentine was the realization that in twenty years she had travelled a long way from the woman who had written that letter. The realization came and went like a flash of light. She folded the letter and laid it down without comment. It was the last of the papers which Mr. Waterson had given to Eustace, and which Eustace had passed to her in silence.

They were sitting round a small table with an inlaid top, which was used for tea. Mrs. Ryven had poured out tea at that table for twenty-one years. She looked at Mr. Waterson's grave, lined face. She could not trust herself to look at Eustace. She heard Ida Cobb make a rustling movement behind her, and instantly the whole tide of her anger and resentment turned against Ida, who never knew when she wasn't wanted. She ought to have left them alone. She ought to have gone with Timothy. It was not her business. She wasn't a Ryven.

Eustace Ryven pushed back his chair and got up. The movement broke a strained silence. Mrs. Ryven also rose.

Ida Cobb rustled again. How like Helena not telling her anything—making her feel she wasn't wanted. Goodness knew it had been inconvenient enough to come down. But had she hesitated? Marjory had wanted the car, and she had told her quite firmly that she couldn't have it. "I must go to Aunt Helena." That was what she had said at once. She tossed her head and rustled protestingly.

"Ring, Eustace," said Mrs. Ryven.

## Chapter Nine

VALENTINE PULLED her hand away from Timothy's. There was a cold feeling deep inside her; when they talked about Aunt Helena it got worse. She didn't want to talk about Helena any more. She pulled her hand away.

"Who was the man who opened the door?"

"Who opened the door? Oh, Bolton—he's the butler. He's been here since the year one."

"Oh"—her colour rose—"I've always wanted to see a butler!"

Timothy burst out laughing.

"Why?"

"There was one in *Lady Catherine's Secret*. It's a lovely book. Edward said it was trash—but it isn't. Have you ever read it?"

"No."

"I'll lend it to you. I brought it away from the island."

"And there's a butler in it?"

"Yes." She leaned forward and spoke breathlessly. "*Yes*. And it was really *him*—no, *he*—I mean *he* was really the one who sent the warning, only no one knew—at least they didn't know till the very last page."

"It sounds frightfully exciting. I'm afraid Bolton's not so exciting as that."

He looked up at the sound of the opening door.

"What is it?"

Bolton stood there, pale and grave, his extreme decorum shadowed by a sense of catastrophe. After thirty years the family was so much his family, and the house so much his house, that a change of ownership seemed to him to demand some of the funeral gloom which is its normal accompaniment. He said,

"Mrs. Ryven would be glad if you will come into the drawing-room."

As they crossed the hall, Valentine felt Timothy's hand on her arm. He had an unformulated feeling of resentment against Helena. Why had she sent Bolton? Why couldn't she have come herself? She was making an occasion of it. Helena always made occasions of things.

He opened the door and took Valentine into the room.

Mrs. Cobb described the meeting to her family late that evening. Marjory sat on one arm of her chair and Reggie on the other, whilst Henry Cobb, on the opposite side of the hearth, made comments which occasionally merged into the scraps which he always liked to read aloud to her from *The Times*. There was a little fire, and the room had a pleasant, well-worn air of comfort.

Mr. Cobb was a stout, comfortable man with a round bald head, a round clean-shaven face, and round shell-rimmed spectacles. Marjory had on her pretty new evening frock because she was going on to a dance with Reggie. Mrs. Cobb had not changed, and the children, one on either side of her—she always thought of them as "the children"—kept on telling her how untidy she was.

"Just like a hen, darling—a disgraceful, dissipated old hen with straw in its hair."

"Marjy! How can you?" Mrs. Cobb's protest was a feeble one.

Reggie prodded her with a jutting hairpin.

"Looks as if she'd been sleeping out in a haystack—doesn't she?"

"Reggie, dear boy, that hurts! And you're not listening. Of course Helena was wonderful—"

"Ain't she wonderful? Ain't she beautiful? I'll—tell the world."

Reggie and Marjy sang this in chorus.

"Really, children!" said Mrs. Cobb.

"It's rough on Helena," said Mr. Cobb. He turned a page. "Hullo! I see Cheesman's standing for the Wurrel division."

"I'm as sorry for Helena as anyone," said Helena's sister. "But, you know, Henry, she makes things rather *awful*—I don't mean in a slangy sort of way—but I'm sure this afternoon if it had been a funeral it wouldn't have been nearly so gloomy. I kept feeling as if I ought to be wearing black."

Marjory stroked her mother's cheek.

"And you look such a fiend in black, darling."

"You're interrupting," said Reggie. "Cough it up, Mum! What happened when they met?"

"Well, Timothy brought her in—and I must say I felt sorry for the poor child, because there was Eustace looking too gloomy and handsome, and Mr. Waterson exactly as if he'd just finished reading the will, and Helena—"

"Being wonderful!" said Reggie with an irreverent cackle.

Henry Cobb looked mildly over the top of his glasses.

"The last Conservative majority was two thousand and eighty-one—but of course that was on a split vote."

Marjory kissed the tips of her fingers at him.

"Lovely! Run away and play, darling! It's rude to interrupt—and you've often told us how nicely you were brought up."

"And she really did look scared," said Mrs. Cobb. "She's the prettiest child, but she looked scared to death. And she stopped just inside the door and clutched Timothy as if he was her only hope. And then all of a sudden she let go of him and ran to me and flung her arms round my neck."

"Good for her!" said Reggie.

"My dears, it was dreadful! Because she took me for Helena—Henry, I do think you needn't go on reading the paper!"

"I'm not reading it. I can't, my dear, whilst you all make such a noise. I'm just glancing at it, glancing, you know. And by the way, Monty Askew is advertising that house of his—draughty old ruin—and he's the face to ask six thousand for it!"

No one took any notice of Monty Askew.

"Wasn't it dreadful?" said Mrs. Cobb. "She flung her arms round my neck and she said 'Aunt Helena!' And of course I was going to explain, but I thought I'd better kiss her first. And Helena was most unreasonably annoyed."

"What a jest!"

"Reggie! My *dear* boy! You wouldn't talk like that if you'd been there. Helena was too dreadfully dignified and imposing about it. I must say—" She pressed her lips together and restrained herself, but her cheek bones turned pink.

"Oh, Mum, do say it!"

"No, Marjy." Ida Cobb tossed her head. "I'm *sorry* for Helena."

"What happened?"

"Well, I was just going to explain, when Helena said in her platform voice, 'You are making a mistake, Valentine. *I* am your Aunt Helena—and I should have preferred to have been the first to give you a welcome.'"

"And then?"

"Well, Valentine just turned round and looked at her, and you could see her face fall. And she said, 'Are you?' And then Helena kissed her forehead—"

"Darling, she *couldn't*! You can't kiss a person's *forehead*—not off the stage."

"Helena did—she took her hand and she kissed her forehead. And she led her up to Eustace as if he were the Pope or something and said, 'This is your cousin Eustace.' And Eustace shook hands with her in a hushed sort of way."

"How *grim*!" said Marjory in heart-felt tones.

"Of course I'm very fond of Eustace," said Mrs. Cobb. "But I must say he's a little overpowering, and even Helena can't pretend that he has any small talk. I don't know what we should have done without Timothy, I came away as soon as I could—"

"Now here's an odd thing," said Henry Cobb. "Here's a fellow writes to the paper to say that snails breed four times a year. Did any of you know that?"

"Henry!"

"Ouf!" said Marjory.

"Well, my dear, he says so, so I suppose they do."

Ida Cobb waved the snails away.

"Of course Helena will marry her to Eustace."

"An excellent if rather obvious solution," said Mr. Cobb in an abstracted manner.

Reggie whistled. Marjory Cobb jumped off the arm of her mother's chair.

"Well, I admire Eustace," she said. "I wouldn't marry him for the world, but I do rather admire him. He's got pots of money—at least he *had* pots of money—and instead of having a good time with it, he practically lives in a slum."

Reggie got up too.

"Eustace don't know how to have a good time," he said. "Come along, Marj, it's time we got going."

Mrs. Cobb looked at them fondly as they went out together; Reggie, thin, nondescript-coloured, with a monkey-like capacity for grimace; Marjory, a little pale thing with oddly marked eyebrows, not pretty, but rather uncommon. She would not have changed either of them for Eustace Ryven; and it is certain that Eustace would never have sat on the arm of her chair and thrilled her maternal soul by poking in her hairpins and calling her an old hen. But all the same, she would have got on better with Helena had Marjory been a beauty, or Eustace plain.

The front door banged.

"Helena will certainly marry her to Eustace," said Mrs. Cobb in a tired, fretful voice.

## Chapter Ten

VALENTINE LAY AWAKE through the hours of her first night at Holt. It was not only her first night at Holt, but her first night in a house.

She had a room with three windows, and the windows and the chairs and her bed were all dressed in shiny chintz patterned with blue and yellow and crimson birds. There was a blue carpet on the floor, and a white fur rug in front of the fireplace; and there were a great many pieces of shining furniture. They were made of a wood that looked like dark, rippled water. And there were two looking-glasses; a long one hung between carved wooden poles; and another, a gleaming oval in a dark frame, on a table between the windows.

She had asked to have the windows open, and when the light was out, she pulled back the cold, shiny curtains so that the air, the wet dark air, could come right into the room. She did not sleep, because her mind was full to the brim. The house—her thoughts about the house lay uppermost. In Honolulu she had been in shops, and in an hotel for an hour or two. Holt was quite different. It was not as large as the hotel, but somehow it seemed to be larger, because no two rooms were alike. All the rooms had a strange crowded feeling; not because they were overfilled with furniture, but because so many people seemed to have lived in them. The portraits of these other people hung upon the walls—people who had been born at Holt; girls who had left it to be married; women who had come into it through marriage; men, women, and little children who had lived out long lives at Holt. She had wanted so much to come to her own people, but she felt something between excitement and awe in the presence of these pictures. They were the first portraits that she had ever seen, and they seemed to her to be very real, and the people they portrayed very near, very sensibly her people and near—and so many.

Helena Ryven had talked about them at dinner, and Valentine experienced a strange discomposure. The smiling lady in rose-coloured brocade had lived to be very sad. The old man with the beard who held a sword in his hand had had three wives. The portrait of one of them hung opposite Valentine. It was the portrait of a child of six in a lace cap and full, stiff yellow skirts; there was an apple in the dimpled hand. "She had ten children," said Helena Ryven.

Valentine lay in the dark and wondered about the yellow-skirted child's ten children. The house seemed full, full, full of people. She looked at her three windows, which she could just make out as three long panels of a darkness that was not quite so black as the rest of the room. The three panels framed the steadily falling rain. They were like three pictures of rain, and night, and soft wet blowing wind. The rain, and the night, and the wind were nearer to her than all the people of Holt.

Long afterwards, Valentine knew that she thought about the portraits because she could not think about Helena Ryven or Eustace. Her mind would not think about them; it went blank and numb and blind at their approach. She could not think about Helena. And she tried not to think about the people in the portraits.

She looked at the rain-pictures and thought how strange it was that the blue and crimson and yellow birds on the shiny curtains should still be there all night though she could not see them. It would be funny, and nice, if they could fly out into the room.

She became a little drowsy as she thought about the birds and pictured them flying quite, quite silently through the dark on gold and blue and crimson wings. She began to drift into a light, half-conscious sleep which was full of dreams. She felt herself moving on a soft, wet breeze with the birds all round her. They were not in the house any longer; they passed the window and were part of the picture of the night. The wind blew them over the tops of the trees; it blew them towards the dawn. Then she heard the sea beating against rock. And all at once she was on the island and Edward was looking at her with a frown, just as he always looked when she was stupid. He began to say something; but the birds came crowding between them with such a twittering that Edward and the island and her dream slipped away from her.

She opened her eyes and saw that her windows framed the dawn. The rain had stopped. There were real birds twittering. She ran to the nearest window and looked out.

It was about four o'clock by the sun, five by the clock. Valentine did not think in hours. The sun was up, but not clear of the trees. This window looked south-east. The trees were edged and laced with gold. The sky, without a single cloud, was a pale, sweet blue, not clear, not misty. It was colour that became with every moment more full of light. The grass was all silvery green, and the woods held dark misty places which the light had not yet reached.

Instantly Valentine became filled with the desire to be out of the house. This desire rushed into her mind like a fresh, invigorating breeze; her thoughts became full of it to the exclusion of everything else.

When she wanted to do something she wanted to do it at once. It simply didn't occur to her to wait or to go through the door and down the staircase into the dark shut-in hall. The window was so much the nearer way; and to Valentine, who had climbed the island cliffs since she was a child, it was quite an easy way.

She did put on some clothes; but clothes were as yet either a vanity or a protection from cold. It was warm already, with the warmth that comes on a still summer day after rain; and as far as vanity was concerned, she was at the moment much more passionately interested in all this new green world than in the adornment of Valentine Ryven.

She discarded her night-gown, chiefly because it was long and would be in her way, but she would not put on any of the dresses which Barclay had given her, because she thought they would get spoilt in those wet, deep woods. It ended in her fishing out one of the island dresses made from the *Avronia*'s sheets; and in this, bare-armed and bare-legged, she climbed out of her window with the help of a waterpipe in the near angle of the wall and the thick brown stem of the old wistaria which almost hid it.

She ran across the paved terrace, down the steps, and reached the long green stretch of turf that fell by an easy slope to the woodland. Last night's rain lay in a thick pearly dew. It bathed her feet deliciously. She ran on, and half way down the slope turned to look back at the house.

In yesterday's downpour she had not really seen it at all. It stood now above her, just touched by the rising sun, and looked at her with rows of blind, curtained windows. It was one of those square Georgian houses, beautiful in proportion and mellowed by sun, wind and rain to a most perfect harmony with its surroundings. The green of wistaria and Virginia creeper covered the entire front.

Valentine looked at it with awe. It held so many stories. Helena Ryven had told her that the house stood on the site of an older one which had been burnt down. Some of the furniture and a few of the portraits had come from this older house. She stared, trying to picture the two houses, one gone into smoke and ash, the other watching her. And all of a sudden she was frightened, and ran without stopping until she reached the trees.

It was more than an hour later that she came to the river. Sometimes she had walked, and sometimes stood quite still watching a bird, a squirrel, or a rabbit. The woods were enchanted woods, full of the loveliest wonders—ferns; lichen; a spider's web with the dew making rainbows in it; shy little furry creatures that could stay as still as she could and run even faster. She was seeing everything for the first time, and seeing it between rain and sun, with the bloom of dawn upon it.

When she came to the river, she remembered Timothy. He lived by the river, he and Lil. There was only one house in sight, a little picture-book cottage, all thatch and gables and pink climbing roses, sitting in a garden quite full of blue and pink and purple flowers. The garden ran down to the water's edge. She wondered if it was Timothy's house.

She sat down on a branch of willow and dabbled her feet in the water.

# Chapter Eleven

HELENA RYVEN RANG Timothy up at half-past seven, and he had only to hear her voice to know that she was angry. Helena angry was Helena even more restrained than usual. A feeling of boredom came over him. When Helena was restrained, it generally ended in his wanting to smash the furniture.

"She's gone," said Mrs. Ryven slowly and distinctly.

"Who has gone?"

"My dear Timothy, I do *not* want to mention names."

"Oh, very well—if this is a guessing game—"

"I want you to go and look for her at once."

"Why me? What's wrong with Eustace? It seems to me—"

"Eustace went back to town last night. He naturally did not wish to stay here. Will you go at once?"

"Good Lord, Helena! I might as well look for a needle in a bundle of hay. If the girl's gone for a walk, why fuss? She'll come back when she's hungry."

Helena's voice became colder.

"I should not have rung you up if it were merely a case of a walk."

"Well—what is it a case of?"

A pause. Then, icily:

"As far as I can make out, she has gone without any shoes or stockings."

"Well, it's nice and warm—she won't hurt."

"I must really beg you to be serious. She must have climbed out of the window, because everything downstairs was shut up. It is extremely important that someone should find her and bring her home at once. We can't have her wandering about without shoes and stockings or anything."

"*Or anything?* My dear Helena—"

"Don't be a fool!" said Helena Ryven. "Please go and look for her. I suppose even you can see that we don't want to set everyone talking."

Timothy got out his car, threw a coat of Lil's into it, and went off to look for Valentine, who might be anywhere within a ten-mile radius, or beyond it, if she got up really early.

That he found her in about twenty minutes was due to the fact that she was looking for him and had remembered approximately what he had told her about the position of his house. She was getting hungry, when she heard the car and moved away from the willow-tree to see where the sound was coming from.

She had come down through the woods to the river. About a hundred yards farther along, a winding road took a bend and ran for a mile or two above the stream. The car came round the bend, slowed down, and stopped.

Valentine called out, "Timothy!" and ran up the sloping bank.

"Oh, my hat!" said Timothy to himself.

Valentine came up to the car, running with an easy grace. Her hair hung in curls of a really startling wildness; her drenched sleeveless smock was stained and torn, her bare legs were scratched, and from one deepish cut a trickle of blood ran down to her wet foot.

She shook the curls out of her eyes, scrambled over the hedge, and jumped down on to the running board with a laugh.

"Oh, Timothy, I was looking for you!"

"Well, you've found me," said Timothy. "Oh, Lord! Where *have* you been? Here—put this on quick!"

He fished out Lil's coat and held it up.

"I don't want it—I'm quite warm."

"Put it on!" said Timothy.

He thrust it on her, and she began to laugh.

"Is it Lil's? I shall make it all wet. Are you going to take me to see Lil?"

"I'm going to take you straight back to Holt. Helena's raging."

At Helena's name she changed, stopped laughing, and drew away.

She said "Why?" in a quick, breathless way; and all at once Timothy didn't want to take her back to Holt—not looking like that anyway.

"Oh, get in!" he said. "Look here, I'll take you back to have breakfast with Lil if you like. I can telephone to Helena, and Lil can lend you some clothes to go home in."

"Lovely! Oh, Timothy—"

"What?"

"I didn't know anything could be as lovely as this!" Then, with a droop in her voice, "Is she angry? Why is she angry?"

Timothy started the car.

"I think she was frightened. She'll be all right by the time you get back."

She gave a sigh and snuggled down into Lil's coat. They were turning and going back along the river's edge. The little picture-book cottage was being left behind. She leaned out to look at it.

"I thought you lived there. I was watching to see if you would come into the garden."

"That's old Trent's cottage. Pretty—isn't it!"

"I wish you lived there. I wish I lived there. I don't think I want to live at Holt."

"Holt belongs to you, Valentine," said Timothy seriously.

She said "No," saw his look of surprise, and found troubled, stumbling words of explanation: "It doesn't belong to me—I don't see how it could. It belongs to all those other people, it doesn't belong to me."

"What people?"

Did she mean Helena and Eustace?

"All the old people. After you went away and Eustace, Aunt Helena showed me their pictures and told me stories about them."

He thought, "Funny child—but rather nice."

"What's bothering you?" he said.

She looked startled.

"Why does that bother you?"

"It doesn't—bother."

"Something does."

He took a quick sidelong glance and saw her flush and look away.

"There isn't room for me," she said in a very low voice.

There was a silence.

Yesterday Timothy had been sorry for her. Today he did not feel exactly sorry. He had been angry and bored—fed up. And then, with extraordinary suddenness, he had stopped being angry and bored. He wondered shrewdly whether it was Holt that gave her the crowded feeling, or Helena. Helena had a way of making one feel crowded.

"Timothy—" said Valentine.

"What is it?"

"Why did you say that Lil would lend me some clothes to go home in?"

"Well—"

"Aren't these proper clothes?"

"They're very wet."

"That's not what you meant." She fingered the hem of her smock where the coat fell away. "It's what I wore on the island. I didn't want to spoil the dress that Barclay gave me. He gave me some lovely dresses. But they all got dirty on the yacht except the one I had on yesterday. So I thought—I was afraid—"

Her flush had deepened. He saw to his horror that her eyes were wet.

"I say—it doesn't matter."

He heard a little woe-begone sniff.

"Edward said I should have to be so very careful when I came to England. He said it was folly to run counter to the established conditions of English society. He said—" Her voice wobbled.

Timothy fairly shouted.

"I say, I'm awfully sorry—but it did sound so funny!"

He looked round at her apologetically and found her laughing too.

"Oh, Timothy, you are nice!"

"Am I?"

He wondered a little what her standard was.

The road began to leave the river. It took an upward slope. The fields on either side of it were Timothy's fields. Now they bent towards the river again. A tall holly hedge rose like a black wall on their left.

Timothy turned in between grey stone pillars.

"Is this your house?"

He nodded.

The drive was like a green tunnel. Under yesterday's rain it would have been black. To-day the sun shone through the crowding foliage like light coming through a stained glass window.

The car came out of the tunnel and stopped in front of a low white house with a thatched roof. The walls were almost hidden by climbing roses, and a very large lavender bush bloomed on either side of the front door.

Timothy Brand had inherited from his father one of those old small manor houses which are fairly plentiful in the south of England. The land that went with it had steadily dwindled in value, and if Mr. Brand had not been able to leave his son some hundreds a year from other sources, Timothy would have been forced to take his farming tastes to one of the Dominions.

As Valentine jumped out, the door opened and a girl in a bright blue cotton dress ran to meet them. She had fair hair rather like Timothy's, and a peaked thin face which looked pretty when she was flushed with excitement; her eyes were a very bright pale blue. She looked at her coat on the strange girl. And then Valentine made one of her quick movements.

"Oh, Lil! You are Lil, aren't you? Timothy has brought me to breakfast. And I've made your coat wet—and Timothy says you'll lend me some proper clothes."

"She's drenched," said Timothy. "Take her away and give her something dry to put on."

Valentine followed Lil Egerton up a staircase with heavy oak newel posts into a whitewashed bedroom that had bright blue curtains at the casement windows.

Lil stared as the coat came off. What clothes!

"Have you been in the river?"

"No—only in the woods. I didn't think there was anything so lovely—" She broke off, slipping out of the wet smock and displaying a pink Parisian undergarment to Lil's astonished eyes. "And there were creatures—do you think I had better wash my feet?—There was one with a bushy tail that ran up a tree and held up his paws and made such a funny scolding noise. Do you think he was a squirrel? Edward told me about squirrels, but I've never seen one. Oh, thank you! It was the long thorny things that scratched me."

"What does it feel like?" said Lil suddenly.

She had poured water into a bowl and was watching Valentine's quick movements.

"What do you mean?"

"Everything," said Lil with a wave of the towel she was holding. "I wanted to see you before you got used to it all. I'd have given anything to be there when you arrived yesterday, but of course Mrs. Ryven—"

"Why do you call her Mrs. Ryven?"

Lil tossed her head.

"I'd like to see her face if I were to call her Helena!" She laughed. "She's Timothy's half-sister, and I'm Timothy's half-sister. But she's always taken particular pains to make it quite clear that I'm not a relation, so I wondered when I was going to be allowed to see you."

Her antagonism to Helena Ryven was so plain that Valentine was abashed. She took the towel and sat down on the floor to dry her feet. After a moment she looked up sideways, as a bird looks at a crumb which he does not feel quite sure about.

"I've never talked to a girl before."

"How do you get on with Mrs. Ryven and the great Eustace?" Lil never took hints; when she wanted to know things she asked about them and went on asking.

Valentine finished drying her left foot in silence.

"Well—how did you get on with her? Of course Eustace is frightfully good looking. But I never know what to talk to him about—he won't be bothered, you know. Did he talk to you?"

Valentine looked up with a faint, fleeting gleam in her eyes.

"He said, 'How do you do, Valentine?' and he shook hands with me. And directly after Timothy had gone he said 'Good-night, Valentine,' and he shook hands again. He has a very large hand to shake—hasn't he? And then he got into his car and went back to London."

"And left you all alone with Mrs. Ryven? Goodness! How frightful!"

Valentine stood up.

"She was very kind. She told me stories about the house."

She came down to breakfast with a neat shining head, curls disposed in an orderly fashion, eyes and cheeks very bright above an old brown jumper of Lil's. She wore shoes and stockings, and an air of being very clean and on her best behaviour.

The dining-room was small and rather dark because the old panelling drank up the light and the ceiling was low and crossed by three black beams. There were two little windows with diamond panes, and Timothy's grandfather had cut through the wall to make a rather incongruous French window which opened on the garden. All through the summer this window stood wide open to a path paved in the middle and edged with cobble stones. On either side of the path was a wide border ablaze with flowers, and the path, with its brilliant borders, ran down a gentle slope to the river's edge.

Valentine ate brown bread and honey, slice after slice, and talked about the island. She told them how Edward had planted maize and rice, and how hard it was at first to get them to grow.

"Was that all you had to live on?" It was Lil who asked the questions.

"At first—oh, at first there were the things on the ship. And afterwards there were cocoanuts—and of course we had the hens—and we caught fish."

"How did you have cocoanuts when you were coming from New Zealand?"

Valentine sucked a sticky finger.

"Everyone asks that. They were on the ship. Edward said they came from Honolulu. The ship touched there and came to New Zealand, and she was going back again. And there were still some cocoanuts left, so Edward planted them, and they grew."

Lil continued to look at her with an interest that sharpened her features and gave her an air of being rather hungry.

"What *did* you do all that time you were alone on the island? I'm sure I should have gone out of my mind. Three months and nobody to speak to. It must have been too awful! Wasn't it?"

Timothy saw the colour go out of Valentine's face. She looked out of the window at the bright flowers. She seemed to have become in one moment too remote to reach. He scowled at Lil, kicked her under the table, and said the first thing that came into his head.

"Lil can't imagine anyone being able to go for half an hour without talking."

He wanted to change the subject, but he could not think of anything to say.

Valentine turned her head slowly. Her eyes were dark and mournful. She spoke to him, not to Lil.

"I don't like to talk about being alone." Her lip quivered. "Why does she ask me about it? Everyone does. But why do they? If it had happened to them, they wouldn't want to talk about it." There was no anger in her voice; it was just slow and sad.

"You shan't talk about anything you don't want to," said Timothy. "Shall she, Lil?"

He kicked her again, and she coloured high but did not speak.

A little wavering smile curved Valentine's mouth. She drew a long sighing breath.

"I do wish I could eat more honey—but I can't."

Timothy burst out laughing; it came so suddenly, and was said with so much earnestness.

"I've got to take you home."

"Can't I stay here?"

"Not to-day. Colonel Gray is coming to see you."

"Who is Colonel Gray?"

"He's your trustee. He has charge of your money, you know."

"Have I got money?"

"Yes—a great deal." He found her eyes fixed on him with a hesitating question in them. He went on quickly, "Colonel Gray will explain it all to you. That's why he wants to see you."

Valentine sprang up and ran to the open window. The air was full of warmth and light. There was a scent of lavender in it, and a scent of roses. The borders were full of flowers whose names she did not know. She would have liked to walk in the garden and learn the names of all the flowers. She turned back regretfully.

"I like your house much better than Holt," she said.

## Chapter Twelve

COLONEL GRAY COULD NOT have said what he expected Maurice Ryven's daughter to be like; but vague alarming visions came and went in the recesses of his mind, whilst isolated words such as squaw, wigwam, tomahawk, and other equally irrelevant expressions rose occasionally to the surface like bubbles rising through muddy water.

When he saw Valentine he experienced such a shock of relief that he became almost effusive. Maurice's daughter! Well—well. Dashed pretty girl! Not like Maurice—not in the least like Maurice—not like any of the Ryvens. But when Mrs. Ryven presently made the same remark, he discovered a likeness to old James Ryven. He was so pleased with his discovery that he talked about it at some length.

"And now, my dear—I beg your pardon, but I ought to have known you when you were a child, and it slipped out. I knew your father when he was a child, anyhow. Well, what I was going to say was this. We've got to have a little talk—a business talk, you know. Dry stuff business, but we can't get on without it, and I think we'd better just come along into the library and get it over."

Valentine regarded the library with awe. It had never occurred to her that there could possibly be so many books in one room. They went up to the ceiling, and down to the floor, and all round the walls, except just above the grim black marble mantelpiece, where an ancestor in armour looked down on them with a stern, unseeing stare. He was William de Ruyven, and he had come over with William of Orange. He looked as if he would have had very little patience with his descendants.

Valentine sat with her back to him. Colonel Gray was rather frightening to look at, but not nearly so bad as the ancestor. He had a long bony nose, a red weather-beaten face, and a stiff white moustache; but his little grey eyes looked quite kindly at her, and she liked his fluffy hair. She could not imagine the ancestor looking kindly at anyone, so she kept her back to him whilst Colonel Gray explained to her that he and Mr. Waterson were her trustees, and what a lot of money she had.

He explained very carefully what a trustee was, and he spoke very loud as if she were deaf.

"Now my dear, do you know what coming of age means?"

"Oh, yes—Edward told me all that sort of thing. You come of age when you're twenty-one."

"Ah!" said Colonel Gray very briskly and smartly. "Ah, now! There we are! That's just what I want to explain to you. The fact is, you do not come of age when you are twenty-one—at least not so far as your money is concerned."

"Edward said—"

Colonel Gray tapped the table.

"I said as regards your money. Let me explain. In the ordinary sense you come of age when you are twenty-one, but the whole of your property remains in the hands of your trustees until you are twenty-five. Your great-grandmother brought a lot of very valuable London property into the family, and it's a good thing for you, my dear, that your cousin, Eustace Ryven, only came into it four years ago instead of nine, or there would have been precious little of it left. What with pulling down and rebuilding, and buying up neighbouring properties and pulling *them* down, he's run a pretty rig already."

Valentine lifted her dark blue eyes to his face.

"Did Eustace have my money?"

Colonel Gray went on explaining, very loud:

"When your father died in New Zealand, the property devolved upon you—and when you were supposed to have been drowned, it passed to Eustace. Mr. Waterson and I will now take the legal steps to put you in your proper position."

Valentine went on looking at him.

"Am I taking the money away from Aunt Helena and Eustace?"

"Not from Mrs. Ryven." Colonel Gray coughed.

"From Eustace?"

He coughed again.

"You must understand that it never really belonged to Eustace Ryven."

"I don't want to take anything away," said Valentine earnestly.

Colonel Gray drew out a violent-coloured bandanna and blew his nose. He always blew his nose when he was embarrassed. He didn't like Eustace Ryven. But undoubtedly the situation was a difficult one. He was willing to concede that it pressed rather hardly on Eustace.

Valentine waited until he had finished blowing his nose. Then she said, even more earnestly than before,

"Can't I give it back to him?"

"Certainly not, my dear—quite impossible."

"Can't I give any of it back?"

Colonel Gray shook his head.

"You can't touch it, my dear. You can't touch a penny of it without my consent and—er—Waterson's."

"I want to give him half," said Valentine. "I think that would be quite fair."

Colonel Gray rubbed his nose furiously with the green and purple bandanna.

"We couldn't hear of your giving him a penny—legally, you know, my dear, legally. We couldn't possibly do it "

He wished that she would take those very clear dark eyes off his face. Fine eyes—dashed fine eyes—pretty girl—not a bit like Maurice—must take after the mother—nice feeling—does her credit. He could see her wrinkling her forehead.

"Isn't there any way I can do it?"

"Not unless you get married," said Colonel Gray.

"What happens if I get married?"

"Well, in the case of female heirs, it's the old 'come of age or marry' clause—dashed stupid clause too—direct invitation to fortune-hunters, to my mind. But there it is—if you get married, you get control of your property at once. So if you want to give half of it away to Eustace Ryven—there you are. Only I fancy your husband would have a word or two to say in the matter." He laughed heartily, a good deal pleased at having reached firmer ground. "And now, my dear, let me give you a piece of advice. Don't you go worrying yourself about Master Eustace, because this is about the best thing that could have happened. He's got some bee in his bonnet about the London property, and he's been so busy trying to get rid of it that if you had turned up a year or two later, there mightn't have been much left. Anyhow, you don't need to worry about him. He's got a good two thousand a year of his own. Luckily for him he can't touch the capital, or he wouldn't have it for long."

Two thousand pounds seemed a very large sum to Valentine. Money was something you did sums with, turning pence into pounds, and pounds into francs, and marks, and dollars. When Mrs. Ryven took her shopping later on, she found herself being told how much things cost.

"You'll have to learn to manage money, Valentine. It would be a good plan if you had an account book and wrote down just what you are spending. I think we had better get one."

They bought a blue one with red edges, and a bright green pencil. The book was ruled, and the pencil had a tin protector with an india-rubber in it.

Valentine was immensely pleased. She wrote down everything they bought, and when they got home she added up the three columns and was very much surprised to find how much they came to.

After dinner she sat with Helena Ryven in the drawing-room and listened whilst Helena talked. Already the visionary Aunt Helena, the Aunt Helena who had stood for home and love and welcome, had become a faint, fading image. The real Aunt Helena was not in the least like the picture. She was kind, practical, efficient; she was different. Valentine did not want to touch her or be touched by her; she did not even want to talk to her.

Mrs. Ryven wore a handsome dress of wine-coloured brocade. She sat in the sofa-corner and knitted until the coffee came, and as soon as she had drunk her coffee she began to knit again. She was going to teach Valentine to knit. She was going to teach her how to sew properly. She was going to teach her how to keep house. She was going to teach her how to write and answer invitations. She was going to teach her her catechism.

"You have a great deal to learn, Valentine," she said; and Valentine felt unaccountably depressed.

Mrs. Ryven went on to speak of the responsibilities of wealth.

"The Ryvens have always taken their responsibilities seriously. Eustace—" She paused and bit her lip; it vexed her that it should have trembled. She could not quite bring herself to speak to Valentine of Eustace's great plans, which Valentine herself was bringing to wreck. "Your great-grandmother, Henrietta Ryven—she was Henrietta Marchmont—was one of the first women of her class to interest herself in the political status of women, and one of her daughters was amongst the first half-dozen women graduates."

Valentine wished she had gone on speaking about Eustace; she was more interested in Eustace than in her great-grandmother Henrietta.

"There is a miniature of her on the mantelpiece. She was a very remarkable woman."

Valentine stood by the little warm fire and looked at Henrietta Ryven's pale, bony features. She had a high pale nose, long pale cheeks, a thin pale mouth, and very, very neatly braided hair. She made Valentine feel cold in spite of the fire.

"Great possessions mean great responsibilities," Mrs. Ryven was saying; and all of a sudden Valentine flashed round with her hands out and her eyes shining.

"Oh, Aunt Helena—I don't want it! I don't want any of it! I don't really! I don't want to take it away from you and Eustace."

Mrs. Ryven put down her stocking. What a stupid, undisciplined scene! She spoke in her restrained voice:

"I think it is a pity to talk like that. Sensible people make the best of an awkward position—they don't talk about it, because talking about it only makes it more awkward for everybody. If you will think for a moment, you will see this for yourself."

Valentine sat down on the hearth-rug. She felt that she wanted to stay near the fire.

"Edward said it was better to talk things out." Her voice shook a little with eagerness. "He said it was a mistake for people to be afraid to say things."

"I don't think there is any question of people being afraid."

"Yes, there is. I want to say things. But I'm afraid—you make me afraid. But I want to say them. I want to give the money back. I want to give half of it back to Eustace, and Colonel Gray says I can't until I'm twenty-five."

"My dear Valentine—"

("Why does she say 'dear' when she hates me?")

"Really, my dear Valentine!"

"He says I can't unless I get married—and he says perhaps my husband wouldn't let me. But I think Austin would."

Mrs. Ryven was startled into a quick natural exclamation:

*"Austin?"*

Valentine was flushed and earnest.

"He didn't want to marry me because of my having a lot of money, so perhaps if I was going to give it back—"

"What are you talking about?"

"About Austin Muir. He was on the yacht."

"Who is he? What does he do?"

"He was Barclay's secretary. But he's going to be secretary to his cousin, whose name is McGlashan, and who is a member of parliament for Glasgow."

"Good heavens!" said Mrs. Ryven.

"Austin says he is a very rising man."

Mrs. Ryven gazed at her.

"Has this young man made love to you?"

"He kissed me," said Valentine with unchanged colour and pellucid eyes.

"Any young man will kiss a girl if she lets him." Mrs. Ryven's voice was severe.

"Timothy didn't," said Valentine dreamily. "But he's rather old, and a sort of uncle. And Eustace didn't—did he? And Austin only kissed the back of my head."

"Did he ask you to marry him?"

"Oh, no, he didn't. He said he wouldn't because of the money. And I said I didn't want to either, because I don't think I want to marry anyone for a long time. I don't know anything about babies—and Edward said they were terribly difficult to bring up—he said he had a dreadful time bringing me up with tins and goats. So I really don't want to get married yet—and Barclay said he thought I had much better not."

A black fur rug lay before the fire. Valentine, in a pale green frock, sat back on her heels surrounded by the soft black fur. Her brown curls shone in the firelight which glowed behind her. The evening light came in through the long windows, the light of a fair, clear day that would pass presently through sapphire dusk to a moonlit night.

As Valentine talked, her face had no changes. It was a child's face, serious, interested, and unembarrassed.

"I think," said Helena Ryven, "that Mr. Barclay was very wise."

"But if I don't marry someone, Aunt Helena, I can't give the money back to Eustace."

Mrs. Ryven lifted her eyebrows.

"I think you don't quite understand, but it is really better not to say things like that. Eustace—" She considered her words carefully. "Eustace would dislike it very much indeed."

Valentine's little quick movement and her "Would he?" came together.

"Of course he would. It doesn't do to talk about money like that. Eustace has, I hope, done his duty at Holt—he has, I think, done something more than his duty. He has taken his responsibilities very seriously. Well, it seems that they are no longer his responsibilities— they are yours. You can no more give them away—" She paused, then went on again with a little more colour in her voice: "You *can't* give them away—but you can fit yourself to carry them."

Valentine looked back at her with a trace of bewilderment.

"I don't know how."

"You can learn."

"Will Eustace teach me?"

Mrs. Ryven laid her knitting on her knee; her hand was not quite steady. She did not answer at once. Then she said,

"You can ask him."

## Chapter Thirteen

Valentine wrote next day to Austin Muir. She wrote on the new paper she had bought. It was straw coloured, and it had her initial in one corner. She wrote:

DEAR AUSTIN,

I have never written a letter to anyone before—not a real one—only what Edward made me write so that I should know how. When are you going to come and see me? I want to see you very much.

She looked at this sentence for some time with a frown, then wrote on:

I want to see Barclay too. This is a very big house, but it does not feel as if I would ever get used to it. But Edward said one could get used to anything. I have got a trustee. His name is Colonel Gray. He says I have a great deal of money, and I would like to give it back to my cousin Eustace—or I think I might keep some of it. But I would rather Eustace had the rest, because he is used to it, and Aunt Helena says he has taken his responsibilities very seriously. He has pulled down a lot of old houses that belonged to us in London because they were too old and dirty for people to live in, and Aunt Helena says twenty people slept in one room. She says the only reason Eustace would mind about the money is because he can't go on pulling down houses. I would go on doing it if I knew how. But Colonel Gray says I can't do anything at all until I am twenty-five unless

I marry someone. If I get married, I can give the money back to Eustace, so I have been thinking perhaps it would be a good thing if I got married. Perhaps you would like to marry me if I haven't got any money, or only a little, because I suppose I would have to have some money because things add up so when you buy them. I went shopping yesterday with Aunt Helena, and I wrote everything down in an account-book and it came to eighty-seven pounds three and two pence half-penny, so I had better keep some of the money and let Eustace pull down houses with the rest. There is a great deal.

It took Valentine a long time to write this. She sat very upright and wrote very carefully and neatly in a clear, unformed hand. She wrote in pencil because, so far, her efforts to use pen and ink had resulted in a mess which she regarded with distaste. She was sure that it would have shocked Eustace very much.

When she had finished her letter she read it through, and when she had read it through, she tore it up. She did not know that she was going to tear it up, but quite suddenly her cheeks were hot and her fingers were tearing the paper.

Later on she wrote another letter, quite a short one:

DEAR AUSTIN,

When will you come and see me? I want to see you very much, and I want to see Barclay. Aunt Helena would like to meet you both.

She got as far as this, and considered the signature. You said "Yours sincerely," and "Yours very sincerely" to your acquaintances. Edward's instructions had been clear and practical. And you said "Yours affectionately" to your relations and friends. And if you loved someone very much, you could put "Your loving Valentine"; and she had planned to put "Your loving Valentine" if she even wrote to Aunt Helena, but that was long ago. She wondered about Austin Muir. She was not sure whether he was a "Yours affectionately," or whether she would put "Your loving Valentine." She hadn't ever been at all loving to him, because they had always quarrelled; only when he said he was going to go right away and never see her any more, she had felt as if she couldn't bear it.

She couldn't make up her mind about the signature. In the end she wrote:

> I don't know the right way to finish this.
>
> VALENTINE.

She went out into the garden after that. The long herbaceous borders fascinated her, but she wanted to know what all the flowers were called, and there wasn't anyone to tell her. Flat pink and yellow rosettes growing up a tall spike; blue things like little hoods; round indigo-blue balls stuck full of spikes; and sheets of rose and lemon and flame-coloured flowers which made funny faces and opened their mouths when you squeezed them.

She was on her knees smelling a rose, when Timothy came through the door in the red brick wall. She was so pleased to see him that he would have been flattered if she had not immediately explained the reason.

"Now you can tell me the names of all these flowers! I did so want someone to come. Aunt Helena's gone to London. Don't you think it stupid not to know the names of things? I have to say 'the round red thing,' or 'the yellow one'—and they've all got names, haven't they?"

When she had learnt the names of a dozen flowers she sat down on the step of the sun-dial where four borders met. Grass walks ran between them, and an old rose-red wall covered with pear, greengage, plum, and nectarine kept the winds away.

"I came to see Helena, and I ought to be getting back," said Timothy.

He was squatting on the grass with his arms about his knees. The sun shone very pleasantly. The garden smelled of lavender, and thyme, and southernwood, and damask roses.

Valentine did not speak, but her eyes said, "Don't go"; they looked soft, imploring, and a little shy, as if she were a child, and he a playfellow just found.

"When will Helena be back?" said Timothy.

"I don't know."

The sun-dial was made of grey stone. It had a slender shaft. One shallow step led up to it. Valentine sat on the step with her lap full of flowers. She wore a thin green dress that was just the colour of willow leaves. She had on new shoes and stockings. Her hair was beautifully brushed, and her hands were beautifully clean. Timothy remembered a bare-legged, muddy gipsy with a wild tangle of curls and a smudged face. He was a good deal tickled.

She was counting over the names of the flowers—snapdragon, hollyhock, viola—Then suddenly she sat up very straight.

"Oh, I wonder if my letter has gone, because if it hasn't you could tell me how to finish it."

"What do you want to know?"

"It's to Austin, and I don't know what to put at the end."

Timothy controlled an inclination to grin.

"Well—that depends."

"Yes, of course it does. But I don't know what I ought to put."

"Depends on how well you know him."

"I don't think I know him very well—he isn't the sort of person who lets you know things. I know Barclay, but I don't know Austin. Austin doesn't let you look when he's thinking."

Timothy was entertained.

"And Barclay does?"

"Oh, yes—he lets you look all the time. I always knew when he was cross, and when he was pleased, and when he was fond of me."

"Well," said Timothy, "how would you write to Barclay?"

Valentine smiled. Her lips were very soft and red, and when she smiled, the upper one lifted a little and showed how white her teeth were.

"I haven't ever written to Barclay—I haven't ever written a letter to anyone before. That's why I wanted to know."

"But if you did write to Barclay?"

She smiled a little more.

"I think I should say, 'Darling Barclay,' and I think I should finish up, 'Your loving friend, Valentine—' I love Barclay," she added seriously.

"And do you love Austin?"

To his horror, she blushed scarlet.

"Oh, I say—I was only ragging. I'm most awfully sorry—I really am."

"How funny!" said Valentine. She put up a slim brown finger and touched her glowing cheek. "I don't know why." She looked at him in a puzzled sort of way, "Is my face red? It feels all funny and hot."

"It's pink," said Timothy.

She touched her cheek again.

"It's going away now. You haven't told me what I ought to put to Austin."

"I don't see how I can tell you."

"I did think about 'Yours sincerely.' And then I thought about 'Your loving Valentine.'" She put both hands to her face. "Oh, it keeps on doing it! I wish it wouldn't!"

Timothy felt himself unable to share the wish; she blushed delightfully, the natural rose deepening to carnation. He thought Austin Muir ought to feel very much flattered.

"I wouldn't bother about it," he said. "You look ripping when you blush. Lots of girls get red in the wrong places, you know."

"Don't I?"

He shook his head.

"Now—about this letter. How *did* you sign it, if it's not rude to ask?"

"I just put 'Valentine.' Is that all right? Because you see—" She stopped and took a long breath.

"I'm afraid I don't."

"He said"—she wasn't looking at him any longer—"he said he couldn't—he didn't want to. Oh—"

"Valentine! What's the matter?"

"I don't know." But she put out her hand, and when he took it her fingers clung.

"What is it, Val? I say, don't cry!"

"I don't know. He said he couldn't come and see me, or write, or—or anything, because he hadn't any money, and because, he said, I was going to have such a lot."

Timothy whistled.

She pulled away her hand and rubbed her eyes with it.

"I thought he was going to be my own real friend. I do want to have a real friend of my own. And he said he couldn't marry me because of the money. But I don't want to marry anyone."

Timothy found himself sitting beside her. He got out his handkerchief and began to dry her eyes with it. Her skin was most astonishingly soft and fine under the sunburn. There were little blue shadows beneath her eyes. The tears kept brimming up against her dark lashes and flowing over. He had never dried a girl's tears before. Lil only cried when she was in a temper. He found it an absorbing occupation. The absent Austin appeared to him to be either an extraordinarily noble fellow of the strong silent sort, or else the world's prize mug. He rather inclined to the latter view.

"I say—I wouldn't cry any more."

Valentine sniffed hard.

"I don't know why I did. I don't ever. Edward said female tears were an abomination. He said they were a grossly immoral method of getting one's own way. May I have your handkerchief to blow my nose? He said a lot more things like that that I can't remember. He never let me cry. He said it made men take to drink."

"I shall plunge into *The Spotted Cow* on my way home and go on the binge."

A look of bright interest came into Valentine's eyes.

"That's a new word! Barclay didn't teach me that one. I *love* it. Does it mean getting drunk?"

Timothy grinned.

"In this instance it would. But it really only means going on the spree and having a beano—"

"Tell me lots more words like that! I do love them!"

"You'll get them mixed up with the names of your flowers. Think of Helena's face when you call a nasturtium a beano!"

"I won't—I won't!" Then with a shadow on face and voice, "Would she be—vexed?"

The laughing brightness had gone out of her eyes. How quickly she changed, and how sensitive eyes, lips and colour were to her change of mood. He was reminded of a day of ruffling wind and racing cloud—one of those very early spring days of sun, wind, rain, and sudden soft balm.

"What is it?" he said, and saw her colour brighten.

"I don't like to vex her," she said in a small wistful voice.

"My dear child—don't be a goose! Why should you vex her? I was only rotting."

Valentine leaned forward, her elbows on her knees, her chin in her cupped hands. Her eyes regarded Timothy mournfully.

"What is it, Val?"

She went on looking at him with a sort of steadfast sadness that he found rather piteous. Then all at once she said in a quick whisper, "She tries to like me," and her hands came up and covered her mouth as if she had said something dreadful.

Timothy felt oddly moved. He took refuge in being angry with Helena. And just because he was angry with Helena he had to defend her.

"What on earth put such an idea into your head?"

She took her hands from her mouth and made a gesture with them as if she were giving him something.

"Oh, I didn't mean to say that—it jumped right out of my mouth."

"Things do." His eyes teased her a little, kindly. "But it isn't your saying it that matters—what matters is that you should think it. Why do you?"

She spoke in flushed distress, impetuously, the words coming, now in a rush, and now haltingly word by word.

"Austin said—it would be like that. He said she wouldn't love me. I always thought she would—I always thought about her on the island—I never thought she wouldn't love me. And Austin said how could she when I was taking everything away from her and Eustace? He said she couldn't possibly. But I thought she would." She paused, took a choking breath and repeated, "She tries to like me."

Timothy's heart gave a jump. He concealed as carefully as possible an extreme tenderness for all young and helpless things—wild creatures, kittens, children. He concealed it so well that only Lil really guessed at it; and he was painfully aware that she considered it "soft." He found Valentine very young, very much the wild, innocently daring, shy, bold, alert, sensitive creature that those other young wild things were. She had never been tamed; but she was fearless because she had never been harmed, and shy because she did not know her ground— bold one moment and shy the next because of her ignorance. And on the surface of her nature, quite unassimilated, the maxims and axioms of Edward. He found the whole thing rather moving.

He was sitting beside her on the step. He looked away from her, frowning a little. It was no use telling her lies. He said at last,

"Give her a little time, Val."

Valentine said, "Yes—"

"You see," pursued Timothy, frowning at an innocent delphinium, "you see, you've been thinking about her all these years, but she hasn't been thinking about you—she didn't know you existed."

"It isn't that," said Valentine. The sorrowful certainty of her voice convicted Timothy of subterfuge. "It isn't that at all. You see, I *am* taking everything away from her and Eustace. May I talk to you about it? Because I can't talk to Aunt Helena—she says people don't talk about that sort of thing—she says it isn't done. Always when there's something I very dreadfully want to do, someone tells me that it isn't done—Austin was *dreadful* about it. But if I can't talk to anyone about it, it feels like something hurting all the time—and when I wake up in the night it hurts more."

Timothy moved a little farther off, because he was afraid that he would put his arm round her, and he didn't think it would be fair; besides, someone might come. This was the very first time he had thought about putting his arm round her. When he moved away from her he took the first step that leads from pity to love. He said, in his kind, quiet voice,

"Of course you can talk to me about it."

"Can I? I've been thinking about it such a lot. Colonel Gray says I can't give any of the money back. He says I can't do anything at all until I'm twenty-five—and I shan't be twenty-one till March, so it's a very, very long time to wait—isn't it?"

"Eustace couldn't take what doesn't belong to him, Valentine," said Timothy seriously.

"It would belong to him if I gave it back."

She was brightening again—sun, wind, rain, and little racing clouds. He shook his head.

"He couldn't take it. So I shouldn't worry about not being twenty-five. You'll get there all in good time."

"He wouldn't take it for himself—Aunt Helena said that too. It wouldn't be for him; it would be for all those poor people who haven't got proper houses to live in. They can't wash, and they can't keep clean, and they're all crowded together in dreadful dirty rooms, and they haven't enough to eat." Her face was quite pale, and there was horror in her eyes. "He wouldn't take it for himself, but he would take it for them."

"But you can't give it to him, Val."

Valentine put up her hand to her throat—the instinctive movement of fear. She was frightened but she didn't know why. The pulse in her throat beat hard as she said, "I could if I got married."

Timothy was half shocked, half touched.

"Good Lord! You're not thinking of getting married?"

"I don't want to—at least I think I don't want to. But I'm thinking about it, because then I could give the money back. Colonel Gray said I could do what I liked with it if I got married." Her tone was eager.

"Oh—" said Timothy; it was a sort of grunt. "And whom do you propose to marry?"

"Austin won't," said Valentine. "At least I don't think he will—he said he wouldn't. And I don't know anyone else, except Barclay, and he's so old. Do you think I ought to marry Barclay?"

Timothy found the situation a little beyond him. He got up, took Valentine's hand, and pulled her to her feet, scattering her flowers.

"I don't think nothing about it, as my old nurse used to say. Look here, you stop thinking about it too. The more you think, the less you'll know. Come along down and have tea with Lil. She's all alone, because I've got to go into Renton to see a horse."

After tea Valentine sat in the garden and watched Lil sew. She used too long a cotton and took quick, jerky stitches. All her movements were rapid and rather awkward. She wore a very bright pink dress, too bright for anything but a flower.

"I'm making my trousseau," she announced.

"Are you going to be married?" Valentine was full of interest.

"I suppose so—some day. I've been engaged five years. He's in Canada. Hasn't Mrs. Ryven told you about it?"

"No—she hasn't."

"How like her!" Lil took a vicious stitch. "She disapproves of me, and she disapproves of my engagement. It puts her in rather a hole though, because she's always gone on like mad about my being a burden on Timothy; so she's torn between wanting to see me off his hands so that he could make a good match—as if anyone could ever get Timothy to make a good match!—and feeling how dreadful it is for her half-brother's half-sister to marry a farmer's son." The long cotton knotted, and she broke it with a jerk. "She needn't think I don't see through her," she concluded.

Valentine looked at the river. The water did not seem to be moving at all. It held a smooth, unbroken picture of grey willows and green rushes. She wished very much that Lil would not talk about Helena Ryven. She said,

"Is he really a farmer's son?"

"Yes, he is," said Lil defiantly. "His father had one of Timothy's farms. As a matter of fact an uncle took him away and half adopted him—sent him to a public school and all that. He'd made money. And then he died and never left Jack a penny. So like a relation! And Jack came back here to help his father—that's how we met. And when his father died, he went to Canada, because he said he wasn't going to have me looked down on for marrying him."

Lil's eyes were a very hard, bright blue. Valentine looked away. She said in a slow, dreamy voice,

"Five years is a long time. Do you love him very much?"

"Oh, *love*—" Lil was biting off a new thread; as she pulled on the cotton, the reel slipped from her lap and rolled away down the paved path—"I don't know about love. I want to get married."

A little line came on Valentine's forehead just below the eyes. It gave her a puzzled look.

"There's a lot of rubbish talked about being in love," said Lil. "Real life isn't like novels—I don't want it to be myself. Jack's a good sort and he'll make a good husband. Even Timothy says that."

"When are you going to be married?"

Lil laughed.

"This year—next year—sometime. I used to think it would be never; but the land he took up is beginning to pay all right now, so I suppose it'll be sometime."

Valentine watched a little breeze come ruffling down the stream. It moved the thin grey willow-leaves and the tall pointed rushes, and at once all their reflections moved too and made a blurred pattern. She liked looking at the river.

# Chapter Fourteen

Mrs. Ryven was talking to her son in the room which he had used as an office for the last four years. It was very plainly furnished, and the best chair—she had taken the best chair—was only moderately comfortable. The windows looked on a dingy street, and a perpetual hum and rattle came from the thoroughfare beyond. It was a great deal hotter than it had been at Holt, and there was no freshness in the air.

"What will you do, Eustace?"

Helena Ryven had come up to town to put the question, but she had been sitting in her uncomfortable chair for half an hour before she asked it.

Eustace was obviously very busy. He sat at a littered writing-table, and every now and then the telephone-bell rang and a brief and sometimes unintelligible conversation ensued: "No—tell him quite impossible.... No, certainly not.... No, it would be quite useless."

Twice Katherine Hill had come in from the outer room to refer to him for the wording of some letter of extra importance. As Helena greeted her, the thought passed through her mind that Eustace would miss such a capable secretary; only to be followed by the piercing second thought, "He won't need a secretary now—*his work's gone.*"

It was when Katherine came in the second time that it struck her that the girl looked as if she needed a holiday. Of course she was always pale—that type never had any colour. But ... She watched her standing at Eustace's elbow. The heavy intellectual face had an odd stiff look. The rather square figure was more upright than usual, and when for a moment she glanced past Helena at the window, those deep-set, thunder-coloured eyes looked as if they had not slept. "She'll feel it too," Helena thought; and when the door closed behind Miss Hill she said at once,

"What are you going to do, Eustace?"

Eustace pushed back his chair and surveyed her calmly.

"I shall join the Community at St. Luke's. Harden will be very pleased to have me, and as I can live on very little, I shall just be able to finish the work on those last three houses. Katherine and I have been working it out, and it's an immense load off my mind. Of course the scheme passed in April goes by the board."

"And Miss Hill? What will she do?"

"I don't think she has quite decided. I shall not, of course, require a secretary." He had the air of closing the subject. "And your plans? Have you made any, Mother?"

Helena Ryven did not answer for a moment. She was struggling with the feeling that this interview would be easier if either or both of them were less under the necessity of behaving well. If Eustace could have broken through his strained pride and railed at his luck, or—impossible vision—had come to her for comfort—The thought broke off, too weak and insubstantial to carry such a load of improbability. It broke and faded. Yet at the back of her mind there was a verse from the Bible: *"As one whom his mother comforteth."* Eustace did not want to be comforted, or if he wanted it, was shut away behind iron walls of reserve. He looked ill. It was no good. They must just go on as best they could. She said in her usual, pleasant, well-bred voice,

"I am thinking of staying at Holt for a time. Valentine seems to wish it, and it will look better from every point of view."

"You won't find it too trying?"

"I don't think I ought to consider that. Except for these special circumstances, I should be the natural person to be with her. Colonel Gray seemed very grateful."

"Naturally."

"Yes—it relieves him of an awkward responsibility, and it will give Valentine a better start." Her voice changed; a little more life came into it. "She's really wonderful."

Eustace did not answer. He turned to the table and wrote rapidly for a moment. As he looked up again, his mother was saying,

"When are you coming down?"

"I? Never." There was both pride and distaste in his voice.

"I want you to reconsider that."

He shook his head.

"Can you afford to indulge a personal feeling at the expense of your work?"

"How does my work come in?"

Helena chose her words carefully.

"Valentine is inclined to be deeply interested in it. She will have a very large income for the next five years, and at the end of that time she will be free to make any dispositions she thinks fit. She is, at the moment, a warm-hearted, impressionable child. I should like you to come to Holt and tell her what you have been doing with regard to the slum property."

Eustace pushed back his chair and walked to the window. He was so near to Helena that she had only to lift her left hand from the arm of her chair and it would touch him. She had the feeling that he was a very long way off. When he turned round, his face had changed. It was less set.

"If she could really be got to take an interest, it would be something. Old Gray wouldn't let her do much out of income though. He's a mass of prejudice, and he'll have control until she's twenty-five."

"Unless she marries," said Mrs. Ryven. There was no expression whatever in her voice.

When she had gone, Katherine Hill came back with half a dozen letters for him to sign. Eustace wrote his name at the foot of each in a beautifully clear hand. When he had finished, he looked up. She was standing at the other side of the table, facing him, the tips of her fingers just resting on the bevelled mahogany edge. Her eyes were cast down. He reflected that Katherine was the only woman he knew who could remain perfectly still and perfectly silent. Other women fidgeted, moved things, patted their hair. If he kept Katherine waiting for half an hour, she would not move at all. He found his mother's question on his lips.

"Have you settled anything yet—about yourself?"

Without looking up she said "No—" in that rather deep, slow voice which was not like anyone else's.

He sat there with the signed letters in his hand and made no comment.

Katherine Hill lifted her eyes and saw what Helena had seen, and a little more. He looked ill; there were lines—quite new; his face had sharpened; he held himself as if he were carrying something heavy; the hand that was holding the letters held them over-tightly. She thought he had not slept since Valentine Ryven came to Holt.

"And you?" she said.

"I told you my plans. I am going to St. Luke's. I can still give service."

A flash came and went in Katherine Hill's dark grey eyes. They were so dark, the iris so heavily ringed with black, that they looked black. But black eyes are brilliant and hard; it is only those dark grey eyes that have the trick of tragedy. That flash between the thick black lashes lighted sombre depths.

"Why don't you fight the case?" said Katherine Hill.

"There's no case to fight—there's no doubt at all. She is certainly Valentine Ryven."

"That's what you all say. But how do you know? She's got a good case, and she's got Mr. Waterson on her side; but I've never heard of any case so good that a clever lawyer couldn't find a hole in it. You're taking it lying down." She repeated the last words on a deeper, almost violent tone, "*Lying down.* Don't you want to fight? I should if I were you. I should want to fight to the last ditch. If I lost, I'd have the satisfaction of knowing I'd put up a good show."

"No, I don't feel like that." His tone was quiet and meditative, the greatest possible contrast to hers. "I don't feel like that—and I couldn't fight a claim which I am quite sure is a just one."

Katherine had not moved at all. She said,

"No—" with a leap in her voice, "you don't care enough to fight for anything."

"Don't I?"

"Do you? I don't think you do, or you'd *fight*—fight and be beaten—but *fight*!" She leaned just a little forward upon her hands—strong white hands, beautifully shaped and very strong. "I came along Parkin Row this morning, just to look at it. I looked at it—all those damned filthy refuse heaps of houses festering in the sun—all those horrible crushed, draggled women—all those verminous children. They can just go on as they are because you're too proud to fight!"

Eustace leaned back in his chair.

"That is not true. I would fight if there was any case. There isn't."

"There's always a case! A lawyer would find you one. You haven't tried—you're just taking old Waterson's word." She paused and then spoke his name strangely poignantly—"Eustace!"

Eustace Ryven was conscious of a sort of weary surprise. Katherine had never called him Eustace before. Until six months ago he had called her Miss Hill. Then, in an extra press of work, she had imported a friend to help them out, and with the friend saying "Katherine" all day long, he had slipped into saying it too. But she had never called him Eustace. He was just not quite conscious that it was months since she had called him Mr. Ryven. He was feeling too tired to speculate on why she used his name now; he was too tired to admit a new idea, combative and disturbing, into the arena in which he had already fought himself to a standstill. He was concerned, deeply concerned, to maintain a calm, indifferent front. Not to the world, not to Helena, not to Katherine, would he show the wound through which interest, zest, all that he really cared for, was slowly draining away.

He shook his head and, with the feeling that he must end the scene, took up a packet of envelopes and began to fold the letters he had signed.

Katherine lifted her hands off the table. The deep smouldering fire showed in her eyes.

"Of course there's an easy way out for you," she said. She spoke low and steadily, her voice held in so that it had no vibration—a ghost of a voice.

*"I?"* said Eustace; and just for a moment his pain showed.

"You've only to marry her," said Katherine Hill. And with the last word she turned and went out of the room; the door shut quietly behind her. A moment later the outer door shut too.

Eustace stayed without moving for half an hour. Then he addressed his letters and stamped them; after which he locked up the office and walked to his flat, posting the letters on the way.

Life seemed a tolerably drab affair.

## Chapter Fifteen

AUSTIN MUIR ANSWERED Valentine's letter by return of post. It was the very first letter that she had ever received. The housemaid brought it up to her when she came in to draw up the blinds and to say that her bath was ready. The blinds were already up, because, whatever the weather was, Valentine liked as much of it indoors as possible.

Austin's letter came after a night when the moon had walked beautifully over the black woods, and turned the dewy lawns into sheets of silver water. Then, with the dawn, there was a clouding, and the sun came up in a mist, all red, and for the space of half an hour the sky ran scarlet. After that a still grey day, just trembling into rain. The windows were damp when Agnes stood by them for a moment arranging the curtains. Then she went out and left Valentine alone with her letter.

Valentine took one jump out of bed and ran to the window.

The letter wasn't very thick. It must be from Austin, because she had written to him. It couldn't be from anyone else—oh, it couldn't. But if it were—

She sat down on the wide window-ledge and tore open the envelope very carefully, because she had never opened one before and it would be dreadful if she hurt Austin's letter. She wondered which day he would come. She wondered whether Barclay would come with him. Her fingers shook with excitement as she took out the letter and unfolded it.

"Dear Valentine"—Austin wrote a very neat upright hand—

DEAR VALENTINE,

It was good of you to write, but I think I had much better not come and see you. It is better that we should not meet. If you don't realize that now, you will very soon. I've got my way to make, and we are not at all likely to come across each other again. Barclay has gone to America on business. I expect to be very busy from now on, as the General Election has been definitely decided upon. I will say good-bye now. Yours sincerely,

AUSTIN MUIR.

Valentine read the last words through two large unshed tears. He had promised—and he wasn't coming. It didn't even sound as if he wanted to come. He wasn't her own best friend—he wasn't her friend at all; he was "Yours sincerely." And Barclay had gone to America.

She let the letter fall and went down beside it on the floor all in a heap, her arms on the sill, her face pressed down on them, quivering. The two unshed tears burned hot and wet against the back of her right hand, but no more came. It would not have hurt so much if she could have cried. But what she had told Timothy was true—unhappiness stayed in her heart; it had no easy outlet in tears.

She began to think miserably about the money. It was because of the money that Austin wouldn't come. Eustace didn't come either. Perhaps that was because of the money too—and Aunt Helena. She began to hate the money very much; and, for the first time, she thought back and saw the island as a place where she had been happy, a rock in a blue sea. She had had something there which had been taken away from her now. Helena Ryven—when she was on the island she always had her picture of Helena, wanting her, loving her—her picture of a playfellow—Eustace—a family like the nicest family in her nicest book. That was on the island.

She had stood on the deck of the yacht, whilst the island slipped away into the sunset, and dwindled, and was gone. She had not even watched it go; she had been looking so eagerly towards England. And in England, instead of finding the dream come true, she found that money mattered much more than anything else; it mattered more than people loving each other—and much more than being friends. She hated it with all her heart.

It was after breakfast that she asked Helena Ryven when Eustace was coming to Holt.

"I don't know, Valentine."

"I would like him to come."

"He is very busy."

"What does he do?"

"I told you the other day what he had been doing. In his altered circumstances, he cannot of course go on with his plans of rebuilding the slum property. All the work has to be cancelled. It is naturally giving him a good deal to do."

"Will he come when he has finished doing it?"

"I don't think so."

Mrs. Ryven was at her writing-table in the little room which had always been her own sitting-room—a pleasant room furnished with quiet good taste. From the mantelpiece a row of miniatures gazed with simpering, high-nosed approval; the men in stocks, and well-frilled shirts, and coats of sage or prune or scarlet; and the ladies powdered, high-busted, *fichu*'d, and of an unearthly delicacy of complexion. On the chairs pale, dimly patterned linen covers. On the walls soft colour prints. At the windows straight wine-coloured curtains. Everything in the room seemed a long way off and a long time ago. Helena Ryven made one feel a long way off.

Valentine understood that Eustace Ryven would not come to Holt because she had taken Holt away from him. She said what was in her mind:

"He won't come here."

Mrs. Ryven frowned. She took an envelope and addressed it. When she had stamped her letter she turned round. Valentine was standing by the mantelpiece; she looked pale and dejected.

"I have to go to London again to-morrow." she said. "Would you like to come with me?"

"Oh, yes!" The dejection vanished; the blue eyes brightened. "Oh, Aunt Helena, how lovely!"

"We could lunch with the Cobbs," said Helena thoughtfully.

Valentine sprang at her. She stopped just short of an impulsive embrace and stood with her hands clasped at her breast.

"And see Marjy and Reggie?"

"Probably. I believe Reggie comes home to lunch."

"How lovely! And—and—shall I see Eustace?"

The silence did not really last very long. Then Mrs. Ryven said,

"I thought perhaps you might care to see something of what Eustace has been doing. After all, he has been in some sense your"—she paused, rejected the word steward, and, reflecting that she had only Valentine for an audience, used rather deliberately the grandiloquent, "viceroy—he has been your viceroy, hasn't he? Would you like to see what he has been doing?" Her voice sounded warmer, perhaps because her mind was not quite at ease.

Valentine flushed delightedly.

"Oh, yes! Oh, *yes*, Aunt Helena!"

Timothy and Lil came up to dinner that evening. Mrs. Ryven allowed her gaze to rest for a marked moment upon the bright green dress which Lil had evidently made herself. It was very bright and very short, and Lil had been very much pleased with it until Helena looked at it like that. It was not a frowning look or a disagreeable look; it was just a look. Yet Lil was instantly aware that her frock was not all that she had thought it, and that Helena, as usual, considered her lacking in taste and a social handicap to Timothy. Her colour rose unbecomingly and remained high.

At dinner she talked a good deal about Jack Harding, choosing the moments when the servants were in the room.

"He's getting on splendidly," she declared as she helped herself to the *entrée*. "I went to see Mrs. Hambrough the other day—you know he's her favourite nephew—and she's so pleased with the way he's getting on that she's going to give us one of her famous eiderdowns—every bit made with her own feathers. She only gives them to relations she approves of, because they take ages to make and all the feathers have to be picked over by hand." She turned to Valentine with a pleasant consciousness of having scored off Helena. "She's Mr. Harding's sister—a darling untidy old thing. Her husband has one of your farms."

Mrs. Ryven began to discuss prayer-book reform in a quiet well-bred voice.

After dinner she asked Lil to sing. Something indefinable in her manner conveyed the impression that she preferred Lil's music to Lil's conversation as being the lesser of two evils. Miss Egerton, in reply, jerked the piano open, drew off two much disapproved of bangles, which she put down with the largest amount of jingle, and banged out her preliminary chords in a way that made Timothy frown.

Valentine had never heard anyone sing before. She wasn't quite sure that she liked it; it gave her a curious shaken feeling; the air round her seemed to be shaking too, quivering as the hot air used to quiver when the sun beat on the island.

Lil had a good untrained voice, fresh and perfectly in tune. She sang 'Billy Boy', and 'Green Broom', and the pretty country variant of 'The Keys of Heaven' called 'My Man John':

"Oh, madam, I will give to you the keys of my heart,
To lock it up for ever, that we never more may part.
If you will be my bride, my joy, and my dear,
And you will take a walk with me anywhere.
"Oh, sir, I will accept of you the keys of your heart,
To lock it up for ever, and we never more shall part.

And I will be your bride, your joy, and your dear,
And I will take a walk with you anywhere."

When she had finished singing, she stayed at the piano, playing any scraps of tune that came into her head. She had stopped thumping. She loved the piano at Holt far too much to go on thumping it. She thought, as she always did, "I should like to steal it," and went on playing because she couldn't make up her mind to stop.

Mrs. Ryven crossed the room and began to look for something in the drawers of a walnut tallboy. She proceeded to sort through a tangled mass of wool. Maggie Brown's stockings were finished, and she wished to make certain whether she had enough of that particular wool to make her another pair.

Valentine got up out of her chair and knelt on the hearth-rug close to Timothy. There was a little fire, and she wanted to get near it. She also wanted to talk to Timothy, because she simply had to tell someone about Austin's letter. That was the funny thing; she had lived for twenty years on the island with Edward, and she hadn't ever wanted to tell him anything. It wasn't that nothing ever happened, because things did happen—very exciting things happened. It was very exciting when Sophronisba hatched out thirteen chickens; but she hadn't wanted to go and tell Edward about it. It had been rather fun waiting to see when he would notice the chickens for himself—Edward wasn't at all a noticing person. But now she wanted someone to tell things to. Perhaps it was because she had always planned to tell things to Aunt Helena— only you couldn't, you simply couldn't.

She knelt beside Timothy and said in a little shy voice,

"I wrote to Austin."

Timothy looked kindly at her. She had on a blush pink frock with frills. She was looking pale; she had hardly spoken; he had been wondering what was wrong. He looked at her kindly and wondered whether it was Austin's name or the firelight which made her seem less pale all at once.

He said, "Did you?" and she nodded.

"Yes—I wrote to him, and he wrote to me." She paused, and added, with a drop in her voice, "It's the first letter I've ever had."

"Was it a nice one?" said Timothy, very much as he would have said it to a child.

"No." Then, after a pause, "It wasn't nice—not at all."

"Wasn't it? I'm so sorry."

"*He* isn't sorry," said Valentine." He said Barclay had gone to America. And he says he won't come down and see me, though he really promised he would." She blinked vigorously. "*He did*. He promised he'd come—and now he says he won't. He says he had much better not come—he says it is better that we should not meet—and he says we are not likely to come across each other again."

Timothy felt an unregenerate desire for five minutes' conversation with Mr. Austin Muir. He felt that he could say quite a lot of things in five minutes that would help to relieve that young gentleman of the good opinion which he obviously had of himself.

"Look here, Val," he said, "I shouldn't worry about him."

"I'm not worrying. But it hurts—here." She pressed a hand against her pale pink bodice. "There isn't anything to worry about, because it's all settled. He won't ever come and see me now, though he *did* promise." She fixed her eyes on Timothy. They were round, and dark, and solemn. "I know why he won't come."

"Why?"

"It's because of the money. He said so on the yacht—he said I'd be too rich. That was when he kissed me." Timothy felt unaccountably angry. What a blighter! "He wouldn't have kissed me if he hadn't been fond of me, Timothy—would he?"

"Well—" said Timothy. He had on more than one occasion kissed damsels for whom he had no very special affection. This did not, of course, interfere with his conviction that Austin Muir was a low hound.

"It was the back of my head he kissed, really," said Valentine, still gazing at him anxiously.

In addition to being a low hound, Timothy now considered Austin Muir to be a damned fool.

"Perhaps that makes a difference," said Valentine.

"Perhaps it does," said Timothy with a gravity that did him credit.

Valentine shook her head.

"I don't think so really. I think he was fond of me, but he wouldn't let himself be because of the money. I think he thinks too much about money—I told him he did. Having a lot of money doesn't stop you wanting to be happy, and it doesn't stop you wanting people to be fond of you. Aren't people ever fond of a girl who has a lot of money?"

Timothy looked at her. His eyes twinkled and said something, but she didn't quite know what it was. It was a kind thing. She thought Timothy was kind. His eyes twinkled, but he said in quite a solemn voice,

"I don't think you need worry about that."

"Perhaps I'm not the sort of person that people are fond of." This was a dreadful thought, but it had occurred to her more than once lately.

"Perhaps you are," said Timothy.

"Do you think I am?"

"I shouldn't wonder." Then, just as Helena came back with her arms full of wool, he bent forward and whispered, "Don't be a goose!"

## Chapter Sixteen

NEXT DAY Valentine went up to London with Mrs. Ryven. They went by train because Helena considered driving a waste of time. Valentine would have liked to go in the car; the train was exciting too, but she had the wonderfully keen sense of smell that wild things have, and the smoke from the engine offended it.

The day was clear and fine. The smoke which smelt so nasty was blown across a cool blue sky that was blurred by no other cloud. The wind came lightly out of the east and brought a sparkle of cold to meet the warmth of the sun. Valentine wished the roof off the train so that she might see the bold, clear arch of the sky. She wanted to feel quite close to the blue, and the wind, and the sun.

The day was going to be one of those days that you never forget, even when you are quite, quite old. Sometimes they come suddenly, and sometimes you know about them beforehand—and it is much, much nicer when you know about them beforehand. The day that Austin came to the island was one of the sudden days, and the day that Edward—fell. They begin like other days, and you don't know that anything is going to happen until it happens; and then you know that you aren't going to forget it any more, even if you live to be as old as the very oldest people in the Bible. The other sort of day, the sort that you know about beforehand, is a much better sort; you keep on getting happier and happier, and more and more excited—only sometimes the thing isn't as nice as you think it is going to be. Coming to Holt had been like that—and getting her first letter.

Valentine sat in the train opposite to Helena Ryven and wondered how she could read when there were so many exciting things to look at, and wondered what London was going to be like, and whether Eustace was going to like her a little, and what the day was going to give her to remember.

Mrs. Ryven held up a book between herself and Valentine. She read a paragraph, and by the time she came to the end of it, something was saying in a just perceptible undertone, "It's not fair." After which she had to stop reading and reiterate her excellent reasons for taking Valentine to see her own property, the property from which so large a part of her income was to be derived. No one should own property and remain ignorant of its condition. If owners were forced by law to inspect all properties held by them at least once a year, slum property would rapidly disappear. Most of it belonged to quite well-intentioned, kind-hearted people who would be horrified at the conditions for which they were responsible.

This line of thought having induced a calm consciousness of virtue, Mrs. Ryven resumed her book. By the time that she had read another paragraph, the faint voice once more disturbed it with the same accusing whisper, "It's not fair."

Helena was not accustomed to contradiction. The voice angered her. She argued it down, bringing up so many moral and religious reinforcements that anything less tenacious than a conscience would have been beaten off the field. The voice became so faint that she no longer heard it; but she could not quite reach the conviction that it was silenced. It had retreated to the extreme limits of consciousness. To keep it there taxed and over-taxed her will.

Valentine spent a rapturous morning. The things that she remembered afterwards stood out from the general sea of happiness like islands—some big, some small. No one can tell what another person's unforgettable things are going to be. Valentine's were the towers of Westminster Abbey; the Quadriga against the sky, cloud-grey against the blue, racing as clouds race, high up, wonderful, rejoicing;

a baby in a pram with yellow curls all over its head and a black woolly monkey cuddled in its arms; a scarlet bus plunging along full of people; sparrows, grey-brown and dusty, impudent, full of gaiety, flirting their tails, chasing one another, fighting, pecking, running almost under people's feet. These—and the shops.

Helena took her into a great jeweller's. She left some pearls to be restrung, and the man behind the counter brought out wonderful sparkling stones set in wonderful shapes of flowers and stars, and showed them to Miss Ryven who was a great heiress and whose romantic story had begun to reach the public. He looked at her with a great deal of interest, both personal and professional, and for half an hour he laid beautiful things on a velvet cushion and talked to her about them. Helena looked on. She was doing nothing; it was being done for her.

Later on they were looking at brocades. Mrs. Ryven had made a purchase, but she did not seem to be in any hurry. She let Valentine stand entranced before a rainbow cataract of shimmering silk and tinsel. One piece was all pink and blue and green and gold like the waves of the sea under the sunrise. She had seen those blue and rose and golden waves when dawn came up over the island. This lovely stuff was like a picture of all those island dawns.

"Do you like that?" said Helena Ryven.

Valentine looked at her with remembering eyes.

"Edward said it was a sea of glass mingled with fire," she said. "It's in the Bible. He said—"

Mrs. Ryven was sharply shocked. She was one of the people who think it the height of irreverence to quote from the Bible, except on Sundays and on solemn occasions. With the desire to check any further remarks of the sort, she said quickly,

"I asked you if you liked this brocade. Would you like to buy a length for an evening coat? You can, if you like." She paused and added with intention, "You can buy anything you like. Have you realized that, I wonder?"

Valentine was silent. Helena had made her feel as if she had missed a step somewhere and come down with a jerk.

"Well?" said Mrs. Ryven. "Would you like to buy it?"

The distressed look that had touched Valentine's eyes fleeted again. She said an odd thing, a thing that pricked Helena Ryven rather sharply, though she could not have said why. She said,

"No—I don't think so. I can remember it. I would rather remember it."

"Why?"

"If you remember things, you have them always."

Ten minutes later, in the fur department, she was an excited child again, slipping on one soft coat after another and whisking round in front of a big mirror in an attempt to see front and back at the same time. Helena was reminded of a kitten chasing its tail. Pleasure, excitement, and the warmth of the fur had brought the brightest carnation to Valentine's cheeks. Her eyes shone, and she kept up a flow of happy, laughing talk. It lasted all the way to the Cobbs.

Mrs. Cobb kissed her very kindly. Marjory touched her cheek with her own pale, smooth one. When Reggie held out his hand, Valentine put up her face quite simply, and it was Reggie who blushed a little as he kissed her, though his eyes twinkled in enjoyment of his Aunt Helena's obvious annoyance. If Helena had not been annoyed Ida Cobb would have allowed herself to be a trifle shocked.

Valentine enjoyed her lunch-party very much. She had had a lovely, lovely morning; she had bought the most beautiful furry coat; and now she was having lunch with Aunt Ida, who was kind, and with Reggie and Marjory, who had kissed her as if she belonged to them. She told them about her fur coat, and Marjy was very, very much interested, and Reggie said all sorts of silly amusing, teasing sorts of things; and after lunch Marjy took her up to her room and showed her all her clothes. It was lovely. She thought what a lot she would have to tell Timothy when she got back.

And she never told Timothy at all, because the afternoon took all the happiness and the lovely dancing feeling that she had had in her heart, and made her feel ashamed of them, so that she could never speak about them, or be pleased, or tell Timothy.

They called for Eustace, and they went down into the places where Eustace worked. They were all places that belonged to the Ryvens. They belonged to *her*. Dirty houses and dirty narrow streets. Dirty men and women. Dirty children and dirty babies. And everywhere the horrible smell of dirt. The afternoon had its unforgettable things as well as the morning. They were quite different things.

Helena Ryven had wished to provide an object-lesson and to point a contrast, but she had only a vague and insensitive notion of what the effect of this object-lesson would be. Valentine had the child's mind, sensitive as the unexposed photographic plate is sensitive, and as ready to hold impressions; but she had also the more alert brain, the stronger reasoning power, and the quickened emotions that belong to the woman.

She received impressions which she could never forget.

They went from Lentham Court to Basing Buildings, and from Basing Buildings to Parkin Row. Echoes and snatches of what she said to Eustace, and of what Eustace said to her, kept repeating themselves in Valentine's mind:

"Why does that baby look like that?"

"Because it has never had enough to eat."

"Why?"

"The man's out of work—he drinks."

"Oh, why does he? Edward said—"

"If I lived where he has to live, I should probably drink too. Two families in one small room—ten people. The public house is decency and comfort compared with it."

Up a stair, slippery with grime, foul to the smell. Rooms worse than the stair. A new-born baby wailing. Down again and on.

Mrs. Ryven in her quiet usual voice: "You were going to do this street next, weren't you, Eustace? Were you able to cancel the contracts?"

"Yes—everyone's been very decent about it."

"What was he going to do?" said Valentine in a whisper.

"He'll show you." Mrs. Ryven looked at her hard. "What's the matter? Are you not well?"

All the carnation colour was gone.

"I think I'm going to be sick," said Valentine in a trembling voice.

Mrs. Ryven dealt with this firmly.

"Nonsense! Pull yourself together! I didn't think you'd be so foolish." She spoke to Eustace in an undertone. "Eustace is going to show us the last block of re-built tenements. You'll find those pleasanter."

The sick feeling passed a little, became less of a physical sensation. The re-built tenements were clean and airy.

"Eustace—can't you possibly go on pulling those dirty houses down?"

"They're not mine," said Eustace Ryven with a groan in his voice.

"You were going to."

"Yes, of course."

"And you can't—because of me?"

He said, "It's not your fault." He did say that.

Valentine felt a passionate gratitude.

"If I begged and *begged* Colonel Gray?"

Eustace shook his head.

"It's no use—he can't do anything. Even if he wanted to, he couldn't—and he doesn't want to. What exists is good enough for him. He's the type that thinks change of any sort is the worst of all evils. You can't do anything with that frame of mind—it's completely impervious to any new idea. But in five years' time you'll be independent of him— you can pull down Parkin Row then. The trouble is you won't."

"I will." The earnest voice made the words sound like a vow.

Eustace Ryven shook his head.

"Five years is a long time. You'll have learnt how to spend money by then, and you'll have got accustomed to spending it. Besides, you'll probably marry."

Her face flamed just for a moment.

"But if I get married, I can give it back."

Eustace actually laughed.

"I can see your husband letting you!" he said.

"*Wouldn't* he?"

He shook his head again.

Helena Ryven interposed with a question about the hot water supply.

They drove back to the station. Valentine no longer saw the streets or the people; she saw only Parkin Row and the baby who had never had enough to eat. What she saw caused her the most dreadful suffering; and the suffering was weighted and fastened down upon her heart by a crushing sense of responsibility. To the island-bred child, the dirt, the crowding, and the noisome air of Parkin Row were a great deal more dreadful than they would have been to the ordinary girl—and to the ordinary girl they would have been bad enough. She had never seen dirt, foulness, poverty, or disease before. She saw them now as things for which, in some dreadful unescapable way, she was responsible. If she hadn't come back from the island, the houses would have been pulled down and the people would have had clean places to live in. It was her fault.

She sat up a little straighter in the taxi beside Helena Ryven. If a thing is your fault, you are bound to do something about it—Edward always said that. She had got to do something, and there was only one thing that would make it possible for Eustace to go on pulling down those dreadful houses and building new, clean ones in their place. He couldn't go on unless he had the money; and she couldn't give him the money unless she married someone. She saw the whole thing quite plainly. The only thing she didn't see was whom she was going to marry. She had planned to marry Austin, and Austin wouldn't. Barclay had said he would always be there if she wanted him. But Barclay had gone to America; and she had got to marry someone at once so that Eustace needn't stop pulling down houses and building them up again. Besides, Eustace said that perhaps her husband wouldn't let her give the money back. It would be dreadful to marry someone just for nothing at all; because she didn't, *didn't* want to get married for a long, long time.

The taxi stopped, and they got out. All the time that they were crossing the crowded station, Valentine's thoughts went on.

They passed the barrier and got into the train. Mrs. Ryven bought a couple of papers and arranged herself comfortably in a corner seat. Valentine sat opposite to her. And as Helena unfolded a rustling sheet between them, the great idea came into her head.

A preliminary quiver ran through the train; the engine shrieked. A late passenger ran panting down the platform, wrenched the door open, and plumped into a seat. Mrs. Ryven glanced at her, wondering why people did not allow themselves time to catch a train. Then her eyes were back to her paper and she became plunged in a *cause célèbre*.

Half an hour later the train slowed down preparatory to stopping at Durnham. Helena put down her paper and looked up. Valentine's place was empty, and the door into the corridor half open. She leant forward and looked down the narrow passage. Valentine's green dress was in sight. Mrs. Ryven was rather short-sighted, but she saw the green dress, and the girl's figure turned away from her at the end of the corridor. And then the train stopped and people began to pour into it. An elderly man came into the carriage and sat down opposite Mrs. Ryven.

"I beg your pardon—this is my niece's place," she said, and he apologized and moved up, leaving the corner free.

Helena began to feel more than a little vexed. Valentine ought to come back and keep her seat whilst the train was in the station.

Presently they moved again. Mrs. Ryven read for a little longer, and then got up and looked out into the corridor. There was no one there.

Ten minutes later she was in a state of very considerable alarm. Valentine was not on the train at all, and at least three people had noticed a girl in a green dress leaving it at Durnham.

Helena looked at her watch. It was seven o'clock. They would stop again in twenty minutes. She took out her time-table and consulted it. She could not get back to Durnham before nine. If she were to telephone for the car, it would hardly save any time at all. She decided to wait for the train.

It was actually a quarter past nine when she got to Durnham, and it took her nearly half an hour to find anyone who remembered a young lady in a bright green dress who had got out of the London train two hours before. It was a porter who remembered, and he was quite positive that the young lady had crossed the platform and got into the Lexington train, which was waiting there.

Helena took a ticket to Lexington, with bewilderment and anxiety struggling for the upper hand. The anxiety came uppermost. The girl had had a shock. She, Helena, had deliberately subjected her to this shock. Suppose it had unbalanced her. Such things happened. She began to recall with horror that Valentine had not spoken a single word after they got into the taxi together.

Lexington is a large junction. Trying to trace a green dress seemed to be a pretty hopeless business. This time it was the waiting-room attendant who remembered it.

"Oh, yes, ma'am—set here for half an hour she did, and told me she was expecting a gentleman to meet her. And he met her, and they went off together.... No, I couldn't describe him, because I can't rightly say I saw him."

"You didn't see him?"

"Not to say *see*. She was setting here and asking me if I knew Liverpool—because that's where she was going—when all of a sudden the door opened and she says, 'There he is!' and off she runs."

"But you didn't see him?"

"No more than a bowler' at and an 'and."

The journey to Liverpool was a nightmare. Helena, tired, remorseful, and thoroughly alarmed, arrived there at midnight. At the third hotel she visited, her urgency produced a waiter who remembered serving a lady in a green dress; she had arrived with a gentleman at ten o'clock and they had had coffee in the lounge; he thought they were staying in the hotel.

Reference to the register showed the last entry as Mr. and Mrs. Trotter. For a moment Helena Ryven saw it through a thick mist. Then she had herself in hand again. She asked questions.

"Had the lady a wedding ring?"

"Oh, certainly."

"Was she in the hotel?"

The waiter didn't think so. They were talking over their coffee and he could not help hearing what they said. Also they had asked him whether they could come in late. He thought they were going out to visit friends. They might have returned or they might not.

Helena found herself addressing the night porter.

The night porter could only say that he had not seen them come in; and on the top of his saying so the swing-door opened, and into the rather dimly lighted hall came a dark young man in glasses and a girl in a green dress. She was of about Valentine's height and of about Valentine's figure. But she wasn't Valentine.

## Chapter Seventeen

IT WAS NOT VALENTINE who had left the train at Durnham. Valentine had never reached Durnham. When the great idea entered her mind, it took command of it to such an extent that she acted exactly as if everything that she had to do had been carefully planned. She got up out of her seat, passed through the half open door into the corridor, opened the outer door, and jumped out just as the train began to move.

She was not seen, because everyone who might have seen her was looking in the opposite direction. On the other platform a woman was running to catch the train; she was panting and wrenching at the door of Mrs. Ryven's compartment at the moment when Valentine shut the door behind her and began to walk quickly towards the barrier.

The train throbbed, clanked, and gathered speed. Valentine did not even turn her head to look in it. She had her ticket, because Helena, in an educational mood, had made her take it herself. The little snipped square was in her hand. She presented it at the barrier, and the man said,

"You've missed your train."

He said it rather severely, and she felt obliged to explain:

"I didn't want to go by it really."

"Next one doesn't go till seven-twenty, and you'll have to change at Durnham."

Valentine thanked him politely and put the ticket away in her purse. Then she walked to the line of waiting taxis, gave Eustace's address just as she had heard Helena Ryven give it, and in a moment was being driven out of the station.

It was all quite, quite easy. The horrible sick feeling had gone, and the weight on her heart had lifted. If she married, she could give the money back; and if she married Eustace, there would be no difficulty about giving it back. This was the great idea that had come into her head as she sat in the train. She would marry Eustace; then the money would all belong to Eustace again.

She felt very happy indeed, and she hardly gave a thought to Helena Ryven. Great ideas are like that; they catch you up and whirl you away so fast that you have no time to think about other people. Also somewhere deep down in her mind was the unformulated impression that Aunt Helena might say "No," or that Aunt Helena might say "Wait." She might say "No," because she did not really like Valentine, and she might say "Wait," because that was what she nearly always did say. Valentine was tolerably sure that Aunt Helena would not feel very enthusiastic about a great idea unless it were her own great idea. She wasn't troubling at all about Aunt Helena. She was going to see Eustace, and she was going to find out whether he would like to marry her at once, so that he could have the money and go on with his work.

She felt no embarrassment, because people under the influence of a great idea are never embarrassed. She was going to his flat. She wanted to see him alone, and she wanted to see him at once. The great idea made her feel that she could not possibly wait till to-morrow, or the day after, or next week. She was going to see Eustace at once, and when they had got everything fixed up, he could telephone to his mother and tell her all about it.

The taxi drew up, and she got out and paid the man as composedly as if she had been going about London by herself for years. Eustace's flat was on the fourth floor. She walked up the stairs because the automatic lift was out of order, and when she had almost reached the fourth floor she heard someone behind her, running. Next moment a man rushed past her and on, taking three steps at a time. She heard the click of a key, and, running too, came up on to the landing to see the door of Eustace's flat standing ajar.

It was Eustace himself who had passed her then. She had been almost sure of it; but the stair was dark, and he was gone so quickly.

She pushed open the door and came into the small empty hall. When she and Helena Ryven had been there earlier in the day, they had waited in the sitting-room, whose door stood half open just in front of her.

She went into the room and threw a quick look round it. Eustace wasn't there. There were the chairs they had sat in—worn leather chairs, one a little larger than the other; and there was a crumpled newspaper on the floor, and one or two matches in the grate. Eustace wasn't there.

She turned and went towards the door of the room, and just as she reached it, Eustace ran through the hall and out of the flat, banging the door behind him. Valentine ran after him. But the catch of the door puzzled her, and by the time she got it open, there wasn't even the least sound of his footsteps to be heard, though she hung over the well of the lift and listened.

Presently she went back into the flat and shut the door again. It didn't really matter. She would look for the servant and tell her she wanted to wait till Eustace came in. In two minutes she realized that there was no servant; the tiny kitchen was empty, and though there were two bedrooms, only one bed had been made up. She stood for a moment looking round Eustace's room. It was very bare and plain, and it smelt of boots. Valentine didn't think she liked the smell of boots very much. She went back into the dining-room and sat down to wait for Eustace. Presently she fell asleep.

It was some hours later that she woke up with a start. Something had waked her, but she didn't know what it was. She sat on the edge of the leather armchair, blinking a little under the electric light and staring at the black oblong which was all the open door could show her of the dark hall. Then the telephone bell rang again, and she knew what it was that had waked her.

She jumped up, put on the hall light, and took up the receiver with a little thrill of excitement. Telephones were most frightfully exciting things. She listened, and heard a woman's voice speaking:

"Is that you, Eustace? Katherine speaking. I thought I'd just catch you. You didn't sign one of that last lot of cheques—I've only just discovered it. I know you work late. I hope I didn't haul you out of bed."

Anyone a little more experienced than Valentine might have thought Miss Hill rather too explanatory. Valentine did not think anything at all. She said in a sleepy voice,

"Eustace—hasn't—come back yet. Is it very late? I've been asleep."

There was a pause. Then Katherine Hill said sharply,

"Who is speaking?"

"I'm waiting for Eustace," said Valentine. "Who are you, please? Because I can take a message." This came word for word out of Helena Ryven's last lesson in telephone manners.

There was no answer. The humming of the wire had stopped.

Valentine asked her question again. Then she yawned and hung up the receiver. She wondered when Eustace would come back, and went down the passage to the kitchen to see what the time was by the funny round clock on the dresser. It was a quarter past one.

She had just taken a peep into Eustace's room to see whether he had come home without her hearing him, when the telephone bell rang again. This time there was a lot of buzzing, and someone asked her three times whether she was 0008. Then, very faint and small, Helena Ryven's voice:

"Eustace—"

Valentine dropped the receiver and backed away from the telephone. She stood in the middle of the hall and looked at it with round, frightened eyes. A gurgling, crackling sound came from it, broken every now and then by a long thrum.

Valentine stood quite still until the thrumming and the gurgling died away. Another sound took its place. This sound came through the door. Someone was on the landing.

This time Valentine knew how to manage the catch. She flung the door open and ran out with Eustace's name on her lips. And it wasn't Eustace at all. The door of the opposite flat was open; two women in evening wraps were just going in. They turned and looked at Valentine curiously.

Valentine came to a standstill a yard away from the door she had opened.

"I'm so sorry," she said, "I thought it was Eustace."

"I see," said the younger woman. She had red hair and green, malicious eyes. Valentine didn't like the way she looked at her at all.

The red-haired girl turned to the other woman, a large blonde creature artificially pale.

"She thought it was Eustace," she said with extreme gravity. Then her eyes danced back to Valentine.

"I'm waiting for him," said Valentine. And because the girl looked at her like that, two bright carnations flamed in her cheeks.

"She's waiting for Eustace," said the red-haired girl in the same solemn tone. Then she began to laugh, and Valentine ran into the flat and slammed the door with all her might.

## Chapter Eighteen

IF EUSTACE RYVEN had not forgotten to provide himself with a pocket handkerchief that Thursday evening, a great many things might have happened differently. He came running back, having gone no farther than the corner of the street. He passed Valentine on the stairs without noticing her in the least, and banged the door of his flat behind him without any idea that he was closing a door in his life.

He went on his way to St. Luke's. Thursday evening was devoted to boxing, and he spent the next two and a half hours imparting the elements of the noble art to a crowd of eager boys. After which he went back with Harden and sat talking over his plans with the one man on earth who had the power to loosen his tongue.

Harden had been head of the Community of St. Luke's for two years. He was not so much a man as a dynamic force, unresting, dogmatic, and of an optimism unquenched by a twenty years' struggle against the grinding poverty of the slums. He was small, dark, bright of eye, and quick of movement. He let Eustace talk for a while, and then cut in, his voice as dry as might be.

"In any country but this the whole thing would be settled with the greatest ease—you'd marry your cousin and there'd be an end of it."

Eustace looked at him for a moment in silence before he said,

"What sort of end?"

Harden gave one of his quick shrugs.

"Oh, one of the best, I should say. Parkin Row would come down, and about six or seven hundred people would get a new start. That's not an end of course—it's just a beginning. The end—" He paused and threw out his hands with a jerk. "The end—isn't yet."

Eustace made no comment. About ten minutes later, in the middle of a conversation about drainage, he said,

"Were you serious just now, Giles?"

"Horribly, I expect," said Harden with his staccato laugh.

"About my cousin—you're the second person who has suggested to me that I should marry her."

"I never suggest. I merely say that if we were in some other country, the marriage would be arranged as a matter of course. England's the best country in the world; but our institutions are not practical. That's the worst of belonging to a sentimental race."

Eustace refused to be drawn.

"You haven't answered my question. I didn't come here to talk about national characteristics."

"Did you come here to talk about your cousin?"

"Perhaps I did."

Harden got up.

"If you're really asking my opinion, I'll give it you. You're in such an unfair position, and the way out is such an obvious one, that I really don't see what there is to talk about."

There was a little pause. Then Eustace said slowly,

"Would it be—fait?"

Harden laughed.

"Have you by any chance been reading novelettes? Fair? What d'you mean by fair? Fair to the girl?"

"Perhaps."

"Well—" said Harden deliberately, "if she gets a kind, sober, God-fearing husband, she gets what any woman round here would go down on her knees and thank God for. *Wouldn't* she?" He shot out the question with a sort of galvanic energy, his small black eyes for a moment fixed and intent.

"Perhaps," said Eustace again.

"Then what d'you mean by fair? It isn't as if you'd a fancy for another woman."

"And if I had?"

Harden looked at him sharply.

"Well, personally, I shouldn't feel justified in gratifying my 'fancy' if it were going to cost some hundreds or some thousands of poor devils their chance of a decent life."

Eustace looked up quickly.

"It strikes you like that?"

"It strikes me like that."

A moment passed.

"About those drains—" said Eustace.

It was two o'clock when he let himself into his flat. The light was burning in the hall, and he looked about him with a puzzled frown before he switched it off. He couldn't remember having put it on. It had been daylight when he went out. But the hall was always dark. He must have put it on without thinking. All the same it puzzled him.

He felt his way to his room, undressed, and lay awake until the early dawn showed him a blue misty sky looking over the top of the tall houses opposite.

In the dining-room Valentine slept dreamlessly, curled up in the largest leather chair. The dawn that brought sleep to Eustace woke her; but before waking her it brought her a dream—one of those fleeting dreams that touch the still half sleeping thought.

It was a dream about the island. She was quite alone in the dark inner cavern where she had found her pink shells, and all the floor of the cavern was heaped with shining pearls. All the pearls in the world were there, and all the colours of the rainbow dazzled on them under a milky veil. *But it was dark in the cavern.*

She came awake, and felt the light on her face; and suddenly she was so hungry that she didn't know what to do. It was still dark in the passage. She went along it with her fingers on the wall until she came to the door of Eustace's room. It was shut. She was sure that she had left it ajar. Eustace must have come home while she was asleep. She turned the handle very gently and looked in. Eustace was lying on his side with his face hidden against his arm. He looked very large. She shut the door and went on down the passage.

There were eggs in the kitchen, and a loaf and some butter. When she had eaten two eggs and a great deal of bread and butter, she felt better.

She had discovered a pot of strawberry jam, and was engaged in trying to balance a strawberry on a wobbly bit of bread, when Mrs. Fleming walked in.

The strawberry overbalanced. Valentine gave a little shriek and caught it just in time. When it was safely in her mouth, she began to notice the immobility of Mrs. Fleming, and the redness of her face, and the way she stared.

"Lor!" said Mrs. Fleming. "Of all the starts!" She had held her breath until she could hold it no more, and the remark had the effect of a small explosion.

Valentine finished sucking her finger.

"How did you get in?" she inquired.

Mrs. Fleming stiffened.

"How did *I* get in? How did *I* get in? Why, same as I always do—with the key what I has a-purpose. And may I arst if you're stayin' 'ere, miss?"

"No, I'm not staying—at least I don't think so. Eustace isn't up yet, so I don't know."

Mrs. Fleming's sharp little grey eyes fixed Valentine in a stare of frank curiosity just tinged with hope. Charing was dull work—not that she called herself a char; she was a "daily," and more than equal to putting anyone in their place if they called her out of her name. A bit of scandal would liven things up, besides providing her with an opportunity of feeling superior to the gentry; so there was a tinge of hope in the inquisitive eye.

"May I ask where you slep', miss?"

"In the dining-room," said Valentine, waving the sucked finger in the air to dry it.

"An' either she's the boldest, brazen-faced 'ussy as ever I should wish to see—an' 'eaven knows there's plenty of 'ussies to be see'd for anyone as isn't as stone blind as any old Balaam's ass—or else she's one o' them born innocents that didn't ought to go hout without 'er mother, an' 'er grandmother, an' 'er great-grandmother's cat." This, after work was over, to a fellow "daily," Mrs. Diggs by name, a frail and lachrymose creature who wiped her eyes before replying:

"An' what's the use of being an innocent young creature, Mrs. Fleming, with the world full of men?"

Mrs. Fleming sniffed.

"Oh, lor, Mrs. Diggs, 'ow you do go on about the men! Can't say I mind 'em myself—but then I've 'ad luck. An' what I says is this—get 'em in 'and an' keep 'em in 'and, an' they'll come an' feed out of yer 'and same as a lot of puppy dogs. But let 'em once get out of 'and, an' you may whistle for 'em—for they 'aven't got no sense, men 'aven't,"

"Well, I dunno about that," said Mrs. Diggs.

Mrs. Fleming had plenty to say to Mrs. Diggs afterwards; but at the time she confined herself to looking sharply at Valentine whilst she removed her battered black hat and drab waterproof and put on a checked apron which had seen better days. Valentine sat on the kitchen table and looked on whilst she made tea.

When Eustace emerged from his room, the sound of voices in the kitchen puzzled him vaguely. He had his bath, and as he returned, the voice of Mrs. Fleming could still be heard. She appeared to be embarked on a sustained narrative. Her voice was very shrill and penetrating. He frowned and shut the door with something of a bang.

Mrs. Fleming, thawed by hot tea, was engaged in giving Valentine the full and complete history of her courtship and marriage. She made toast and fried bacon at the same time.

"An' I says to 'im, 'Now,' I says, 'you just got to choose whether you'll 'ave your public 'ouse or whether you'll 'ave me.' An' mind you, miss, I don't say as h'orl barmaids is no better than they should be, but

I do say, an' willing to swear, that that there Kate Smith at *The Bull* was the very image of Jezebel out of the Old Testament, an' wot I couldn't bring myself to name in front of a young lady. So I spoke plain enough to George Fleming, an' thought it my duty—lovely bit o' bacon this is by the smell. I'll say this for Mr. Ryven, 'e always gets the best—'George,' I says, and me donkey was up, I can tell you. I says to 'im, 'George, you can 'ave me or you can 'ave that ginger-'aired Jezebel, but you can't 'ave both of us, not unless you go for a 'eathen Turk or a Mormon, an' then, I dessay you might 'ave a dozen, or *more*—only one of 'em won't be me, George, an' that I tell you straight. So you can just choose,' I says."

Mrs. Fleming turned over all the bacon with a wump, and a loud sizzling arose from the pan.

Valentine was thrilled.

"Oh, do go on! What did he say?"

"Seein' as me name's Fleming, 'e said what 'e oughter say. 'Maud,' 'e says, 'wot are you gettin' at?' 'e says. An' I says, 'George Fleming, I'm a-gettin' at *you*.' An' 'e says, 'Me pore mother always said as you were'—which a more interferin' woman I never 'opes to see, not this side of the grave. An then I says, 'You come along o' me, and we'll put up the banns an' you can sign the pledge at the same time. No more public 'ouses for me,' I says, 'an' no more ginger-'aired Jezebels for you, George Fleming.' An' I 'ope to goodness that Mr. Ryven isn't going to be late, for bacon kep' is bacon spoiled."

Valentine slipped down off the table and ran out of the room. She had heard what Mrs. Fleming had not heard, the opening and shutting of Eustace's door and the sound of his footsteps going in the direction of the dining-room.

Mrs. Fleming left the bacon and put her head round the kitchen door. She was in time to see Eustace Ryven's face of petrified astonishment. Then Valentine passed out of her sight round the corner. Mr. Ryven followed her. The dining-room door was shut. She began to dish up the bacon in a frantic hurry.

In the dining-room Eustace's surprise was becoming rapidly merged in annoyance.

"You left my mother?"

"In the train."

"She doesn't know where you are?"

"Oh *yes*—I think she does."

"Why do you think so?"

"Because—" Her tone became a little guilty, and she looked at him between her eyelashes. He was so large, and of course she ought not to have dropped the receiver and run away when she heard Aunt Helena's voice.

"Well?" He sounded very impatient.

"Because—she telephoned."

"Telephoned—here? When?"

"In the middle of the night."

"Good heavens! She must have been frantic. Did you tell her you were here?"

Valentine backed a little away from him, as she had backed away from the telephone.

"No—I didn't."

"But she must have heard your voice when you answered. Didn't she recognize it?"

"No—she didn't."

"She didn't recognize your voice?"

"I didn't say anything."

"Good heavens! Why didn't you?"

Valentine made a little gesture with her hands as if she were throwing something away.

"I didn't—I dropped it."

"You dropped the receiver?"

She nodded. A faint gleam showed under the dark lashes, mournful yet defiant.

"Why on earth?"

"I didn't want to talk to Aunt Helena."

The handle turned, and the door burst open, propelled by Mrs. Fleming's knee. She had three smuts on her right cheek and a very large smudge on the left side of her nose. She held the bacon dish in one hand and the teapot in the other. "An' if hever I see a gentleman put hout, it was 'im. Frowning 'orrid 'e was, and she a-saying something about her h'arnt and looking at 'im as if butter wouldn't melt in 'er mouth. 'H'arnt hindeed!' I says to myself, and I goes out a-leaving the door open. An' I give you my word, Mrs. Diggs, I 'adn't gone not 'alf a yard before I 'ears it slam."

Eustace turned from the slammed door.

"What's the meaning of all this, Valentine?" he said severely.

"There's toast, and marmalade, and butter, and the milk, and the hot water still to come. I'd rather tell you after she's brought them."

Even under the pressure of a great idea, it is difficult to propose marriage to a large scowling gentleman whilst a sharp-eyed "daily" brings in breakfast piece by piece.

Mrs. Fleming's next entrance found Mr. Ryven frowning on the hearth-rug. "An' she a-setting in a chair with 'er 'ands in 'er lap a-looking as if she were saying 'er catechism."

"I don't hold with Church catechisms meself," said Mrs. Diggs in her disconsolate voice. "We was brought up Chapel, and brought up strict, an' if my pore mother could ha' known—"

Mrs. Fleming was not in the least interested in Mrs. Diggs' mother.

"An' when I went in with the 'ot water, which I lef' to the last, they 'adn't moved—not a hinch they 'adn't."

When Mrs. Fleming had gone away for the last time, Eustace broke the silence.

"I must go and telephone to my mother—she must be terribly anxious."

Valentine continued to sit with her hands in her lap. Everything was being quite different to what she had thought it would be. Everything was being very depressing. The question now was, should she ask Eustace to marry her before he ate his bacon, or afterwards? Half cold bacon was another rather depressing thing. She did hope he wouldn't be very long telephoning.

He wasn't very long. But his return added no cheerfulness to the situation. He shut the door and said in a portentous voice,

"My mother is not at Holt—she did not return last night. And as you left the receiver off the telephone, she has, of course, been unable to communicate with me. Will you have some bacon?"

Valentine decided not to ask him to marry her till after breakfast. Without actually formulating her hope, she did trust that breakfast would prove a softening influence. She said,

"No, thank you, Eustace."

"You must have some breakfast. You should never leave the receiver off the telephone."

"I won't again. I've had two eggs and some strawberry jam. I hope you don't mind—I was so very hungry."

Eustace ate all the bacon in a rapid, gloomy manner, and broke two pieces of toast into little bits, which he scattered on the table. He then swallowed a cup of tea and pushed back his chair.

Valentine had not moved. She felt a passionate desire to put off proposing to Eustace.

"Won't you have any marmalade, Eustace?"

"No!" said Eustace impatiently. "I want to know why you ran away from my mother."

"Won't you have another cup of tea?"

"No! Why did you run away?"

"I wanted to come and see you."

He was standing in front of the empty fireplace, yards high, and frightfully cross. Valentine shut her eyes and thought about the baby that never had enough to eat.

"I wanted to see you," she repeated in a little voice.

"You had just seen me."

"I wanted to see you alone."

"You wanted to see me alone?" His tone was full of angry surprise.

Valentine kept her eyes screwed up and nodded.

"I had to."

"Will you please explain?"

"I'm going to."

She put her hands up to her face, not covering it, but, as it were, holding on to herself.

"Well?"

"I couldn't bear it." The last word came with a gasp.

"What do you mean?"

"The houses," said Valentine with a sob. She opened her eyes and looked at him earnestly. "The more I thought about them, the more I couldn't bear it. I want you to be able to pull them down."

Eustace frowned in rather a different way.

"It's not your fault," he said grudgingly.

"It would be my fault if I didn't do anything."

"I'm afraid there's nothing you can do."

"There is!" said Valentine. There was a rush of colour into her cheeks, and a rush of feeling into her voice. "Oh, there is! Only I can't do it without you."

She had twisted sideways in her chair and was looking full at him, her eyes were dark, her hands framing her flushed face.

"I'm afraid—" said Eustace.

The great idea glowed suddenly into fervour. Valentine sprang up and ran to him.

"Don't you see? Oh, Eustace, how stupid you are! You can't stop helping all those poor people—you can't let them go on living in those dreadful houses!"

"I can't help it," said Eustace rather bitterly. "You can't help it either."

"But we can." She took his arm and shook it. "We *can* help it! If we get married, you can go on pulling down houses just as if—"

The bell of the flat rang a loud, insistent peal. Valentine let go of Eustace's arm and looked involuntarily towards the door. Eustace began to say something, and stopped. They heard Mrs. Fleming pass through the hall, humming in a cracked, flat voice; and they heard the front door open. Next moment the dining-room door opened too. Mrs. Fleming appeared for a moment with a very dirty duster in her hand.

"Miss 'Ill," she said, and stood aside with reluctance.

Katherine Hill came into the room.

## Chapter Nineteen

To KATHERINE the little domestic scene looked like a picture painted on the air; it appeared to have no actuality. The two chairs pushed back from the breakfast table; Eustace and this very pretty girl standing together. She could not relate this in any way to the Eustace Ryven with whom she was familiar. The picture was related only to the voice that had answered her in the night—a girl's voice—this girl's voice.

She came forward quite composedly. No one, to look at her, would have guessed that the room and its inmates trembled before her eyes like a mirage that is shaken by the first breath of a storm.

Valentine looked at her and thought, "Why is she so unhappy?" And as the thought went through her mind, Katherine was speaking:

"I tried to get you on the telephone last night. You didn't sign Barrett's cheque. I thought it would save time if I brought it down. He's rather in a state about it as he's got some big cash payments to make to-day."

Valentine slipped out of the room. Katherine affected her strangely; she felt attracted, repelled, and startled. The thing that startled her was the smouldering something which she had seen for an instant as Katherine's glance passed over her. It was not anger, dislike—hatred even; but a spark of fury ready to break into a blaze. She ran down the passage to the kitchen, and felt safer.

When she was gone and Eustace was bending his long back to sign the cheque, Katherine said abruptly,

"Who's that?"

He finished his signature, "Eustace Carrington Ryven," and said without looking up,

"My cousin."

"She answered the telephone last night?"

"I suppose so. There—that's all right. Only don't blot it—the ink's wet."

Miss Hill took the cheque, folded it, and put it away, all in a series of jerks. The air about her still shook.

"Is she staying here?"

He moved away from the table impatiently.

"She ran away from my mother and came here last night when I was out. It's very awkward."

"Very." Her tone was cool and dry, her eyes just not aflame— waiting. "It will provide you with an excellent excuse for marrying her."

Eustace turned a startled face on her—startled, and angry.

"Katherine!"

"Eustace—"

"Katherine!"

"Are you not going to marry her?" She said it because the pain at her heart was so intolerable. Now he would contradict her—*now*.

She waited in that shaken room. Two chairs—a man—and a girl— Eustace and the cousin who had robbed him—Eustace and the cousin he was going to marry. She hadn't really believed it; she had only been afraid of it. No—she had never known what fear was until this moment. She waited until fear had turned into a burning pain. There was no fire in the eyes that she turned to him; only the black, blank certainty of pain.

"You're going to marry her."

"Perhaps—Katherine—I don't know." The words came indistinctly. He wasn't looking at her. Then, in a louder voice, "I don't know. Why do you ask? I—" He broke off and turned away, leaning with his elbow on the mantelshelf and staring down at the empty grate.

Katherine picked up the bag which she had laid on the table. She went to the door and took hold of the handle. Then the impulse that had carried her there failed. There was a minute of silence. It seemed like a long time. Eustace spoke again:

"One can't always—think of oneself."

"Oneself?" said Katherine Hill. Her voice was low and shaken; there was a protest, and a question in it—an anguished protest, and a hopeless question.

Eustace did not turn.

"Oneself—or one's—other self. Harden said last night—" His voice failed. Then he said very indistinctly, "One can buy happiness—too dear—at least I *think* so."

Katherine set her back against the door and lifted her head. An open battle would never find her without courage. She spoke quite quietly, but with a hard, determined ring in her voice:

"I don't. There isn't any price that would be too great."

"I think—there is."

"You think so because you want to think so, or else because you've got all your values wrong. You're making money mean too much, and yourself too little. What is it going to profit you or anyone else— or *anyone else*—if you gain the whole world and lose your own soul?"

Eustace experienced a faint antagonism. If Katherine had wept, or if she had continued to look at him with miserable, stormy eyes, his heart would have softened to her, though his resolve would not have weakened; but at the hint of dictation he felt himself stiffening to fight her. And then all at once it came over him how strange it was that he and Katherine should find themselves in the midst of such a scene as this. They had worked together for four years, and in those four years of work and friendship not a word of love had ever passed between them. Not a word? Scarcely even a thought—or if a thought at all, one so near to being unconscious that it could only be realized in retrospect. Yet now they were talking as if they were lovers taking an agonized farewell. There was no tie to break; yet something was breaking as they looked at each other now.

Katherine said, *"Eustace,"* and the dominant tone angered him again.

"I've no right to think of myself," he said.

"You're letting yourself be obsessed by the money." Her hand tightened on the door-knob. "Money's like that—it hypnotizes people, and they think that nothing can be done without it. But the greatest things in the world—all the really great things—have been done by people who had no money." She paused, and said with a sort of desperate force, "That's true, Eustace."

He looked at her, frowning.

"Talking won't rebuild a slum."

"There is a faith that moves mountains."

"I haven't got it," said Eustace wearily.

"We might find it together. I'm going to say what I think, because if I don't, I shall feel a coward all my life—and I'd rather be dead. I believe there's no limit to what two people could do together if they were one and—happy—and willing to give their happiness."

Eustace looked away.

"My dear, that's talk. I want to pull down Parkin Row. Talk won't do it." There was a tired finality in his voice.

The passion went out of Katherine. She could have fought anger, but not this weary conviction. Her battle was lost, but she lacked the strength to go. Going would hurt so much. She had no strength left to endure it.

# Chapter Twenty

In the kitchen Valentine sat on the dresser and watched Mrs. Fleming wash the floor. She slopped nearly a pailful of water over it, and then splashed in it with the dirtiest cloth that Valentine had ever seen. She called it a rubber, but she didn't rub with it; she just splashed. Valentine was glad that her feet were well above the mess.

"Lor! It's 'ot!" said Mrs. Fleming, pushing back her hair with her wet hand. "But I'm never one that skimps me work, 'owever 'ot it may be."

"Mrs. Fleming," said Valentine, "did you love your husband very much when you married him?"

Mrs. Fleming sat back on her heels. She had a sharp pointed nose, red where the bone showed through, a sharp pointed chin, and pale determined lips; her eyes were pale too, and her mouse-coloured hair was extraordinarily wispy.

"Love?" she said. Then she repeated the word in a higher key, "Love? I'm a respectable woman I am."

"Yes," said Valentine, "of course you are. But didn't you love him very much—I mean when you tried to get him away from the ginger-haired girl—didn't you love him then?"

Mrs. Fleming was plainly scandalized.

"I wanted to do 'er down, and do 'er down I did—*proper*. Wished she'd never been born, I should say, by the time she'd 'eard what I'd got to say about 'ussies that tries to come between a pore soft 'eaded chap and his lawful young lady. I put it across 'er straight, I did. But as for a lot of fancy rubbidge about *love*—why, I don't 'old with it. An' if you'll take my advice, miss, you'll put all such nonsense out of your 'ead."

"Do you think it's nonsense?"

Mrs. Fleming turned the pail upside down with a clatter.

"Empty-'eaded rubbidge is what I should call it. When a girl's looking for a 'usband, what she wants is a steady young man that's taking good money an' that'll bring it 'ome to 'er of a Saturday night. She don't want one of the matey sort, because that sort's just naturally bound to 'ave a drink with every pal 'e meets. What she wants is someone who'll do as she tells 'im. 'E may kick at first but it's my belief as a woman that gives 'er mind to it—"

The front door bell rang very loudly, and Mrs. Fleming jumped.

"Oh, lor! An' me with me 'ands like this! I s'pose, miss, you wouldn't go to the door for me?"

Valentine jumped down on to a chair, made a spring for a dry patch near the door, and ran down the passage.

The bell pealed again as she reached the hall, and as if it had summoned her, Katherine Hill came out of the dining-room. She was alone. She held her head very high, her face colourless, her eyes burned out. She looked at Valentine, and Valentine looked at her. Then Katherine went to the door and opened it.

Mrs. Ryven was just lifting her hand to ring for the third time. Katherine walked past her as if she had never seen her before, and Helena took a step forward and saw Valentine.

She said, "Thank God!" and came in, shutting the door behind her.

The relief was overwhelming. The last few hours had been really dreadful ones. They had taken the smooth colour from her cheeks and set dragging lines at the corners of her eyes and mouth. She looked travel-worn, and her hat was a little crooked.

Valentine was struck to the heart. She said, "Oh, Aunt Helena!" and then, "I didn't think you'd mind."

"Not mind? Are you quite a fool? Where have you been?" She spoke roughly, shaken out of her well-bred calm. Now that the strain was over, she was trembling with anger. "Where's Eustace?" she said, and went towards the dining-room.

Valentine felt a dreadful sense of guilt. Aunt Helena was all dusty, and her hat was crooked, and she had a smut on her cheek. And she was angry—she was certainly very, very angry. It was dreadful.

"I had to come—" She faltered. "I had to come and see Eustace."

Mrs. Ryven stopped with her hand on the door.

"And why, pray?"

"I had to. I didn't feel I could wait. I had to find out if he would marry me."

Helena Ryven was not often taken aback; but she was at a disadvantage. She gasped.

"Eustace! You!"

And then, unbelievably, she felt the sharpest stab of triumph.

"What do you mean, Valentine?" she said in a controlled voice.

Valentine's eyes were wet.

"If we get married, I can give it back, and he needn't stop pulling down houses."

Mrs. Ryven spoke lower.

"You said that to him?"

"Yes, Aunt Helena."

Lower still, because she could not keep her breath steady: "What did he say?"

"He didn't say anything. *She* came."

"Katherine Hill?"

The door was opened from the inside. Eustace stood there, tall, pale, and severe. Mrs. Ryven passed into the room and shut the door.

Valentine did not know what to do. She didn't want to go back to the kitchen. There was a chair on the other side of the hall. She went over to it and sat down.

She could hear Mrs. Ryven and Eustace talking in the dining-room, first one voice and then the other, but no words. There was something odd about hearing people's voices when you couldn't see them; it made you feel lonely. Yet on the island she had not really been lonely. She had been alone. There was a difference between being alone and being lonely.

She found herself thinking about Katherine Hill. When Katherine passed her in the hall, it was like a cloud of unhappiness going by. She went on thinking about Katherine.

Presently Eustace came out of the dining-room. He went down the passage towards the kitchen, spoke to Mrs. Fleming, and came back again. Valentine got up, and he shook hands with her politely, and said, "Good-bye—I'm afraid I've got to go out. Mrs. Fleming will look after you and my mother." Then he went away. Valentine watched the door shut behind him.

Helena Ryven took her back to Holt after she had had a rest and a bath. She told her that she was too tired for conversation, and she let Valentine see how entirely she was to blame for her fatigue.

After they arrived at Holt Mrs. Ryven went to her own room. The feeling of being in disgrace got stronger and stronger.

After tea Mrs. Ryven reappeared. She was now sufficiently restored to point out to Valentine how badly she had behaved and how much trouble she had given. Valentine said she was very sorry. She was wondering very much about Eustace. Most of the time that Aunt Helena was talking, she could not help wondering about Eustace. He had shaken hands with her and gone away. He had never said whether he was going to marry her or not. It was very difficult to attend to what Aunt Helena was saying. But of course she was sorry. She said so. Then she said,

"Am I going to marry Eustace? He didn't say."

Mrs. Ryven made an impatient movement. Really the girl was too impossible.

"My dear Valentine, you mustn't say things like that."

"But I want to know. I asked him, and he didn't say."

"Valentine," said Helena Ryven, "I want to ask you very seriously not to talk like that. It is not fair to yourself, and it is certainly not fair to Eustace, who would be horrified. Marriage is a serious thing. Girls don't ask men to marry them, my dear. Don't you know that?"

Valentine coloured a little, as a child colours when it is found fault with. They were in the drawing-room, with the windows open to the sunny evening air, Helena upright in a chintz-covered armchair, Valentine on the window-seat with the sun on her curls and on her bare brown neck. She had changed the green dress for a rose-coloured one.

"Don't they ever?"

"Nice girls don't," said Mrs. Ryven. She still looked tired, but she had recovered her air of superior calm.

"*But,*" said Valentine, "*but*, Aunt Helena—Eustace didn't come to Holt. And if he didn't come, he couldn't ask me to marry him—could he?"

"I think, my dear, we won't talk about that. In fact, I want you to promise me that you won't talk about it to anyone." She paused and added, "Eustace is coming down to-morrow for the week-end." Her voice was quite smooth, but her heart was full of triumph. Eustace was coming back to Holt. The week-end was merely a symbol. She looked at Valentine almost kindly.

Valentine meanwhile was considering. If Eustace was coming for the week-end, perhaps he would tell her whether they were going to be married. She felt that she would like to know. It would be nice if he came and they were all friends. And if she was engaged, she would have an engagement ring. And when she was married, she would have a wedding dress, and a veil, and orange-blossoms. It was very exciting. A soft, pleased colour replaced the flush that Helena Ryven's rebuke had brought to her cheeks. She fixed an interested look on Helena's face.

"When you were married, did you have orange-blossoms?"

Mrs. Ryven lifted her eyebrows.

"Yes—it was the fashion."

"Isn't it the fashion now?"

"I believe so."

After a pause Valentine began again.

"Did you love Uncle Edmund very much when you were married?"

"People don't ask that sort of question, Valentine."

"Don't they? I asked Mrs. Fleming, and she said she was a respectable woman. Isn't love respectable?"

"I don't think it's very nice to talk about it."

"Mrs. Fleming said she didn't hold with love. Don't you hold with it either?"

"My dear! What an expression! You shouldn't talk to women like that."

Valentine moved a little, following the shifting sun.

"In books people who are going to be married love each other very much. But Mrs. Fleming said that all a girl wanted was a steady young man who didn't go into public houses. Eustace wouldn't go into a public house—would he? Is he steady?"

Mrs. Ryven got up.

"My dear, you really must not quote the charwoman to me. When Eustace marries, his wife will be a very lucky woman."

## Chapter Twenty-One

EUSTACE CAME DOWN next day, and stayed for a week, during which Mrs. Ryven kept the house full of people. There were people to lunch and people to tennis, and there were two rather stately dinner parties.

Helena saw to it that Valentine wore her prettiest frocks. She praised her with a sort of cool candour, and was pleased to find the neighbourhood favourably impressed. When all is said and done, a pretty girl with a romantic story can hardly fail to make a good impression.

Kind Lady Needham declared herself charmed with "poor Maurice's daughter." "And surely, my dear Helena, Eustace is, may I say—I'm sure I'm such a very old friend—attracted. What an excellent thing it would be!"

The blunt Miss Bulger—Agneta Bulger, the golfer—wrung Mrs. Ryven's hand and said in hearty tones, "Good for you, Helena, my dear! I always said you were a sport. Are we to congratulate Eustace?"

Mrs. Ryven allowed herself to say, "Not yet." But she smiled.

Even Mrs. Wendle's sharp tongue had nothing worse to say than, "Well, I congratulate you on *la belle sauvage*. Is it your doing? Or did she reach you civilized?"

"Valentine is very well educated," said Mrs. Ryven. "I believe Mr. Bowden was a very distinguished man."

"Edward Bowden? Oh, yes—I believe he was. My brother James knew him—a distinguished crank. Well, I'll say this for the girl, she doesn't look like a blue-stocking. Are she and Eustace going to make a match of it? Or is that too obvious?"

This time Mrs. Ryven did not smile. She said Valentine was a dear girl, and she allowed her glance to rest upon her affectionately.

Valentine only saw Timothy once all the week and then only for a few minutes. He came in to say that he and Lil were going up to town to stay with his mother's people. There had been a letter from Jack Harding, and Lil was to go out as soon as she could get ready.

"Is she pleased?" asked Valentine.

Timothy nodded.

"Harding's a good chap—he'll make her a good husband."

"Is he steady?"

Timothy laughed; the question came so primly.

"Very."

"That's what matters most," said Valentine earnestly.

"It's not a bad thing."

"It matters more than being in love. Being in love is only in books—isn't it?"

*"Valentine—"* said Mrs. Ryven in a warning voice; she had caught a word or two. She got up and joined them.

"Aunt Helena doesn't want me to talk about love," said Valentine.

Timothy said, "Shame!"

Afterwards he was to wish that he had walked Valentine away from Helena and got to the bottom of that prim, anxious questioning. He went away, and, busy and preoccupied as he was, there were moments all through the week when he saw Valentine's blue eyes shadowed and earnest. They had no business to hold a shadow in their depths.

At the end of the week Eustace's engagement to Valentine was given out. They had been together continually, and so much in public, that the announcement took no one by surprise. Valentine found herself treated with an unvarying grave politeness which she supposed to be the proper thing.

Eustace never alluded to her visit to town. On the last day of his stay he asked her to marry him, and when she said "Yes," he kissed her forehead somewhere near her left eyebrow. And then he went and told Aunt Helena, and Aunt Helena kissed Valentine's cheek.

It wasn't at all like a proposal in a book. Eustace didn't say, "I love you," or, "I can't live without you," or even, "Darling!" He said, "Valentine, will you marry me?" and she said, "Yes." And then neither of them seemed to be able to think of anything else to say, so he kissed her forehead, and then went and told Aunt Helena. It was all very solemn and depressing. But she began to cheer up after he went away.

That night she dreamt about the island.

Timothy heard the news when he got back. It staggered him. He had not always admired Helena, but he had not thought her capable of this. It shocked him a good deal. He went to Holt with a smouldering anger under his usual cheery manner. As luck would have it, he found Valentine alone, and some of his anger changed into surprise when he looked at her. She wore a pink dress. Her eyes shone, and her cheeks blushed. He didn't quite know what he had expected, but not this.

"Timothy, I'm engaged! I've got a ring—it's just come—Eustace sent it. It's a lovely pearl. Look at it! Isn't it lovely? I'm so glad you've come—I did so want to show it to someone. Isn't it lovely?"

"Top-hole," said Timothy.

Valentine gave a gurgle of laughter.

"Oh, what a lovely word! May I learn it?"

"I give it you for your very own," said Timothy—"with my blessing. You can have it for a wedding present." He smiled, but his eyes were intent; they saw nothing but a child's pleasure.

"Six people have written to me already to say how lucky I am. They all say things about Eustace. One of them said he was one in a thousand. Do you think that any of them will write to Eustace and tell him that I am one in a thousand?"

"You're one in ten million," said Timothy, and he said it lightly; but his heart contracted.

"Am I? Am I really?"

"Yes," said Timothy. His lips were stiff. One in ten million? She was the only one in the world. There was no other Valentine.

He heard Helena's voice in the hall. He said quickly, "Are you happy, Valentine? Are you happy?" And Valentine said, "Yes."

Then the door opened.

Valentine was happy for a week. Everybody she met said nice things. Aunt Helena was pleased with her. She had a lovely ring. And the houses in Parkin Row were going to be pulled down.

At the end of the week Eustace came down again, and as soon as Eustace came down, she began to stop feeling happy. He kissed her when they met and when he went away, and when he said good-morning and when he said good-night. He nearly always kissed the left side of her forehead. He had to bend down a long way to do it because he was so tall.

Valentine began to wonder why people in books liked being kissed. She didn't like it at all. She asked Helena Ryven.

"Will Eustace go on kissing me after we're married?"

"My dear, I do wish you wouldn't say things like that."

"But will he?"—with mournful persistence.

Mrs. Ryven's conscience gave her a sharp stab. She said, "My dear, what a lot of nonsense you talk!" and went out of the room.

Valentine began to dream about the island nearly every night. She was always alone there. During the long evenings when she sat in the drawing-room between Aunt Helena knitting, and Eustace immersed in a book, she found herself thinking with longing of bed-time; because when she went to bed she would sleep, and be alone on the island—hot sun overhead; a wide blue sky, and a wide blue sea; the shimmer of the sun on the sea, gold on blue; and no one—no one at all—to call her, or to kiss her, or to say "Valentine" in the voice that meant she had done something that "wasn't done."

## Chapter Twenty-Two

EUSTACE AND VALENTINE were to be married in September. "Long engagements are such a mistake," Helena wrote to Ida Cobb, who read the letter aloud at breakfast in the intervals of pouring out tea. She made the worst tea in England, as her son and daughter continually assured her. Henry Cobb did not complain, because in twenty-five years you can get used to anything—even dish-cloth tea.

Mrs. Cobb read Helena's letter aloud.

"Long engagements!" she said—fifty years ago she would have been said to have bridled—"Long engagements indeed! She knows that the only chance to get them married at all is to get them married quick."

"Oh—scandal-monger!" said Reggie.

Henry Cobb looked mildly over the top of *The Times*.

"My dear, it's a most suitable marriage. Hullo! I see that ass Merrydew has been writing to the papers again—traffic noises this time—complains he can't sleep at his club in the afternoon because of the flappers' hoot—wants to have all women under thirty refused a driver's licence—"

"Read your paper, Henry!" said Mrs. Cobb. "Helena's absolutely unblushing about this marriage. I loathe suitable marriages."

Reggie made a note on his cuff.

"That's to remind me to make an unsuitable one, darling. What shall it be? A dope-fiend? Or the dustman's daughter? I live to please! Meanwhile another dollop out of the garbage can!" He passed his cup.

Mrs. Cobb said "Reggie!" in a perfunctory way.

Marjory leaned forward, took a lump of sugar, and began to crunch it.

"Must have something to take the taste away," she murmured. "That last cup was *foul*. You know," she went on, with both elbows on the table, "you know, Eustace is all right if you get far enough away from him. His feelings are like the waves that that wireless man was talking about the other night—if you're too close there's nothing doing; but they come down hot and strong in Australia."

"You've got it all wrong," murmured Reggie. "Never mind—the female brain should never be overtaxed."

Marjory took no notice.

"That's Eustace all over—I thought of him at once. He'll freeze that poor kid till she might as well be Canterbury lamb, because she'll be living with him. But if she was in a slum, he'd love her like anything. He *does* love his old slums, you know, and if Valentine was ragged and dirty, and hadn't got an 'h' to her name, she'd come in for her share. As it is, I'm sorry for her."

Henry Cobb turned a sheet.

"My dear, that's rather vehement. Everyone isn't alike, you know—fortunately." He gave his cup a little push. "Has your mother any more tea?"

"If you call it tea," said Reggie gloomily.

"I shall ask Valentine to come and stay," said Mrs. Cobb with the air of one who burns her bridges. "Helena probably won't let her come," she added.

Helena let Valentine come for three days. Eustace's last week-end had not been a great success. She told herself that she would be thankful when the wedding was over. Meanwhile it wouldn't do to have Valentine going about looking droopy, and Marjory could take her to have her riding habit fitted.

Valentine found the three days full of new impressions. Everybody was kind. They said the oddest things to each other, and they weren't a bit polite; but nobody minded. She called Mrs. Cobb Aunt Ida, and Mr. Cobb Uncle Henry. They weren't really her uncle and aunt, but they said it was all the same thing. And Aunt Ida came into her room after she was in bed and asked her whether she'd got everything she wanted, and tucked her up, and patted her shoulder. Mr. Cobb called her "My dear." It was quite a different sort of "My dear" to the one that Aunt Helena said. When Aunt Helena said "My dear," it nearly always meant that she wasn't pleased.

Reggie teased her. He pretended to be frightfully in love with her, and he brought her silly presents that made everyone laugh—a little black woolly dog which jumped when you pressed a spring; and an awful black spider with scarlet eyes, which he hid in her table-napkin; and once, inside a great sheet of tissue paper, what looked like a bouquet until she opened it and found an enormous purple cabbage.

"You're not to torment her," said Mrs. Cobb with the fond smile which she kept for Reggie.

"Torment her?" Reggie was all outraged innocence. "I love her passionately. She's going to throw Eustace over and fly with me—aren't you, ducky?" Then he went down on his knees in the middle of the carpet. "Star of my existence—elope!"

Valentine giggled softly; Reggie looked so awfully like a monkey when he made that face.

"Why?" she said.

"Because I am beautiful," said Reggie, first rolling his eyes, and then bringing them to rest in a squint. "Beautiful," he continued, "not only as regards my classic features, but with the inner, hidden beauty of a noble soul—and if you don't believe me, ask my mo-o-other. Who should know better than a mo-o-other? Haven't I got a beautiful nature, Mum—from a mere babe? You ask her to show you the photograph of me in my vest at one-year-two-months-five-days-four-hours-six-minutes-and-thirty-seconds looking soulful!"

*"Reggie!"* said Mrs. Cobb helplessly.

Valentine would have loved her visit if it could have gone on for ever; but three days of it gave her a dreadfully lonely feeling. They were all so kind. It was like being cold and coming into a warm room just for a minute—you didn't know how cold you were until you came into the warm room, and just as you began to get a little warmer, you had to go out into the cold again. It made it worse. It made it much worse.

The night before she went back, Marjory came into her room and sat on the end of her bed in the dark. It wasn't really dark, because the light from the lamp-post over the way shone in on the ceiling and made a pattern there. It was a pattern of leaves crossed by the window-bars, and the rest of the room was in a sort of dark dusk. All she could see of Marjory was a shadow that was a little denser than the other shadows.

Marjory sat cross-legged on the end of the bed and said in her cool little voice,

"Why are you going to marry Eustace? You don't really want to."

Valentine did not say that she wanted to; she said, "I must."

"Who's been stuffing you up with that? Aunt Helena?"

"Oh, no."

"I think it's 'oh, yes.' You little fool, she wants Holt for Eustace—quite natural, of course, and I'm not blaming her—but why in the name of the Parade of Wooden Soldiers are you playing her game?"

"I must."

"Why must you?"

Valentine sat bolt upright in bed. She told Marjy all about Parkin Row and the baby who hadn't enough to eat.

"And you see, Marjy, it doesn't really matter about Eustace and me—we're only two people; but there are such a lot of people in Parkin Row."

"Does Eustace kiss you?" said Marjy abruptly.

"Yes."

"Often?"

"When he says good-morning—and when he says good-night."

"Do you mind?"

"Yes," said Valentine in the dark.

"Then, my dear kid, how on earth are you going to marry him?"

"Perhaps"—rather falteringly—"perhaps he won't kiss me when we're married."

"Perhaps he will," said Marjory grimly.

"I asked Aunt Helena, and she said I oughtn't to talk about it, and she went away—she does, you know."

Marjory had a vivid picture of Helena Ryven passing by on the other side. She took a long breath.

"Look here, baby—" she began.

## Chapter Twenty-Three

THE EVENING AFTER Valentine got back from her visit to the Cobbs she startled Helena Ryven by asking suddenly,

"Couldn't I go back to the island?

They had finished dinner. The curtains were still undrawn. The daylight was all gone away into a grey mist, and it was much too dark to read or sew. Helena Ryven sat near the window winding wool, whilst

Valentine crouched all in a heap on the window-seat and watched the mist swallow up the woods tree by tree.

Then, suddenly,

"Couldn't I go back to the island?"

Helena was startled out of her routine.

"My dear, how foolish! I think you had better ring for lights."

"No—I mean it, Aunt Helena—I really do mean it. You're so clever. Isn't there any way that I can go back to the island and let Eustace have everything? I didn't want to take anything away—and if I could go back—"

Mrs. Ryven put down her wool and got up.

"No one can ever go back," she said. She crossed the room, switched on the lights, and rang the bell. "You know, Valentine, you really ought not to talk like that—I've told you so before. It's not fair to Eustace."

When the lights sprang on, the misty woods seemed to have been suddenly overwhelmed by the dark; they were there one moment, and the next a black curtain had fallen and blotted them out.

Valentine went on looking into the dark until Bolton came in to shut up the room. When he had gone again, she tried to say in the bright, coldly lighted room what she had not been able to say in the kind half-light. But she only got as far as,

"Isn't there any way?"

Helena Ryven looked up, and down again. Valentine had come back paler than she went; she had been crying. Helena's conscience pricked her, and she silenced it angrily. An attack of stage fright—lots of girls had it, and were happy enough afterwards. She spoke rather sharply.

"My dear Valentine, what is the matter? Do occupy yourself! I can't bear to see people doing nothing. There's all that brown wool to be wound if you want something to do."

Valentine gave up trying to say what couldn't be said. You couldn't say things to Aunt Helena; she wouldn't let you. It was like trying to open a door when you could feel that the person inside was pushing against you with all their might. There could never be an open door between her and Helena Ryven, because Helena would always hold the door against her. She wound the brown wool in silence whilst Helena had angry thoughts about the Cobbs. What had they been saying to upset her like this?

It was after this that Valentine began to go up to London once a week. She told Eustace that she wanted to do something for the poor people; and he said, not very encouragingly, that she was too inexperienced to be of any use. Afterwards he wrote and told her that if she wanted to see something of what was being done, Mrs. Bell, who was an experienced worker, would take her round and explain things. Mrs. Ryven said she did not think that Valentine would be any good at social work, and that she would be better occupied learning how to keep house. However, if Valentine wished to go, she saw no objection; it would at any rate get her into the way of going about by herself. So Valentine went up once a week.

Every time Eustace came down for the week-end, she felt that she must run away. She had dreams in which she ran, and ran, and ran, and ran, and ran. But when she went up to town in the middle of the week and saw Parkin Row, and places that were worse than Parkin Row, she knew that she couldn't run away.

Mrs. Bell was a useful and practical worker, plump, cheerful, and excessively matter-of-fact. Valentine asked her about Katherine Hill, and was told that Miss Hill had got a place as secretary to Lewis Elderthal, the eminent philanthropist.

"Of course her experience with Mr. Ryven would make her invaluable," said Mrs. Bell in a tone which meant that she didn't like Katherine Hill.

"I thought perhaps—now—she would be working for Eustace again."

Mrs. Bell changed the subject.

One day towards the end of August Valentine was waiting in the outer room of Eustace's office. He had kept the office on after all, but he had not yet engaged another secretary, so the room was empty except for Valentine. Eustace and Mrs. Bell had gone to a committee meeting, but Mrs. Bell was coming back. It was a cloudy, stuffy afternoon. The room was airless and smelt of varnish. Valentine hated the office. The inner room seemed full of Eustace, even when he wasn't there; there didn't seem to be any place for her. Mrs. Bell told her constantly that she was not of the stuff of which social workers are made; she turned white and trembled when people described horrible things; and once she had actually disgraced herself by crying. Eustace ought to be marrying someone quite different—efficient, practical, older. Mrs. Bell didn't say this, but it was quite obvious that she thought it.

Valentine herself had stopped thinking. She was going to be married in a fortnight, and she couldn't think about it. It was like being carried down a rushing river towards a precipice; you couldn't stop, and you couldn't save yourself, and you couldn't think.

She was standing at the dusty window watching the people go by in the street below, when the door opened. She turned round and saw Katherine Hill standing on the threshold.

It was curious that her feeling should have been one so near pleasure, for when she had seen Katherine before she had been afraid. Now she wasn't afraid. She felt the same attraction that she had felt before, but this time it was unmixed.

Katherine looked at her in some surprise and stood where she was.

"I came to see Mr. Ryven's secretary."

"He hasn't got one," said Valentine.

"Is he here?"

"No."

Katherine came in and shut the door.

"Are you expecting him?"

"No—I'm waiting for Mrs. Bell."

Katherine had a dispatch-case in her hand. She set it down on the table.

"I'm working for Mr. Elderthal now. I wanted to ask Mr. Ryven's permission to show him the estimates we had for the last block of model buildings." She paused slightly and said in the same tone, "You are Valentine Ryven, aren't you?"

"Yes."

There was a longer pause. Valentine felt as if Katherine's thoughts were beating against her like waves. She felt as if she could love Katherine very much, as if they were meant to love each other; but something held them apart, and there came into her mind the line she had once read aloud about the unplumbed, salt, estranging sea. She looked at Katherine's square, strong face, with the storm-coloured eyes that made it so alive, and she wished very much that it had been the face of her friend. She stood there just looking, not speaking; and Katherine said:

"You haven't had a very long engagement."

"Aunt Helena thinks long engagements are a mistake."

"I see."

She was still looking at Valentine, and Valentine wondered whether she could see how unhappy she was, and how much afraid. The little bare room that smelt of varnish seemed all at once to be quite full of her unhappiness. There was something about Katherine that made you see things which you had only felt before. She became aware that Katherine was unhappy too—not with her own shrinking unhappiness, but with a kind of stormy misery, bitter and tragic and strong.

"Why are you unhappy?"

Valentine shook her head. If she spoke, the stinging tears would brim over and roll down her cheeks; she mustn't cry. She shook her head.

"You *are* unhappy," said Katherine in her deep voice.

Valentine said "Yes," on a soft, trembling breath.

"My dear—why? Doesn't he love you?"

Valentine shook her head again. She put her hands together and let them hold each other; they were cold although the day was so hot.

"Is that why you are unhappy?" The faintest shadow of a smile moved Katherine's lips as she spoke.

Valentine shook her head again.

"I don't love him," she said, and the tears that she had been holding back overflowed. She put up her hands and wiped them away.

"Then why," said Katherine with a gentle persistence, "why are you marrying him?"

Valentine's wet hands dropped from her face.

"I've got to give the money back—somehow—because of Parkin Row—and the other dreadful places. I can't give it back unless I marry him—everybody says there isn't any other way. It doesn't really matter about my being unhappy. I oughtn't to feel as if it mattered—I don't when I've been seeing very poor, hungry people. That's why I come up here. When I see them I feel as if I can do it."

"And when you don't see them?" said Katherine drily.

"Then I don't feel as if I *can*."

There was a pause. Then Katherine laughed.

"It sounds jolly for Eustace—doesn't it? The sunbeam in the home and all that sort of thing! My good child, *have* you thought of what it's going to be like for Eustace?"

It was quite obvious that Valentine had not. Her wet eyes filled with ingenuous surprise.

"No," said Katherine, "I see you haven't. I thought not. You're the virgin martyr. But what about Eustace, marrying a girl he doesn't care for, and who doesn't care for him? What's it going to do to him? ... You don't know? Well, I do. He's never had as many human feelings as he ought to have. His mother brought him up in a sort of glass refrigerator. She thinks it's rather coarse to have feelings—and Eustace would hate to be coarse. Well, if he marries you, he'll settle down in a nice refined, cold hell and do without feelings altogether. And that will be so good for him—won't it?"

Katherine never had very much colour, but as she spoke, her face became quite white. Valentine no longer wished to cry. She felt as if she had had cold water thrown over her. She said,

"Eustace asked me to marry him. He wants to build those houses. He has to think about all the poor people."

"What a well-matched pair you ought to be—both thinking of others! The bother is that I don't see how you're going to set other people right when you're all wrong yourselves. Now I'm not bothering about Parkin Row, or you—I'm bothering about Eustace."

"Are you fond of him?" asked Valentine.

Katherine laughed.

"I think we may take it that I'm 'fond' of him. I expect Mrs. Ryven taught you that word, didn't she? 'Fond' is about as far as she'll go. 'Love' would shock her to the core."

Valentine looked at her wide-eyed.

"Do you love Eustace?"

Katherine's face changed.

"Oh, you *child*!" she said, and said no more.

Valentine flushed.

"No, I'm not—not now. But I wanted to know. I wish—oh, I do wish that you could marry Eustace!"

"Yes. If it hadn't been for Parkin Row and you, I might—I might—" She choked, caught Valentine suddenly by the wrists, and said in a low muttering tone, "Break it off—break it off! Give us all a chance!"

Valentine felt those waves beating against her. They were waves of passionate anger, passionate love, passionate pity. She felt as if she must be broken by them. But she didn't break. If she could be free—if they could all be free—if she needn't marry Eustace—if she needn't marry anyone—if she could go back to the island—if there were any way out. There wasn't any way out. She must go on. The waves couldn't break her.

She looked straight into Katherine's eyes, and she said,

"I can't break it off."

Mrs. Bell came in on the silence that followed, just a little out of breath and looking at her watch.

"I'm so sorry—I was kept. You know what committees are—people begin talking when they haven't really got anything to say. Oh, how do you do, Miss Hill? You're quite a stranger."

She turned back again to Valentine.

"Do you know, I'm afraid you'll have to catch your train. Mr. Ryven said particularly that his mother wanted you to catch the four-thirty. He asked me to see you into a taxi. Good-bye, Miss Hill. Are you waiting for Mr. Ryven? I'm afraid he'll be at least half an hour."

Valentine followed her down the stairs. Half way down she turned with an inarticulate murmur of excuse and ran back. As she pushed open the door, she had a glimpse, just one glimpse, of the face that Katherine wore when she was alone. She did not know that anything could hurt so much.

She ran up to her, and Katherine said,

"What is it?"

"I came back—" Valentine stopped. Then she said, "Oh, Katherine!" and kissed her, and ran out of the room again and down the stairs.

# Chapter Twenty-Four

LIL CAME BACK to pack up before she sailed. She had been away three weeks, and for most of that time Timothy had been away too. He had not seen Valentine since he had asked her if she was happy and she had said "Yes."

He was out when she came down to see Lil, and the two girls spent a long afternoon together. Every few minutes Lil was called to the telephone, or had a note to write, or a parcel to open. The room was full of tissue paper and half-packed boxes. Lil declared herself to be worn out, and looked radiant.

"Don't you mind going away alone?" said Valentine suddenly.

Lil laughed.

"Not with Jack at the other end."

"I remember—you said you wanted to be married. Do you really want to be married?"

"I want to marry Jack."

"Why?" said Valentine.

Lil stared at her with her bright blue eyes.

"Why do you suppose?"

"I don't know—that's why I asked."

"You didn't think of my being in love with him by any chance?"

"No," said Valentine, "because when I asked you, you just said that you wanted to get married."

"So I do. I want to get married because I'm crazy about Jack, and Jack's crazy about me. Why, good gracious, what d'you think it's been like being engaged all these years, with Jack away and everybody sneering and interfering, and Mrs. Ryven going on behind my back about my being a burden to Timothy?" She broke off with a hard, excited little laugh. "My goodness! D'you suppose I'd have stuck it out if I hadn't cared more for Jack than for the whole lot of them put together?"

Valentine considered this whilst she folded and packed two coats and skirts. Then she asked,

"Do you think it's wicked to marry someone you don't love?"

Lil looked at her sharply.

"I don't know about *wicked*. I couldn't do it myself—and I should say it was a mug's game unless you're the sort that doesn't mind things."

Timothy did not come home till Valentine had gone.

"She looks a perfect scarecrow," Lil told him, "I think your sister Helena ought to be ashamed of herself."

"What's the matter?" said Timothy in the most ordinary voice that he could manage.

"Eustace," said Miss Egerton succinctly.

When Lil sailed it wanted only a week to Valentine's wedding day. Timothy could not decently stay away any longer, neither would it be possible for him to escape the wedding. He presented his offering, and had the opportunity of seeing for himself that Valentine looked like someone in a dream, a very sorrowful dream. All her pretty colour was gone, there were dark smudges under her eyes, and she looked frightened.

He followed Helena to the window where she was marking off acceptances on the long list of wedding guests.

"What's the matter with her?" he said abruptly.

Mrs. Ryven raised her eyebrows.

"With whom?"

"Valentine." He had not known that it would be so hard to say her name.

"My dear Timothy, what should be the matter? What do you mean?"

"Look at her!" said Timothy.

Mrs. Ryven looked.

"She's rather pale. Weddings are hard work for the bride, you know. There were fifteen presents yesterday, and twenty to-day. And of course she hasn't had much practice in writing notes."

*"Notes!"* said Timothy. There was a tone of subdued anger in his voice.

His sister stiffened.

"I hope Lil is having a good voyage," she said.

"I was talking about Valentine," said Timothy. Then, after a pause, with a sort of muffled violence, "Helena—she looks damned unhappy."

That night Valentine went to sleep as soon as her head touched the pillow. It was like going down into deep water, slipping down into it and falling, falling, falling.

After a long time the dream began. She always dreamt about the island now. Sometimes she was bathing in the pool, and sometimes she was fishing, and sometimes she was stringing shells. To-night she came slowly up out of the dark water and opened her eyes with a little sigh. She was in the cavern, standing on the fine white sand at the water's edge. And someone had just called to her, for she was listening. She didn't know why she was listening or who had called, but it wasn't Edward. She was quite sure that it wasn't Edward.

She began to climb up out of the cavern, and then all at once she was under the palm-trees and the sun was shining very fierce and hot. And Edward was there, and he said, "Remember, you've given your word of honour." And then she woke up; and just as she woke up, someone called her again, and it wasn't Edward.

She sat up in bed with her eyes wide open, looking into the dark. It was so dark that she couldn't see where the windows were. There was only a soft black wall like the soft black waters of sleep.

She sat up very straight, looking into the dark and thinking about the dream. She had always been alone on the island. It was her island, her kingdom—her lost kingdom. It had been really hers, but she had lost it, and now she could only go back to it in a dream. But there had never been anyone there before except Edward. But it wasn't Edward who had called her—no, it wasn't Edward. She did not know who it was, but it wasn't Edward.

She began to think about Edward. She was glad that he had been there in her dream. What was it that he said? ... "Remember, you've given your word of honour." That was funny, because he had really said that to her once when she had signed the paper and he had put it away, and tied it up, and sealed it, and made her promise that she would never open it unless—She put up a hand to her throat quickly. Just what had she promised? It was five years ago. Just what had she signed? She had almost forgotten. But it was coming back. "Never to break the seals—never to open the packet or to let anyone else open it unless—" Yes—unless what? What was it exactly?—"Unless things are so bad that they can't be any worse, so bad that nothing can make them any worse." And Edward had said, "Remember, Valentine, you've given your word of honour." That was five years ago, and she hadn't thought about it for years, and might never have thought of it again if she had not heard Edward say those words in her dream.

She began to wonder what had happened to the packet. Austin had helped her pack as much as possible into her mother's old trunk, and when that wouldn't hold everything, he had fetched a canvas kit-bag and they had put a lot of papers and books into that. But everything had come to Holt. Barclay had bought her a new box at Honolulu, and the things that were in the kit-bag had been put into it and she had unpacked them all at Holt. But she hadn't seen the packet. She was quite sure she would have remembered it if she had seen it. It was about eight or nine inches long and four or five inches wide, and it was done up in brown paper tied with string and sealed with big blobs of green sealing wax that had come out of Edward's dispatch-box. She had brought the dispatch-box to Holt; it was in her dressing-room now.

She jumped up, put on the light, and opened the connecting door. She would just look and see, but she was sure the packet wasn't in the dispatch-box. She put her hand up to the switch, hesitated for a moment, and then pressed it down.

The light shone on the old battered case that Edward had taken out of the wrecked *Avronia*. She knew that it was nearly empty; she knew that the packet wasn't there; but she threw back the lid and lifted out the trays. There was no sealed packet. There was nothing—only, in the topmost tray, a little end of dark green sealing wax.

Valentine shut down the lid and put out the light.

It was three days later that Austin Muir rang up. Valentine was called to the telephone.

"Mr. Muir would like to speak to you, miss."

Valentine flushed with pleasure, and her heart began to beat. Aunt Helena, and Eustace, and her wedding, and her wedding presents seemed to have been closing in upon her day by day; they kept coming nearer and shutting her in, and shutting everyone else out. When Bolton said, "Mr. Muir would like to speak to you, miss," it was just as if a window had opened somewhere. It wasn't a door—she couldn't get out, she knew she couldn't get out; but it was a window, and you can look out of a window.

The telephone was in a little room all by itself. There was a table and a chair, and the telephone, and on the table the London directory and the local one.

Valentine came running into the room. She pulled the door to behind her, ran to the telephone, and said "Oh!" rather breathlessly.

Austin Muir said, "Hullo! Can I speak to Miss Ryven? Is that Miss Ryven?" and she gave a little unsteady laugh and said,

"No—it's Valentine." And then, "Oh, Austin—how nice it is to hear your voice again!"

Austin said "Oh—" in rather a taken aback sort of way. She knew just how he looked when he said "Oh—" like that—a little bit frowning, as if he wasn't pleased, as if it wasn't quite the proper thing for her to say "How nice!" She didn't care, and she said it again,

"Oh, Austin—how nice!"

Austin Muir cleared his throat.

"I rang you up—by the way, are you married yet? I haven't seen it in the paper, but you said, 'Not Miss Ryven.'"

"But I'm not—I'm Valentine—if I was married a hundred times, I'd be Valentine."

"Are you married?" said Austin a little blankly.

"No—no." She spoke as if she were pushing something away with all her might.

"But you're going to be?"

There was a pause before she said, "Yes." It was no use pushing things away.

"Well, I rang you up because I've got something of yours. I found it by accident the other day."

"What is it? How did you find it?"

"Well—a cousin of mine borrowed my kit-bag to take with him into camp. I turned it inside out to shake the dust out of it, and I found there was a slit in the lining and something had stuck there. It was a sealed packet addressed to you. You remember we used the bag to cart your things down the cliff?"

"Yes," said Valentine. "Yes."

Her heart was beating so hard that when she said "Yes," it sounded as if someone else was saying it a long way off. She didn't know why she should suddenly feel giddy with excitement. She sat down on the chair, and she heard herself say in a different voice, slow and distinct,

"Is it a little packet in brown paper—and is it sealed with green sealing wax?"

And she heard Austin Muir say, "Yes."

Valentine held the receiver very tight. Austin was saying something, but she wasn't really hearing what he said. She was listening to Edward. Five years ago, and Edward was saying very solemnly, "Only if things are so bad that nothing can possibly make them any worse. Remember, Valentine, you've given your word of honour."

Valentine was remembering.

Austin Muir's voice came to her, speaking with some impatience: "Are you there?"

"Yes."

"I couldn't get any reply—I thought we were cut off."

"No."

"Will this evening suit you?"

"I don't understand."

"Then we were cut off. I was saying that as I shall be passing within a mile or two of Holt to-night I could bring you the packet—it would perhaps be better than posting it. I'm bringing my cousin's car up to town for him. Will that be all right?"

Valentine didn't speak for a moment. She wanted to say "Yes, yes, yes, *yes*!" all very loud and joyful, but she couldn't.

"Will that do? Hullo! Are you there? Will that be all right?"

Valentine said "Yes."

## Chapter Twenty-Five

THE DAY WAS unbelievably long. For the last month the hours had been slipping away with a terrible, smooth, unhasting, unresting flow. She had felt them carrying her on like a river that would presently fall in thunder over some black precipice. Now, instead of flowing, the tide stood still; there was no movement, or so small a movement that it seemed like none. The day seemed to stay at noon. She would look at the clock, and go away and do things for a long time, and try to think about what she was doing, and come back to look at the clock again; and the hands seemed hardly to have moved.

Austin had not said what time he would come; but the day would have to be over sometime, because even the sort of day that seems to stop the clocks does in the end come to its evening. Austin would come, and he would bring her packet, which she had promised not to open unless things were so bad that nothing could make them any worse. And they would open it together, because nothing could be any worse than being just on the very edge of that black precipice. This was Tuesday, and on Thursday she was going to marry Eustace. Nothing could possibly be any worse than that. She did not see how the packet could help, but a faint, faint, unreasoning hope flickered in her mind when she thought about it.

She opened wedding presents, and she wrote notes until lunch; and after lunch she tried on her wedding dress, and Felton, Aunt Helena's maid, hung it up in a big empty wardrobe with a white sheet all round it. Then she tried on the veil and the orange blossoms; and Aunt Helena wanted her to have little bunches over her ears, but Felton wanted her to have a wreath. Valentine stood between them in a white ninon petticoat and saw her own white face and troubled eyes under the white veil in the old-fashioned glass. Felton had been with Aunt Helena for twenty years; so she didn't mind having her own opinion and holding to it.

Valentine was cold and tired. She did not say a single word, and presently they took off the veil and went away, Felton standing aside to let Aunt Helena pass.

Valentine waited for the door to shut; but instead Felton came back with her arms full of old lace and orange-blossoms.

"You have a good lay-down, miss," she said, and hovered and seemed about to say something; only just then Aunt Helena called her and she went away without speaking.

The day was like a whole week of days.

Austin Muir did not come until nine o'clock. Valentine had not told anyone that he was coming. If she had said, "Austin is coming," they would have wanted to know why, and she couldn't tell them why.

They were sitting in the drawing-room, when Bolton came in and said,

"Mr. Muir would like to speak to you, miss."

It was just what he had said in the morning, and when Valentine got up and ran out of the room, Helena had no other thought but that she had been called to the telephone.

Valentine shut the door, ran across the hall, and waited for Bolton to come to her before she said, "Where is he?"

Mr. Muir was in the study. Bolton considered it would be best to show him into the study. Bolton was left explaining his reasons; for almost before he had finished saying the word study Miss Valentine was off like a flash.

Austin Muir was standing in the middle of the room, as a man stands when he has just looked in and has no time to stay. He advanced a step and put out his hand conventionally as Valentine whirled into the room. She caught the hand in both of hers and said "Austin!" eagerly, quickly, and the colour came up into her cheeks for a moment. Austin disengaged his hand. He was really a good deal shocked at Valentine's appearance; it made him feel uncomfortable. He began to wish that he had not come. He had, of course, quite got over his fancy for her, and he had expected to see a happy, radiant bride. What on earth was the matter with her? And even as the question rose in his mind, he told himself quickly that he had no desire to know the answer, which was certainly no affair of his. He stepped back and took a small parcel from the corner of the table.

Valentine felt chilled. She had come in expecting something, she didn't quite know what. The moment that showed her Austin standing there, handsome, upright, sunburnt, was a moment of pure pleasure; it was like coming in sight of the house where a friend was waiting for you. But then—where was her friend?

Austin took his hand away. He looked past her. Then he picked up a little parcel and held it out.

"I've brought my wedding present with me," he said, not exactly awkwardly, but with a firm determination not to be awkward.

The parcel was too small. There were no seals. There ought to have been green seals. Valentine said so in a voice touched with bewilderment:

"There were green seals on it. I remember them quite well."

Austin untied the string, took off the paper, and put a white cardboard box into her hand.

"This is a wedding present. I hadn't time to have your initials put on it, but you can get it done later on."

Valentine lifted the lid. Her mind was so set on Edward's packet that her fingers moved mechanically. There was white cotton wool, a visiting card with Austin's name on it:

MR. AUSTIN MUIR

She looked at it helplessly.

Austin, impatient, burrowed into the wool, fished out a small silver cigarette case, and laid it on the card.

"There!" he said.

Valentine looked at the cigarette case. It had little stripes on it, a dull stripe and a bright stripe, a dull stripe and a bright stripe, all the way across. Then she lifted her eyes and looked at Austin. He still wore a slightly impatient air. When you give a present, you expect to have some notice taken of it, you expect to be thanked.

Instead, Valentine said,

"Is it for Eustace?"

"No, of course not. I don't know him. It's for you."

The bewilderment deepened in Valentine's eyes. "I don't smoke." Then, with a little stab of warmth, "You know I don't."

"Most girls do. I thought you'd have learnt by now."

"No—I think it's horrid." Then, with a belated recollection of many polite notes, "Thank you very much. It is very kind of you."

If Austin had loved her, the little polite, weary speech would have struck him to the heart. He did not love her. He thought her frightfully gone off. He was offended at the way in which his present had been received, and he wanted to be on the road again with the least possible delay.

"Perhaps you'd like to change it for something else," he said stiffly. "The name is on the box. And here "—he dived into his coat pocket— "here's the packet that I telephoned about."

Valentine put out both her hands to take it; they were quite steady. She felt cold and tense. Now she had it—a packet about eight inches long, wrapped in rubbed brown paper and fastened with string. There was a big blob of green sealing wax in the middle, and one on either side; and above the sealing wax was her name in pencil—"Valentine."

"Well, I'm afraid I must be going," said Austin. "Good-bye."

Valentine took a step back, and then another.

"But I haven't opened it yet," she said in a surprised sort of way.

He had no idea what she meant, and she began to explain.

"You don't know—I forgot. I mustn't open it by myself—Edward said so. It's something very important, because he made me promise on my word of honour—"

"What did he make you promise?"

Valentine stepped back again and stood leaning against the door.

"Not to open it unless—" No, she couldn't say that to Austin; something stopped her.

He moved impatiently. He was becoming more and more anxious to be gone, to avoid being involved.

"What did you promise?"

"I wasn't to open it alone—I was to open it when my best friend was there. He made me promise that, as well as other things."

Austin gave an embarrassed laugh.

"Well, that's easy, I should say. Your *fiancé's* your best friend, I take it."

Valentine leaned against the door. She was glad it was there. She held the packet against the bosom of her white lace frock; she held it very tight. Austin wished she would get away from the door. There was something up, and it wasn't his business.

"You open it with Ryven," he said. "And I'm afraid I really must be going."

Valentine did not move. She looked down at the packet. Then she said,

"No."

"How do you mean—no?"

"I can't open it with Eustace. I promised—it has to be my best friend—I thought you were my best friend."

Austin stiffened. He had a most ingrained horror of scenes; and something told him there was going to be a scene if he wasn't careful. He put out his hand again.

"Oh, well," he said, "I expect you've got no end of better friends than I am. I shouldn't like to butt in—I shouldn't really. You take my advice and either put the thing in the fire, or else open it with your *fiancé*. And now I've got to go, or James will be thinking I've smashed the car. Good-bye—and change the cigarette case for anything you like."

Valentine looked at him for a moment. He wasn't her best friend—he wasn't her friend at all. She had wanted him to come so much that the day had been like a year whilst she waited for him; and now all of a sudden, she wanted him to go. She walked past him to the hearth and put the packet down on the mantelpiece.

"Good-bye," said Austin at the door.

Without turning round, Valentine said,

"Good-bye."

## Chapter Twenty-Six

AFTER AUSTIN HAD GONE Valentine went back to the drawing-room. She had put the packet into one of the study drawers, because she did not want Aunt Helena to ask questions about it.

There were half a dozen people in the drawing-room. Some Ryven cousins; the Vicar and his wife; an old lady who had been Mrs. Ryven's governess. Not Timothy, who had been asked, but who had found an excuse. Eustace was not coming down till next day, so the Vicar was the only man of the party—kind, dull, prosy.

The cousins were Mrs. James Ryven and her two unmarried daughters. Mrs. James was cousin Laura, a round, good-natured, voluble lady with a passionate interest in bridge and dress. Her daughters disapproved of her—and of nearly everyone else. They were Janet and Emmeline. They disapproved very much of Valentine.

Nobody enjoyed the evening very much. Mrs. James missed her bridge. Helena Ryven was uneasy; Valentine had been out of the room for half an hour, and had come back looking like a ghost. Old Miss Verrey was disappointed at the absence of her adored Eustace. The Vicar was put out because he could see that Mrs. Ryven was not really listening to his long and interesting account of a walking tour in the Black Forest some forty years ago. And his wife was annoyed because he had told Mrs. Ryven the same story the last time they had dined at Holt. Janet and Emmeline Ryven never enjoyed anything. They talked to Valentine because it was their duty to talk to her; and they would have wondered why Eustace was marrying her, if they had not been certain that it was because of the money.

Valentine did not talk very much. She said "Yes" when Janet asked her if she liked reading, and she said "No" when Emmeline inquired whether she didn't think it a great waste of time to read novels.

A steadily weakening conversation lingered until eleven o'clock, when it finally expired. The Vicar and his wife took their leave; the Ryvens and Miss Verrey drifted to their rooms; and Helena Ryven kissed Valentine briskly on the forehead and told her to sleep well.

Valentine went up to her room and sat down on the edge of her bed in the dark. All through the evening she had been longing to be alone; but now that she was alone she was frightened. Austin had gone out of her world, and she didn't know what to do. It was eleven o'clock, and in an hour it would be twelve o'clock; and when it was twelve o'clock it would be Wednesday. And on Thursday she had got to marry Eustace. She felt cold through and through, and she felt stupid, as if she couldn't think or make any plans. Edward's packet was in the top left-hand drawer in the study. She wasn't to open it until things were so bad that they couldn't be worse, and she was only to open it in the presence of her best friend. How was she to open it if she hadn't got a best friend? If Timothy had been there, she could have asked him what she ought to do.

All at once something happened. It happened when she thought of Timothy. It was like waking up out of those horrid dreams in which you can't move or cry out. She woke up, and she knew what she was going to do. She was going to get the packet, and go down to Waterlow, and find Timothy and ask him what she ought to do.

She switched the light on and looked down at her white lace frock. That wouldn't do; she must put on something dark. She slipped it off and opened the wardrobe door. There were a lot of dresses hanging there. She chose the darkest.

The clock in the hall struck the half hour as she opened the bedroom door. She stood on the threshold, listening and looking out. A small light burned in the corridor and showed it empty—panelled walls; dull green carpet; a picture or two black with shadows; the newel-posts at the head of the stairs; and just that one little light. The house was as still as sleep.

She went back into her room and changed her shoes. She couldn't walk to Waterlow in white satin slippers.

Timothy had been sitting up late with his accounts. Things were not doing so badly. An old investment of his father's had turned up trumps. The fear of having to sell Waterlow was no longer before his eyes, and he had been able to give Lil a good send-off. It was all quite satisfactory—and he was quite unable to derive any satisfaction from it.

He put away the ledger and stretched himself. He did not feel in the least like bed. He had gone for a long tramp to tire himself, but he wasn't tired. He felt strung up and in violent protest against this marriage which Helena was pushing on. He couldn't get Valentine's face out of his thoughts; and every time it came, he remembered his first sight of her, her colour, her bloom, her anxious youngness.

And she had told him that she was happy.

He had been working in the dining-room. He went now to the long window that opened upon the garden, and stepped out on to the flagged path. The night was all clear and dark. The untroubled sky held a faint shimmer of stars. The Milky Way showed fainter still, like a dream of other worlds. It was so still that he could hear the flow of the scarcely moving stream. He went towards it down the path between the invisible flowers. But when he reached the river he turned sharply. He had heard something or—someone—a footstep. And then as he turned, someone passed before the lighted window and stood there, holding to the jamb and looking into the room.

Timothy came back up the flagged path with the feeling that fate had played a trick upon him. It was Valentine. And what was he to do with Valentine on the eve of her marriage to Eustace? What could she do to him except wring his heart? And what could he do with her except take her back to Holt? It was all pretty damnable.

She heard him coming, and said,

"Timothy!"

There was recognition, not question in her voice, and when she had said his name she stepped up into the dining-room and stood under the light, waiting for him to come in too. She was bareheaded, and she wore a dress that was the colour of dark red berries. Her eyes dwelt on him, and she held a small brown packet in both hands.

Timothy came in frowning.

"Hullo!" he said. "What is it?" and Valentine said "Timothy!" again.

"Well, what is it? What's brought you here at this hour?"

"Is it too late?" He thought she turned paler. "I thought—to-morrow—would be—too late."

"Val—what is it? How did you come? Is anyone with you?"

"No. I walked. I thought—to-morrow—would be—too late."

"You oughtn't to have come," said Timothy very gravely. "I'll get the car and take you home."

Valentine looked at him piteously.

"You won't—help me?"

"What sort of help can I give that won't hurt you, Val? I'm thinking about you. What sort of help do you want?"

She relaxed a very little and put out her hands with the shabby little packet in them.

"I don't know what I ought to do. Austin wouldn't do anything—he isn't my best friend at all—he wouldn't help me—he went away. But I sat on my bed and thought—I didn't know what to do. And then I thought about you, and I thought you would tell me what I ought to do. So I came."

Whatever he had to pay for it, she had come to him. And what was he going to do? What did she want him to do?

He said that simply:

"What do you want me to do, Val?" And then, "Won't you sit down?"

She shook her head.

"Will you tell me what I ought to do, Timothy? It's about the packet. I couldn't find it after I came from the island. Austin had it. He brought a bag to carry my things to the yacht, and this must have stuck in the lining. He found it, and he brought it to me to-night. But he wouldn't open it with me, because he isn't my best friend. He doesn't want to be my friend at all. He went away."

"Look here, you must sit down," said Timothy. He pulled up a chair and put her into it. "Now!" he said, "What is this packet?"

Valentine told him in a tired little voice.

"Edward gave it to me—oh, a long time ago—years and years ago—I'd nearly forgotten about it. And he said I was only to open it if I was very unhappy—if things were so bad that they couldn't possibly be any worse—and then I was to open it with my best friend. And I thought Austin would be my best friend, because he found me on the island. But he isn't, so I don't know what to do." She spoke almost as if she were saying a lesson. She drooped in her chair and rubbed at one of the green seals with a little brown finger.

Timothy looked down at her. If he went on looking at her, he would touch her. And if he touched her, he wouldn't be able to let her go. He turned with a jerk and went to the window.

"What's in the paper?"

"I don't know. I promised faithfully that I wouldn't open it ever unless—"

She stopped speaking, and a hurrying silence overtook them. It was like water coming down in flood, carrying you away. Timothy stemmed it with a great effort.

"What do you want me to do?"

"I promised," said Valentine. "But I haven't got a best friend."

"Will I do?" said Timothy gently.

Valentine sat up.

"Would you? I didn't think about that. I only thought perhaps you'd tell me what to do. Would you be my best friend?"

"If you want me to be. I'll be anything you want me to be."

She got up and ran to him, thrusting the packet into his hands.

"Open it! Open it! Oh, open it quickly!"

"Wait a moment. You've no idea what's inside?"

"No, I haven't."

"You're sure you want to open it?"

"Yes—yes—*yes!*"

"Then here goes!"

He broke the seals, burst the frail string, and unfolded the paper. It fell unregarded on the floor. The immediate contents were a large yellow envelope and a sheet of paper.

"This is something you've signed," said Timothy.

"Yes—Edward wrote it, and I signed it—oh, years ago."

Timothy looked at the sheet and read:

I promise on my word of honour that I will not open the enclosure, or allow anyone else to open it, unless things are so bad that nothing can possibly make them any worse.

It was signed: "Valentine." Beneath the signature there were a few lines in Edward Bowden's writing:

Remember that knowledge may be avoided, but can't be unknown. Stop and think. Unless any change may be one for the better, don't open the envelope or read the contents.

E. B.

Valentine put her hand on Timothy's arm.

"Open it!"

"What about 'Stop and think'?"

"Open it!"

"Val—are you sure? Are things really so bad?"

Her hand dropped. She stood back.

She said "Yes." Her voice seemed to shrink from the word.

For a moment Timothy's hand closed on the envelope, closed hard. Then he tore it open. There were some folded sheets of foolscap inside, yellow and crumpled. They had been folded for so long that the creases were like cuts. Timothy straightened them out.

"There's a lot of it, Val," he said. "You'd better sit."

She pulled out one of the straight chairs by the table and dropped on to it. Timothy took one too. They were so close to each other that if either of them leaned forward, knee or hand would touch. Timothy sat sideways to the table with the sheets in his hand.

"Do you want to lead them? Or shall I read them out?"

Her eyes widened. They were full of a troubled expectancy.

"You," she said—just one word. Then she put her hands in her lap and waited.

Timothy began to read aloud what Edward Bowden had written. The light was over their heads, high up, a yellowish globe hanging from the black beam that crossed the room. The polished oak of the table reflected the yellow lamp. It was an old table that had borne the christening, wedding, and funeral baked meats of seven generations. The chairs were old too. Timothy's great-great-great-grandmother had sat as a bride where Valentine sat now. She had sat there in a radiance of happy love. Valentine's head touched the tall back of the chair which the bride's head had touched. Valentine's face was sorrowfully pale. Her eyes hoped, and were afraid. Her hands looked white against the lap of her dark red dress. Whenever there was silence, they could hear the flowing of the stream like the flowing of some deep under-current of the heart.

## Chapter Twenty-Seven

TIMOTHY BEGAN to read:

"'Well, my dear, I have tried to play Providence, and if you ever get as far as reading this, I shall have made a bad failure. Now, just once more before you go on reading, I want to ask you to be sure that you want to go on. I suppose you will go on, if it's only out of curiosity. But remember you won't be able to go back. Your whole life will be changed. Is it now so hard that you would wish it to be changed in every relationship, every circumstance? Think a little before you decide.'"

Timothy looked up, his face very grave.

"There's no more on this page. He wanted you to stop and think before you read anything more."

Valentine said, "Go on."

"'Every circumstance—every relationship.' That's pretty sweeping, Val. Do you want to scrap the lot?"

"Yes," said Valentine.

"Sure?"

"Yes."

He took the sheet from which he had been reading and laid it on the table. As his eyes fell on the top of the next page, they became intent. He put out his right hand and laid it on Valentine's knee.

"Val—"

"What is it?"

"I must go on now—I've got to read it to you," he said.

"What does he say?"

Timothy took his hand away.

"He says, 'You are not Valentine Ryven.'"

The words came into Valentine's mind and stayed there, like drops of oil falling into water. They didn't mix with her own thoughts at all; they stayed there as words—cold, strange, heavy words. Then she heard Timothy speaking sharply:

"Val, don't look like that! Are you going to faint?"

People fainted in books. She moved her head and said,

"I don't think so—I don't know how."

And right in the middle of all the strangeness, Timothy laughed.

"That's something to be thankful for anyhow! Valentine—"

She put her hands on the arm of the chair and leaned forward.

"But I'm not."

"Not what?"

"Not Valentine. Edward said so."

"Val—"

"Will you read it again? He did say so—didn't he?"

Timothy nodded.

"Yes, that's what he says—'You are not Valentine Ryven.'"

"Then who am I?"

"I don't know, my dear. There wasn't any other child on board."

"Go on reading—*please*."

Timothy began to read again. He felt overwhelmed and bewildered. How was this going to affect Valentine—her marriage—all of them? The word *mortmain* came oddly into his mind—something in history— something legal—it meant "dead hand." He thought irrelevantly of King John and Magna Carta, and of Edward Bowden stretching out a dead hand to turn all their affairs upside down. He read:

"'You are not Valentine Ryven—and I can't tell you your real name because I don't know it. Your mother came on board the *Avronia* as Mrs. Brown, but that was not her name. I don't know what her real name was, but she was a very unhappy woman who had cut herself adrift from all ties. She came on board and kept her cabin. And on the second day of the great storm you were born.'"

Timothy looked up.

"So that's it! No one thought of that."

Valentine was holding the arms of her chair. Her mind had begun to work. If she wasn't Valentine Ryven—if she wasn't—

She said, "Go on," in a clear, steady voice.

Timothy went on:

"'I've told you about the storm often enough. On the evening of the second day they launched the boats. The first boat overturned. Little Valentine Ryven and her mother were in it. I helped to get them into it myself, and I was flung down and nearly washed overboard, just as I told you. I decided that I would not go in any of the boats. I managed to get to the companion door and to get inside. I was going towards my cabin, when one of the stewardesses caught my arm. She said, "Mr. Bowden, there's a dying woman in this cabin, and I can't leave her. Will you help me to get her on deck?" Then she wrung her hands and said, "She'll die if we move her." I went into the cabin, and I saw a woman lying on the lower berth with a new-born baby in her arm. She looked at me, and she said, "I want to stay here. I don't want to live, and I don't want my baby to live." The stewardess caught my arm and whispered, "I'll try and find the doctor. God knows where he is, but I'll try and get him if you'll stay with her." She ran out of the cabin, and I never saw her again. I don't know what happened to her. I never saw anyone again. The ship gave the most frightful lurch, and I found myself on my knees by the berth, clinging to it. I had to try and prevent the baby from falling out.

"'After a bit the ship righted herself to some extent. I stayed where I was in case it happened again. Your mother talked to me—she was quite sensible. She kept begging me to leave her and save myself. She said she didn't want to live, and she didn't want her baby to live; but she didn't want to have anyone else's death on hex conscience. She told me she had no friends and no money. She said there was no place for her in the world, and no place for her child, or any human being who would pity it or care for it. I am not very easily moved, but it was very moving. She was not very old.

"'All the time she was talking, the ship kept listing over more and more. It seemed likely that she would soon go down and take us with her. I waited a long time for the stewardess to come back. In the end I went to see if I could find her. Everything below was empty, I tried to get out on deck, but one door had jammed, and the other was up over my head with the tilt of the ship. Anyhow it would have been madness, with the gale that was blowing and the angle of the deck. I thought we were going down every moment.

"'I went back to the cabin, and heard you crying. Your poor mother was gone. I took you into another cabin and lay down in a berth to wait for the end. It seems incredible, but I went to sleep, and so did you. When I woke up, the ship was still afloat and the gale not so fierce. I found a tin of condensed milk, mixed some according to the directions, and gave you a few drops at a time.

"'On the third day we grounded on the island and stuck there as I have often told you. I buried your mother in the sea and read the service over her. I hope you won't think I could have done anything else. I baptized you, as a layman has a right to do in an emergency, and I called you Valentine simply because I had been rather fond of little Valentine Ryven. She was a dear child with very pretty ways, and I hoped if you lived, that you would be like her.'"

Valentine leaned forward—a light breathless movement. Her hand touched Timothy's arm.

"Oh, I *am* Valentine! I thought I wasn't anything."

"Yes," said Timothy. He went on reading:

"'I had no idea then of pretending that you were Valentine Ryven. That came later. You not only lived, you throve. You were a strong and healthy child, and I became very much attached to you. I always had a very strong feeling that you were not meant to live out your life upon the island. I used to feel sure that you would be rescued. But I never felt sure about myself. As time went on, I realized that even if I returned to England, I would find my place filled and my usefulness over. I should be hopelessly rusty, and might feel obliged to resign my fellowship, in which case I should be practically penniless.

"'I became more and more concerned about your future. I used to contrast your friendless condition with the warm welcome which had awaited the other little Valentine. Mrs. Ryven had shown me a letter which she had received from her sister-in-law just before she sailed, in which she spoke in the most affectionate terms of "the dear little baby" and the place that would be made for her and her child in the family circle.

"'It was when you were about four years old that I began to think seriously of calling you Valentine Ryven. I was teaching you all sorts of things, and you began to ask questions. I told you about fathers and mothers, and you asked about your own father and mother. I told you then that Maurice Ryven was your father, and Marion Ryven your mother. When you got older, I let you have her papers and her letters to read. I had brought everything I could from the ship, because at first I thought we should very soon be rescued, and it seemed right to save all the papers I could for the sake of surviving relatives.

"'Well, the rest you know. I hope you will never read this paper. If you ever do come to read it, I am afraid you may judge me harshly. I can only say that I slipped into the deception by degrees—I cannot recall any moment of sharp decision. I hope that you will be happy. And if you are not happy, I hope that you will bear unhappiness with courage and not let go of hope.

EDWARD BOWDEN'"

Timothy laid down the last sheet, and found Valentine leaning back again, the breath coming quickly between her parted lips.

"I *am* Valentine!" she said.

Timothy looked at her doubtfully.

"What an extraordinary story! I suppose he knew what he was talking about. He wasn't—unhinged?"

"It's true," said Valentine. "Why do you think it isn't true?"

"Do you want it to be true, Val?"

He wondered whether she had begun to grasp the implications.

"Yes—yes, I do!"

Timothy hesitated.

"Do you understand what it means?"

She answered him at once with a beaming upward glance.

"I shan't have any money."

"Yes."

"And if I haven't any money—" The colour rose bright in the cheeks that had been so pale. "If I haven't any money—I needn't marry Eustace."

Timothy said, "You don't want to marry Eustace?"

"If the money isn't mine, it's his. He can pull down everything he likes. I needn't marry him." She spoke in a voice that seemed to quiver with happiness. Her colour, the sudden brilliance of her eyes, the dew on her lashes, her unsteady breath, gave Timothy a picture which he never forgot. It was just as if a sudden wind of joy had blown her into flame. He had to take tight hold of himself.

Let her break her engagement to Eustace—let her only break it! Then he could speak. It didn't matter whether it was twenty-four hours or half an hour before the wedding; she could break free. But she must do it herself. It wasn't in Timothy's code to come between Eustace and his bride. If Valentine wanted to be free, she must tell Eustace so herself. He had got to stand aside.

He said, "Val—" and his voice sounded stern.

"Why do you say it like that? Are you angry?"

"No. Val, are you going to break your engagement?"

Valentine said, "Yes—yes—yes!" And with the last "Yes" she gave a little happy laugh. "Oh, yes, Timothy."

"Then you must go back to Holt at once. And, Val—listen! You mustn't say you came down here like this."

"Why mustn't I?"

Timothy ransacked his mind for a reason which would convince her.

"You'd get me into trouble," he said seriously.

"Would I? Are you sure?"

"Quite sure." ("And that's true enough," he added to himself.)

"What shall I say then?"

"I can't tell you what to say."

"Shall I show Aunt Helena Edward's letter?"

"I think you ought to show it to Eustace. You needn't show him the bit about opening it with your best friend."

"Why?"

"If you say that, you'll end by saying you came down here. That's why."

"And you don't want me to say that?"

"No, Val."

"Then I won't. But you don't want me to marry Eustace?"

Timothy put a great force on himself.

"I want you to do what will make you happy." He turned away and went to the window. You must go back. I'll get the car."

## Chapter Twenty-Eight

WHEN TIMOTHY CAME back, he found Valentine asleep, sitting just as he had left her, with her head against the tall back of the chair and her hands lying loosely in her lap. He was startled, because all her colour had gone again and she looked wan and piteous under the lamp. He touched her arm, then her hand. It felt cold.

He said "Val—" and laid a hand on her shoulder.

She opened her eyes then. They were wide and blank. The lids hid them again almost at once.

He put his arm round her waist and got her on to her feet, shaking her a little, and she roused enough to stumble as far as the door, when he picked her up and carried her to the car.

He had to drive very carefully because he was obliged to hold her. He began to wonder how he was going to get her into the house without waking anyone. He wondered how she had got out. He dared not drive up in front of the house, but left the car screened from view by the great beech-trees at the top of the drive.

He tried again to wake Valentine. This time he heard her murmur unintelligibly. He shook her.

"Val—wake up! How did you get out? Val! Val!"

He had switched off the lights of the car. The rustling darkness of the great beeches made a roof over their heads. The warm air moved softly.

"Val—wake up!"

She murmured again, then drew a deep breath.

"Val—"

She said "Timothy—" in a sleepy voice.

"Val—wake up!" But he felt her head fall on his shoulder again.

He propped her up in the car and got out. He had seen Lil sleep like this once as a child. There were fire-works, and they had tried to wake her so that she might see them. They had got her out of bed and at the window, and they had sponged her face with cold water; but they had not been able to wake her, and he had carried her back to bed again.

He didn't think it was the least use trying to wake Valentine. She looked as if she hadn't slept properly for weeks. He raged inwardly at the thought. She hadn't been sleeping; she had been strained to the breaking point, and at the sudden relief she had fallen into this deep sleep.

He came out from under the trees, and saw the house like the shape of a black hill against the sky. The sky was black too, but its blackness was all pricked over with stars. The house had no star, no light. It stood like a cliff above him.

If Valentine had climbed out of her window as she had done before, they were pretty well done in. He would just have to ring Bolton up and chance what Helena would say. Then he remembered the Ryven cousins, and blenched. He might have to try his hand at climbing in. He supposed he could climb in if Valentine had climbed out, but he would make sure of the ground floor windows first.

He found the study window open, and was most devoutly grateful. He climbed in, put on the reading-lamp, and went back for Valentine. She had slipped down a little, her arm on the side of the car, and her head upon her arm. Her breathing was deep, gentle, regular. Her hands were warm and soft.

Timothy picked her up, found her lighter than he had expected, and took his way back to the house. He was glad he had thought of putting on the light; it made things much easier, besides giving him his direction. Even if you know a place very well, it is not so easy to find your way in the dark if you cannot use your hands; there is a horrid feeling that you may at any moment run your head into a wall.

Timothy reached over the study window-sill and lowered Valentine gently on to the floor. Then he got in himself, shut the window and drew the curtains across it.

Valentine moved a little, curled herself up like a kitten, and slept on.

Timothy remembered their first meeting in this room. He remembered a great many things. He wondered if he could have faced bringing Valentine back if she were still going to marry Eustace; and quite suddenly he knew that he wouldn't have faced it. He came of a decent law-abiding stock, sober, honourable; but he knew that sooner than let Valentine go to Eustace with that broken, heartbroken look, he would have carried her off—yes, against her will if there had been no other way.

He went to the study door and opened it. The hall was dark, pitch dark; it was like looking into a black cave. He went out and shut the door behind him to see whether he could find his way upstairs without a light, and as soon as the study door was shut, the small shaded light which burned all night at the stair-head sprang into view. He went up the stairs without making any sound. At the top Helena's door faced him. Valentine's room was away on the left. He went to it, opened the door, put on the reading-lamp by the bed, and then returned, leaving the door ajar.

Timothy was nothing if not practical, but he hoped he would never have to be a burglar. This creeping about the house in the middle of the night business and wondering every moment whether Helena, or Laura, or Janet, or Emmeline would come popping out of their rooms, was fairly grim. It would be especially grim if it were Emmeline. Timothy liked Emmeline less well than Janet—and he disliked Janet quite a lot.

He carried Valentine safely up the stairs and laid her on her bed. There was a blue eiderdown folded back at the foot of it. He covered her with it, tucking it round her. She gave a little comfortable sigh, and as his hand brushed her hand, her fingers closed on one of his in a soft clasp.

Timothy stood looking down at her. She looked very young. The light from the reading-lamp came through a parchment shade painted with coloured fruits. It threw a golden light on the pillow and on

Valentine's hair; it gave her skin a warm look, as if she were standing in the sunshine. Her black lashes lay upon her cheek. The eye-lids were faintly shadowed with blue. Her tossed hair made her look most pitifully young. Her lips were just apart. She wore the pure, remote look of the sleeping child.

Timothy drew his finger away very gently. He loved her so much that her youth, and her sleep, and those blue shadows under her eyes moved him to the very depths. He drew his finger away, and saw her hand relax.

He had made up his mind what he must do. He couldn't have the housemaid coming in in the morning to find Valentine asleep under the eiderdown in her red dress. The housemaid must find the door locked; and he, Timothy, had got to climb out of the window. He had a look at the rain-pipe, and thought he could manage it. He locked the door, turned out the light, and climbed out of the window.

When he was half way home he remembered that he had left the studylight on, and burst out laughing. Bolton would scratch his head in the morning.

## Chapter Twenty-Nine

VALENTINE CAME SLOWLY back out of the depths of sleep. She did not wake, but her sleep became lighter, less unconscious. She passed into a dream of the island. She thought she had just come up out of the cavern, because she was standing near the entrance. She had something in her closed hands, held tightly between palm and palm, but she did not know what it was. She thought she must have brought it up from the cavern, perhaps from the deep waters that were in the cavern. Her hands were wet. Then all at once she knew that her hands were wet because she had wept upon them; and in her dream a strange, happy thought pierced her heart like a warm sunbeam. She knew that she need not weep any more. And someone called her, and she woke up.

She was not really quite awake. The light came through her lashes. Her hand closed on something soft. There was a sound of calling in her ears. Someone was calling her, someone was knocking. She opened her eyes and saw the room quite light, and her blue eiderdown pulled up to her chin. She threw it back, looked at her own arm in its dark red sleeve, and sat up.

Someone was knocking at the door.

"Miss Ryven! Miss Ryven!" It was Agnes with her tea.

Valentine looked down at her red dress and remembered that she had put it on to go and see Timothy. She remembered going to Waterlow, and she remembered Edward's letter; but she didn't remember coming back to Holt. When she remembered Edward's letter, she had the same sort of feeling that she had had in her dream, a piercing joy.

The knocking became louder.

She said, "Wait a minute, Agnes," and then she pushed the eiderdown right back and got off the bed.

She became aware that she didn't want Agnes to know that she hadn't undressed. It was only the work of a minute to take off the red dress and her shoes and stockings—How odd! She hadn't even taken her shoes off!—and to pull down the bedclothes so that she could slip into bed as soon as she had opened the door.

She came down to breakfast with colour in her cheeks and light in her eyes. Something sang in her heart. She felt as if she had been in a cage, and as if the door had opened so that she could walk out of it and be safe and free.

Cousin Laura rallied her a little ponderously.

"Aha, my dear! Somebody's coming to-day! Isn't he? Anyone would know that just by looking at you. Now mind you don't go and cover all that pretty colour with powder, because it would be a sin and a shame. I was afraid you were going to be a pale bride, but now we know what was wanted." She laughed good-naturedly. "You needn't blush, my dear. Eustace is a very lucky fellow." She dropped her voice. "Ssh! We mustn't let your Aunt Helena hear that. No mother of an only son thinks any girl quite good enough for him—does she? I haven't got one, or I'd have been as big a fool as the test of them, I daresay. And so will you, my dear, when your turn comes."

Janet and Emmeline disapproved a little more than usual. Their mother was being coarse. They disapproved of coarseness; they disapproved of a preference for sons. They looked down their noses at their toast and marmalade, and refused sugar in their tea. Laura Ryven took four lumps, and they disapproved again. Mother really had no consideration for her figure.

Eustace arrived just before tea.

Valentine had considered whether she would show Edward's letter to Aunt Helena before he came. She decided that she wouldn't. Timothy had told her that she ought to show it to Eustace. She remembered that. She remembered everything until Timothy went to fetch the car, and after that she didn't remember anything at all. She had gone to sleep. Timothy must have taken her home. She couldn't think how her door came to be locked on the inside. She didn't worry about it, or about anything else. She waited in breathless, glowing excitement for the moment when she could tell Eustace that they needn't get married, because she wasn't Valentine Ryven after all.

It made her laugh deep in her own thoughts to see everybody so busy getting ready for the wedding that was never going to be a wedding at all. Her wedding dress and veil were in the empty room next to hers—and she wasn't going to wear them.

"Oh, lovely, lovely, lovely!" she said to herself. She needn't marry Eustace—she needn't marry anyone. The dreadful aching at her heart had gone, and the frightened, *frightened* feeling. She felt as if she could fly, all light, and happy, and joyful.

*"Lovely!"* she said to herself.

She waited till tea was over. Then she came and stood in front of Eustace as he reached from the big armchair to put his cup down.

"Eustace, can I speak to you?"

Cousin Laura looked archly at them.

"What is he to say? Can she? Now I wonder! What do you think, Helena? Is it allowed?"

Eustace rose to his feet, blankly courteous.

"Certainly. Shall we come into the study?"

They crossed the hall. The study door opened and shut again. Valentine looked at the window and saw the sun dazzle on the geraniums in the bed outside. A bird went past like a flash, with the light on his wing. There were butterflies, and bees. There were such a lot of happy, free creatures. And there was the sun, and the wind, and the trees, and clouds, and flowers. She didn't want the island any more. She had only wanted the island so that she could get away from Eustace; and she hadn't got to marry Eustace after all.

Eustace saw that she had a brocaded bag in her hand. She opened it, took out some folded sheets of foolscap, and beamed at him.

"Eustace, we needn't! Eustace, I've had a letter from Edward!"

"From Edward! What Edward?"

"From *Edward*. I thought I'd lost it. I had it on the island. It was all sealed, and it got stuck in the lining of Austin's bag. And Austin brought it to me yesterday. And we needn't get married."

Eustace was standing by the writing-table. He looked very tall, he looked very grave, he looked as if he had not been sleeping. If he had been a less formidable person, he might have been described as cross. He said, in a displeased voice,

"If this is a joke, it is in very bad taste. What are you talking about?"

"About Edward's letter." Her face had fallen. There was something about Eustace that always made you feel as if you didn't know how to behave. She repeated, "I told you it was Edward's letter, and I thought you'd be pleased."

"Why?"

When Eustace said "Why?" his eyebrows went up and he looked just like Aunt Helena. It was rather damping.

Valentine felt puzzled. He ought to be glad because he hadn't got to marry her. He ought to have a joyful feeling too, and he wasn't being a bit joyful.

"Why am I to be pleased?"

It occurred to her that she hadn't really told him why. She began to tell him; but there was such a lot, and the wrong bits kept coming first, like when you have packed a box too full and you keep finding stockings when you want your night-gown.

"I told you about Edward's letter."

"You didn't tell me what was in it."

"I'm trying to tell you, Eustace. And I thought you'd be pleased— about our not getting married, I mean. You are pleased—aren't you? And you won't judge Edward harshly? Because that's what he specially said he hoped I wouldn't do—at the end of the letter after he had explained how he came to say I was Valentine Ryven."

"*What?*" said Eustace in a different tone.

"I don't want anyone to be harsh about Edward, because—"

And then Eustace was standing over her with his hand on her shoulder.

"What are you talking about, Valentine?"

"Edward—"

"He wrote a letter. What does he say in it?"

She looked up at him fearlessly.

"He says I'm not Valentine Ryven."

Eustace let go of her with great suddenness.

"Do you know what you are saying?"

"Yes, of course I do."

"He says you're not Valentine Ryven?"

"Yes."

"Who are you then? There wasn't any other child on the ship."

Valentine sat down on a chair and sorted out the sheets of Edward Bowden's letter. Then she got up and gave them to Eustace.

## Chapter Thirty

EUSTACE RYVEN READ. Edward Bowden's letter sitting at the writing-table. The room had been his, and the writing-table his. They had passed from him to Maurice Ryven's daughter. If this letter held the truth, they were his again. He read the letter from beginning to end, his face set in a grave composure, the hand that lifted each sheet and laid it down again steady and unhurried.

Valentine stood watching him with a feeling compounded of awe and disappointment. When he had put down the last page, he took up the first one again.

This was unendurable. She moved quickly.

"Eustace—"

He said "Ssh," and went on reading.

Was he going to go through it all again? It appeared that he was, a lifted hand enjoining silence.

Valentine began to feel dreadfully discouraged. Why didn't he say something? Why didn't he look pleased?

He read right through to the end. Then he looked up without any change of face.

"We must have legal advice on this of course."

"Why?"

"Colonel Gray must be communicated with. He's coming to-morrow, isn't he? We can speak to him then, and to Waterson."

Valentine tried to think of all the things she had planned to say. They were gone; her mind felt quite empty, with a little wind of fear blowing to and fro in the emptiness.

"You had better let me lock this up. It's not the sort of thing to leave lying about. Has my mother seen it?"

"Not yet."

"But you've told her?"

"No."

He looked rather surprised.

"She ought to be told." He paused, frowning. "I ought really to get hold of Waters on at once. I don't suppose—" He was speaking more to himself than to her.

"*Eustace!*" said Valentine in the loudest voice that she could manage. He ought to speak to *her*—he ought to say he was pleased—he ought to say something—he *ought*.

Something in her voice gained his attention. He looked at her, saw her flushed and in obvious distress, and hastened to be kind.

"There is no reason for you to be upset. This need make no difference so far as you are concerned."

"But of course it will make a difference."

"None that need distress you. If this is true, it will only mean, as far as you are concerned, that you won't have the burden and responsibility of managing a great deal of money. It won't affect you personally."

"I didn't want the money at all, I never wanted it."

"As my wife—" Eustace began; and immediately Valentine's fear became articulate.

"But we're not going to be married now."

She saw Eustace look at her as he always looked when she said something which people didn't say.

"What makes you say that, Valentine?"

"Because we needn't. Don't you see, if I'm not Valentine Ryven, the money isn't mine at all, and you needn't marry me, because it will belong to you anyhow and you can do anything you like with it. Don't you see that?"

She had not the slightest conception of the affront her words conveyed. In her mind the situation was an entirely simple one. Eustace was marrying her to get the money, and if the money wasn't hers, there was no need for him to marry her.

Eustace was most profoundly shocked. He regarded marriage seriously, and he intended to be a kind, and certainly a faithful husband to his young cousin. He was conventional to the point of fanaticism. Marriage was largely a matter of family obligation, a matter of duty; personal inclinations and sentiments were irrelevancies, pleasant and lawful if they coincided with duty, wrong and to be suppressed if they did not; they were not, in any case, integral factors.

When Valentine put her point of view with the naïve crudity of a child or a savage, it was just as if a small glaring light had been turned upon him, and for a moment he saw, not himself, but her concept of him. He was marrying her to get the money; and if she hadn't got the money, he needn't marry her. He turned quite white with anger. Could she really suppose him to be prepared to jilt her brutally and callously on the eve of their wedding?

He controlled his voice with an effort.

"I don't think you know what you are saying, Valentine. There is not the slightest need to alter our arrangements."

"But we needn't be married now—we really needn't. Don't you see?"

"I can see that you have no idea of what you are saying. We are certainly going to be married tomorrow. How can you suppose for one instant—" He checked himself. "People don't behave like that, you know." He walked towards the door. "I think you had better talk to my mother. I'll see her first, and then she can tell you what I've just told you, that there's no need for you to worry. Whatever happens, you won't be affected personally."

He went out.

Valentine stood in the middle of the floor. She felt what the child or the savage feels when its crude simplicity comes up against the barbed iron wire of convention  bewilderment, a puzzled striving, a terror of the unknown. Not for one instant had she dreamt that Eustace would still want to marry her. It was incredible—and incredibly dreadful.

She remained in this bewildered state until the door opened again and Mrs. Ryven came in. Then she looked up questioningly. Aunt Helena would surely be glad. Aunt Helena didn't really like her. She would be glad. She didn't really want her to marry Eustace. She didn't think her good enough.

She looked up, and she saw what Helena Ryven thought she was concealing—triumph. Her step was unhurried, her face quiet and concerned; but the eyes held that spark of triumph, and Valentine saw nothing else.

She sprang forward.

"Aunt Helena, you're pleased! You don't want him to marry me?"

It was the plain truth, stated plainly, and it naturally shocked and offended Helena.

"My dear, don't say things that you will regret. It's such a pity. I have told you that before, and just now it matters a good deal, because we all want to do and say just what is right—don't we? Come and sit down."

Valentine remembered Timothy saying that on the day she came to Holt. People always wanted you to sit down, and then they talked and talked, and you couldn't get away. She sat on the very edge of her chair as if she were prepared to spring out of it at any moment.

Helena Ryven gave her an encouraging smile.

"Now, Valentine," she said, "this has naturally been a shock to you; but you shouldn't—no, you really shouldn't have spoken to Eustace as you did. There are things one doesn't say."

"What did I say?" Valentine's eyes were on her face.

"I won't repeat it. We'll all forget it, I think."

Valentine frowned. It was a puzzled frown, not an angry one.

"I thought Eustace would be pleased. If the money isn't mine, he needn't marry me."

Mrs. Ryven was silent for a moment. She was doubtless praying for patience.

"Listen to me, Valentine, and try, if you can, not to be so childish. If this had happened before you and Eustace were engaged, you might, or might not, have entered into an engagement."

"Oh, we shouldn't!"

"Please let me speak. If it had happened a month ago, Eustace would naturally have been prepared to carry out his engagement; but it would have been possible to postpone the marriage for a little, if that had been your wish. As you are so young, it might have been all for the best. But now, the day before your wedding—believe me when I tell you that it is quite, quite impossible to do anything except go on as if nothing had happened. We shall consult Mr. Waterson, and the necessary legal steps can be taken. You understand?"

Valentine did not understand at all. Her heart was beating dreadfully. She had never found it easy to talk to Helena Ryven. Even if they used the same words, they meant different things. She felt the suffocating pressure of Helena's will. She couldn't speak, because Helena didn't want her to speak. Helena wasn't going to let her speak. She was going to drive her back into the cage and shut the door. She was going to make her marry Eustace.

She felt weak, frightened, and puzzled. Most of all she felt puzzled, because she had been so sure that Helena did not really like her. And if she didn't like her, why did she want to make her marry Eustace?

Mrs. Ryven looked at her with a sort of controlled kindness. It was true that she had never liked Valentine, but she could become fond of her if she no longer supplanted Eustace. She wanted Eustace to marry; and for some years she had been afraid that he would not marry. If this engagement were broken now in a blaze of scandal, he would probably never marry at all—and she wanted grandchildren, and an heir for Holt. She did not like Valentine; but then she liked very few girls. Valentine, at least, would have no modern fads about not having children. She did not love Eustace; and whilst Helena resented this, her reason told her that Eustace would not give the first place in his life to any woman, and that a girl who had few demands to make would suit him a great deal better than one who would expect him to play the lover.

Helena Ryven had the habit of thinking quickly and clearly. She never allowed emotion to interfere with her mental processes. She had seen at once that the marriage must go on, and she felt entirely competent to manage Valentine.

Valentine got up, went back a step, and said in a low voice,

"I don't understand."

Helena followed her and laid a hand on her shoulder.

"Come, Valentine—you've had a shock. But I think better of you than to suppose that you mean to give way. I don't think you care so much for money that you will mind—"

"I don't."

"I am sure you don't."

"I can't marry him," said Valentine. It was very, very difficult to say; but she said it, and felt at once that she might not have said it at all. It was just as if she had tried to make herself heard against the most raging gale that had ever swept the island.

Helena patted her shoulder.

"Now my dear—"

Valentine whirled round and caught her wrist.

"I can't, Aunt Helena! I *can't*!"

Mrs. Ryven looked at her calmly. It was a tiresome scene. But a girl was apt to be over-wrought on the eve of her wedding. She was not seriously alarmed.

"My dear, do think what you are saying. Have we been so unkind to you here? No, don't speak for a moment, but listen. It wasn't really very easy for us, you know. I want you to think what it meant to Eustace to have everything taken away from him quite suddenly, and to feel that his loss was bound to involve others. I think you will admit that he behaved well, that we received you, not only courteously, but kindly. Don't you think you owe us some return? You entered into an engagement with Eustace of your own free will—you were not urged or pressed in any way. If you do not marry him to-morrow, you will be doing him an irreparable injury. I am sure you had not thought of it in that way—and I want you to think of it. Everyone will say that he threw you over as soon as he found that you were not an heiress. It will be considered so disgraceful that he will never be able to live it down. He will certainly never be able to live at Holt. It would be bad enough for any man; but for a man of Eustace's high character and ideals it would be simply annihilating—he would never be able to live it down, and he would never marry." The last words were less calmly phrased. They were the crux of the whole speech.

Valentine heard the even flow of Helena Ryven's voice. It numbed her. Every sentence made it more impossible for her to resist or even answer. The numbness dulled her fear; she began to feel cold and giddy. She gazed blankly at Helena and saw her waver. Next moment she slipped down on her knees and fell forward.

## Chapter Thirty-One

TIMOTHY HAD SPENT a busy day. He kept away from Holt because he did not mean to butt in. He would not feel free until Valentine was free. And she would have to free herself; it wasn't a thing that anyone else could do. He wasn't quite sure when Eustace was expected, and though he was so busy, the day seemed very long.

When seven o'clock came, he could bear it no longer. If he rang Helena up, she would be bound to tell him that the marriage had been put off. Eustace must have arrived hours ago, and the whole thing must have been thrashed out.

He got Bolton, and asked to speak to Mrs. Ryven. It might have been half a minute before she came, but it seemed as long as the whole of the long day.

"That you, Helena?"

"Yes—I was just going to dress. What is it?"

What was it? Hanged if he knew what to say—he hadn't thought. He had made sure that it was Helena who would have something to say. She was bound—

Her "What is it?" sounded impatient.

"Has Eustace come?"

"Yes—he got down for tea. Do you want to speak to him?"

"No."

Timothy took a decision. Helena wouldn't say anything over the telephone, but she'd be bound to say something if he saw her. He said quickly,

"Can I come up this evening after dinner?"

"Come to dinner. I believe I asked you before."

"No, I won't dine. I'll come up afterwards."

"Just as you like."

Could even Helena sound as indifferent as that if Valentine had spoken? He wasn't sure. It was torture to think that perhaps she hadn't spoken after all.

He dressed, ate what his housekeeper put before him, and walked the three miles to Holt because he could not face sitting at home whilst Holt dined.

Timothy came into the drawing-room at Holt and saw immediately that Valentine was not there. There was a fire, though it was a mild night. Old Miss Verrey sat close to it in her long old-fashioned black silk with a wisp of lace at the neck fastened by a brooch which contained her parents' hair. She was sipping her coffee with great enjoyment.

On the other side of the fire Laura Ryven in a bright petunia dress which showed the whole of her spine, or would have showed it if it had not been too plumply cushioned, was playing patience with a coffee-cup balanced on the green baize board which she held across her knees. Patience was a most wretched substitute for bridge, but it was better than nothing.

Helena Ryven was knitting. She wore black velvet and her old filigree pearls.

Janet and Emmeline were also knitting. They wore the dresses which had been their best, not last summer, but the summer before. They had been cleaned, and the stain on Janet's front breadth really hardly showed at all. It was unfortunate that Emmeline should have chosen a colour which had faded in the sun. But materials can no longer be relied on since the war.

Eustace sat beside Miss Verrey, who adored him.

Valentine was not there.

When Timothy had shaken hands all round, he asked where she was. Helena answered at once, "She's a little overdone, and I've sent her to bed. She's got to look her best to-morrow. Won't you have some coffee?"

Timothy helped himself to coffee. He did not sit down, but stood with his back to the fire and looked about him. Valentine had been sent to bed so that she should look her best to-morrow.... Now what exactly did Helena mean by that? Had Valentine spoken, or had she not spoken? Helena's face never told one very much. She would continue to behave beautifully whether the roof fell in or not.

He turned his attention to Eustace. Old Miss Verrey was telling him long rambling tales of his own childhood. He wore an air of aloof gloom. This was nothing new; he nearly always looked gloomy in the bosom of his family. But to-night Timothy thought he discerned a difference; there was a touch of decorum, a hint of restrained satisfaction, which suggested the heir at a funeral. Timothy thought that Eustace knew. Something in him hardened.

He put his cup on the mantelpiece, and approached his sister.

"Helena, could I have a word with you?"

Helena knew too. She didn't start or show anything that anyone else would have noticed, but Timothy, following her into her own sitting-room, was quite certain that he would not have to make any explanations. Helena certainly knew. He spoke on this assumption:

"What are you doing about it, Helena?"

Mrs. Ryven was putting one of the miniatures straight. It depicted Marianne Kinnaird, who had married Maurice and Edmund Ryven's grandfather in the thirties. Her husband frowned beside her on the mantelpiece in an admiral's blue and gold.

"What do you mean, Timothy?"

"Don't you know what I mean? I take it Valentine has shown you Bowden's statement?"

There was just a perceptible pause before Helena answered.

She said "Yes" gravely, and then asked, "How is it that you know anything about it?"

"Valentine showed me the statement—or rather I was there when she opened it. Bowden had made her promise only to open it in the presence of a friend."

Helena seemed to be thinking.

"When was this?"

"I think I won't say. It's not to the point. I take it Eustace knows?"

"Certainly."

"Well, that brings me back to my first question—what are you going to do about it?"

"Do about it? Nothing."

Timothy controlled himself.

"Did Valentine tell you that she wished to break off her engagement?"

"She said something about it. She seemed to think that Eustace was marrying her for her money, and wouldn't want her without it, poor child."

Timothy was thirty-four years of age, and during the whole of that time he had lived at close quarters with his sister Helena; yet it may be said that she staggered him. He wasn't going to lose his temper yet, but there was a gleam in his eye.

"That won't do," he said. "You know as well as I do that she doesn't want to marry Eustace any more than Eustace wants to marry her."

Helena lifted her eyebrows.

"It's a little late in the day to say that—and not, I think, in the best of taste."

Timothy laughed. The laugh was an angry one.

"I want to see Valentine."

"Then I'm afraid you can't."

He changed his ground.

"Look here, Helena, what are you going to gain by forcing that poor child into a wretched marriage? You know she doesn't care for Eustace. You know Eustace doesn't care for her."

"I don't know anything of the sort." She hesitated. "It's not a thing I'd say to anyone else, but as a matter of fact it was Valentine herself who first proposed the marriage. I was completely taken by surprise; and so, I fancy, was Eustace."

Timothy's eyes blazed and his jaw stuck out.

"And who dragged her through those beastly slums and worked on her feelings until she was ready to do anything that would let Eustace get on with his job? You say she suggested the marriage. Can you look me in the face and say you don't know why she suggested it? Good Lord, she was ready to do anything! She was ready to make herself miserable for life if it was necessary. She nearly cried for joy when she found the money wasn't hers, because she thought she'd get free. On the top of that, do you mean this marriage to go on?"

"Why, of course—what else? Really, Timothy! Are you suggesting that Eustace should throw the poor child over at the eleventh hour just because the money turns out to be his, and not hers after all?"

"I'm not thinking about Eustace"—Timothy's voice had roughened—"I'm thinking about her. She doesn't want to marry him, and she shan't."

Helena Ryven looked at him with a faint sarcasm.

"My dear Timothy, you won't mind if I ask you why you consider it your business."

Timothy met the sarcasm doggedly.

"It's my business because I care."

"And no one else does?"

"Not about Valentine. You only care about Eustace, and about what people are going to say."

Helena Ryven flashed into anger. Timothy had always had the power to anger her. She managed other people, but she had never been able to manage Timothy; not even when he was four years old, a blunt, obstinate baby, who always knew exactly what he wanted and couldn't be persuaded to want anything else. She lost her temper and lost her advantage.

"You've never understood Eustace or appreciated him."

Timothy recovered his balance.

"Oh, yes, I have. You're wrong if you think I haven't. I give him marks for what he's been doing in those beastly slums. I can admire him all right when he's sacrificing himself. But you want me to admire him whilst he's sacrificing Valentine. It's not fair, Helena, it's not fair. And what's more, you know it. Everyone has a right to sacrifice himself, but no one has the right to sacrifice someone else. And Valentine's a child that doesn't know what she's doing. Good Lord, Helena, you don't need me to tell you that!" He came up to her with a hard, direct, insistent look. "That's true, isn't it? Don't you know it's true?"

Helena looked back at him indignantly.

"My dear Timothy, we are not on the stage. I gather that you are in love with Valentine. I suppose that is some excuse for the exaggerated view you are taking. But really I think it is a pity that you should make a parade of your feelings like this. In the circumstances, it seems to me to be in atrocious taste, to say the least of it."

"It would!" said Timothy with a short laugh. "I think I'd better talk to Eustace."

He went towards the door, and just as he reached it, Helena called him:

"Timothy—"

"What is it?"

"You can't make a scene now!"

"Can't I? You'll see!" He laughed again. "As a matter of fact, I've no more wish to make a scene than you have. But I shall certainly make one if I don't see Valentine and hear from her own lips that she wants to marry Eustace."

The door close to Timothy opened as he spoke. Eustace came into the room. He looked from his mother to Timothy. Then he shut the door and crossed over to where Helena Ryven was standing with an unwonted flush in her cheeks.

"What's the matter?" he asked.

"Timothy has apparently come here for the purpose of informing us that we do not know how to treat Valentine. He was announcing his intention of making a scene before you came in."

Timothy stood just where he was. He spoke to Eustace:

"I've read Edward Bowden's statement. I came here to ask what you were going to do about it."

Eustace looked as stiff as a poker.

"How could there be any question of what I should do?"

"Look here, Eustace! I only want to know one thing. I take it for granted that you want to marry Valentine. All I want to know is this—does Valentine want to marry you?"

"It is a little late in the day to ask that," said Helena.

"Valentine," said Eustace, "is, naturally, prepared to carry out her engagement. Mr. Bowden's disclosure would otherwise leave her in a very awkward position." He spoke with offence and a certain air of not being entirely sure of his ground.

Timothy advanced a step.

"Look here," he said, "this is without gloves! I'll admit that you're in a damned awkward position, but I'm not going to see Valentine sacrificed to save anyone's face. She opened that statement because she was so unhappy that she didn't know what to do. I think she didn't show you the first page—the page he made her sign—No, I thought not. It was a promise not to open the envelope unless things were so bad that they couldn't be any worse. Well, she read that through in my presence, and she opened it because she felt that nothing could be worse than for her to marry someone she didn't love, and who didn't love her. You don't, you know. You never did. You only wanted to get on with your work. And she, poor kid, thought it was her duty, and was killing herself to do it. D'you know what she said when I'd finished reading the statement to her? She said, 'Then I needn't marry Eustace!' And she meant it."

Eustace was fearfully pale.

"If you and Valentine—" he began.

"What are you going to do about it?" said Timothy.

"If you and Valentine have an understanding—"

"We haven't."

"Then I think you had better leave me to manage my own affairs. Hadn't you?"

"Damn your affairs! You and Helena think of nothing else—your affairs, and what other people are going to say about your affairs. Cut it out, can't you? Valentine doesn't want to marry you, and I'm here to see that she isn't pushed into it."

Mrs. Ryven commanded herself. Her colour remained high, but her manner was assured.

"I think, Timothy, that if you will cast your mind back to the occasion of our last difference, you will perhaps remember that you told me, not very politely, to mind my own business. If I was not permitted to remonstrate with you about your sister Lil's most undesirable engagement, I really do not see how you can consider yourself entitled to interfere in Eustace's affairs."

"It's Valentine's affairs that I'm concerned with, Helena. Eustace can do anything he damn well pleases, but I mean to see that Valentine has a fair show. I mean to see her."

"You can't—she's gone to bed."

"Then in the morning—"

Eustace put his mother aside.

"I think you had better go away," he said. "I have not any desire to press Valentine. I think I am the person to see her."

"The whole thing is absurd! All girls panic at the last minute. Ida nearly ran away." Mrs. Ryven laughed a little. "*Ida!* You're making a mountain out of a molehill."

"I've got to see Valentine," said Timothy.

"In the morning," said Helena Ryven. She thought she could manage that. There would be a rush and a bustle, and even Valentine could hardly propose to go back on her word when the wedding guests were arriving. Besides, she wouldn't leave her alone with Timothy. She said, "To-morrow," and smiled.

"Then I'll say good-night," said Timothy.

Helena's smile sent the blood to his head. He was afraid of what he might do or say. He went to the door, and then turned.

"If I don't see her when I come up to-morrow, I'll stop her on her way up the aisle. If you want a scandal, you know the way to get one," he said, and went out.

## Chapter Thirty-Two

VALENTINE DRANK the soup that Agnes brought her, and she ate some chicken, because Agnes said that if she didn't eat it, Mrs. Ryven would come up. Then she lay down in the dark and presently she slept. She did not know that she was going to sleep. She slipped into it suddenly and was submerged. No consciousness, no dreams; just a blank space. And then a sharp awakening.

A thrill of terror went through her as she opened her eyes. It couldn't be morning already. No, it was dark. She turned on the light and looked at her watch. It was eleven o'clock.

It was eleven o'clock. Everyone had gone to bed. No one would come near her until the morning. This thought was such a relief that she began to think clearly again. She hadn't been able to think; she had only been able to feel that she must do what Aunt Helena wanted her to do. It was a dreadful feeling. The minute she began to think again, the pressure of Helena Ryven's will lessened. No one would come near her for hours and hours. But in the morning they would come, and Felton and Agnes would dress her in her wedding dress, and she would have to go to church and marry Eustace, because if she didn't—There wasn't any "If." Aunt Helena would make her do it.

She wondered if everyone had really gone to bed. And as she wondered, she heard something. It was the tap of a heel on the polished floor just outside the door. There was a second tap, and then silence. Someone was there. Someone was standing outside her door listening.

Valentine was leaning on her elbow, with her watch in her hand. The little table with the lamp on it was between her and the door, and she could see the door. She saw the handle move. And in a moment she had put down her watch and buried as much of her face as possible in the pillow. There was no time to turn round; she had to face the light and the door. She shook her hair forward, brought her hands up under her chin, and lay still.

The door was opening slowly, and a voice said, "Valentine—" It was Helena Ryven's voice. She said "Valentine" again in the low, even tone of someone who wants to find out whether you are awake or not.

Valentine's lashes trembled as her eyelids shut closer. She felt cold and sick at the thought of having to talk to Helena again. You can't talk to a person who is asleep. If she was asleep, Helena would go away.

Mrs. Ryven did not speak again. She came into the room without making any sound and stood looking down on Valentine. The lamp cast a circle of light on the dark polished table, and a diffused golden twilight upon Valentine. She was lying on her side, her hair over her face and her brown hands clasped under her chin, and all that Helena could really see was the curve of her cheek and part of her mouth and chin—a red mouth, a pale cheek, a soft round chin.

Helena had come because it was her duty to see that Valentine was all right. She did not know quite why she stayed. Valentine was asleep, and she certainly had no desire to waken her. Yet she stood there watching for five of the longest minutes of Valentine's life. Her anger with Timothy had passed into a deep resentment. She had justified herself and proved him in the wrong, and she ought to be experiencing the feeling that she had earned a night's repose. She felt no repose. Timothy had said things which she could not ever forgive, because they were the things that her own conscience would have said if she had not held it dumb.

She looked at the pale curve of Valentine's cheek, and in the deep silence of the room the dumb thing spoke and said, "It's not fair! It's not fair!"

Helena put her hand on the switch of the lamp, and darkness rushed down upon the silence. Then she went out of the room, walking softly.

The door shut, and Valentine broke into a quivering sigh. Helena had gone away at last, and she wouldn't come back.

She thought about Timothy, as she had thought about him at intervals all day. But it wasn't any good thinking about Timothy. He couldn't help her; he couldn't stop people saying dreadful things about Eustace. No—Timothy couldn't help her. He was kind. If he could help her, he would come. If he didn't come, it was because he knew he couldn't help her.

Valentine went to the window in her night-gown and looked out. She could see the arch of the sky and the dark mass of the woods. It was very dark. There was no moon, and there were no stars. Last night there had been stars, so many, and so far, and so bright.

She leaned over the window-sill to catch the breeze—a faint, chill movement of the heavy air. She looked down and remembered her first night at Holt, and how she had climbed out of the window in the dawn and gone down through the woods to meet Timothy. The air stirred about her uncovered neck and her bare arms; and all at once her thoughts began to move, and bubble, and spring up in her just as the water used to spring up in the cavern.

Why should she stay here at all? If she wasn't here, Aunt Helena couldn't make her marry Eustace. And if she ran away, everyone— *everyone* would know that it wasn't Eustace's fault.

It is really quite impossible to describe the relief which this thought brought to Valentine. She had been driven back into the cage, and the door had been shut upon her; and now, just when she had given up hope, the door swung open of itself. She could get out and go wherever she liked. She needn't stay a moment.

She sprang back from the window, put on the light, and began to dress quickly, quickly, quickly, with such a living, joyful energy that everything she did was like doing something new and beautiful. She wasn't dressing, she was escaping. She put on the dark red dress which she had worn when she went to Waterlow, and the little hat that matched it, and a tweed coat with a fur collar. And she packed a few things in a suit-case that was light enough to carry. The suit-case was in her dressing-room, half packed with things for her to take when she went away to-morrow with Eustace. She wasn't going to go away with Eustace. She wasn't going to be here to-morrow. Lovely—lovely— *lovely*. The word kept singing itself over in her mind.

The thought of Helena Ryven came as suddenly as a shadow. What was she going to say to Aunt Helena? In books people always wrote a note and left it on the pin-cushion when they ran awaŷ. But she didn't know what to say. In the end her pencilled note was a very short one. It ran:

DEAR AUNT HELENA,

It is very kind of Eustace to want to marry me. But I don't want to—I really don't. I only wanted him to have the money, and if it is his, I needn't marry him. So I am going away. Please tell everyone Eustace wanted to marry me, but I wouldn't.

VALENTINE.

She put the note under her pillow because she thought that was a better place than the pin-cushion. She didn't want them to find it in the first minute they came into the room, but a little later when they weren't quite so angry as they would be at first.

She packed her case and let it down out of the window by a long piece of string. There was heaps of string in the dressing-room, because parcels had been coming all day. When she had let down her case, she locked and bolted her bedroom door, and locked the door into the dressing-room. And then she put out the light and climbed out of the window.

## Chapter Thirty-Three

TIMOTHY CAME UP to Holt at nine o'clock next morning. He put Bolton's distracted air to the account of the wedding; but when Helena came into her sitting-room, his heart jumped. She looked grey, changed, old.

She shut the door and stood against it.

"Where is she? What have you done with her?"

Timothy was shocked.

"Good Lord, Helena, what's the matter?"

She swallowed and put out her hand.

"Timothy, where is she?"

"Who?"

"Don't you know? Valentine—where is she?"

"Helena! Isn't she here?" Then, as she shook her head, "What's happened?"

"Her door was locked," said Helena Ryven. "Agnes couldn't make her hear. I told her to leave her a little. Then I went. We had to break open the dressing-room door."

She tried very hard for composure, but the waiting at that locked door had shaken her. In those few minutes the voice that she had silenced had spoken terrible things. It was not silent now.

Timothy was consumed with anxiety, but he found it in his heart to pity Helena when he felt her hand tremble on his arm—Helena's strong, calm hand.

"Timothy, don't you know where she is?"

"She isn't in her room?"

"No. We broke in the door. She must have got out of the window." She shuddered. It was she who had passed the frightened maids and looked down from the window, not knowing what she might see below. If she had deserved punishment, that moment rendered it.

"Where's Eustace?" said Timothy.

"Telephoning. He rang you up, but you had started. He's getting through to Ida—she may have gone there."

"Yes. What about the station?"

"No, they haven't seen her—she can't have gone by train. Timothy—she didn't go to you?"

"No."

"On your word of honour?"

"I tell you she didn't."

He made a movement towards the door, and Helena cried out and held his arm.

"Where are you going?"

"To look for her."

"Timothy—wait! Don't be in such a hurry."

Her hand shook, but she made a great effort at self-control. After all, nothing had happened. She had only run away as she had done before. They would find her. Nothing could have happened.

As they stood there close to the door, it opened. Bolton almost ran into them. He had Valentine's note in his hand, a little folded sheet. After thirty years of service, Bolton entered a room in a hurry, and presented a note without waiting to put it on a salver.

"Agnes has just found this under the pillow, ma'am," he stammered.

Helena took it, opened it, and clutched Timothy's arm as she read. Then she drew a long breath.

"It's all right." And as Bolton withdrew, she let go of Timothy and sat down in the nearest chair. An extraordinary sense of relief swept over her. She repeated the words that had dismissed Bolton, "It's all right."

Timothy put out his hand.

"May I see?"

And as he took the note, Eustace came in, haggard and distressed.

"She isn't at the Cobbs'. They'll ring us up if they hear anything."

Timothy handed him the note. He read it, frowning.

"We've been to blame—we've been horribly to blame, I suppose. But why couldn't she say this instead of running away?"

Helena's glance avoided him. It remained fixed on the note in his hand.

"She's all right," she said. Her voice was louder than usual. "She must be all right."

"Yes—yes, of course. I'm glad she's written. Of course she's all right. But what are we going to do?" He put a hand behind him and shut the door. "Whom have you told?"

"All the servants know," said Helena.

"The Ryvens?"

"No—not yet. At least I don't know. I suppose everyone knows. Everyone will have to know." She stood up in a sort of nervous haste. "We'll have to tell people. But what are we going to say?"

She looked from Eustace to Timothy, and it was Timothy who answered her.

"What's the matter with telling them the truth? If you want my advice I should say, just tell everyone what's happened. If you don't, they'll ferret round until they find out a great many things that never happened at all."

He went to the door, but Helena stopped him for the second time.

"What are you going to do?"

"I told you. I'm going to look for her. Do you mind if I see Agnes? I want to know what she's got on."

Agnes was not very helpful. She had been crying, and was still on the verge of being hysterical, as much from excitement as from anxiety. To be the first to discover that a bride has vanished on her wedding day is enough to excite the calmest housemaid who ever made a bed. To Timothy's "Can you tell me what Miss Valentine was wearing?" she responded with a flurry of words punctuated only by a sniff or a hiccuping sob.

"And I'm sure I couldn't say, sir, not to be certain, for there was a whole lot of things as come the day before yesterday, which she chose in London along with Miss Marjory, and she unpacked them herself—leastways I was there part of the time, only Mrs. Ryven called me, so I can't say I took particular notice. But there was hats and dresses, and I consider there was a tweed coat, only I couldn't swear to it, sir."

"Well, is the tweed coat missing?"

"I couldn't say, sir."

"Well, suppose you look."

Agnes looked. Timothy looked too. There was no new tweed coat, and there was no dark red dress such as Valentine had worn on the night that she came to Waterlow.

"Can you tell if there's a hat missing?"

"No, sir, I can't."

"Or a suit-case?"

"I don't know, sir."

"Well, think. Come along, Agnes, this is important! You just stop sniffing and think!"

Agnes began to sob.

"I was packing her suit-case last night, and I'm sure I never thought—"

"Where were you packing it?"

"In the dressing-room," said Agnes with her apron to her face.

Timothy flung open the dressing-room door.

"Where? Show it to me!"

Agnes sniffed, between offence and sensibility.

"It's gone, sir."

"Sure?"

It was the first thing that Agnes had been sure about. She had left the half packed case on the chair by the window, and it was gone.

Timothy raced down the stairs and put his head in at the sitting-room door. The atmosphere was heavy with gloom. Helena and Eustace faced one another across the hearth-rug in solemn converse.

"I'm off," said Timothy. "Buck up, Helena! She's taken a suit-case."

## Chapter Thirty-Four

VALENTINE LEFT the house behind her and entered the thick darkness of the drive. It was very still under the beeches; still, and warm, and so dark that at first she walked slowly and held her free hand stretched out before her. Down by the gate the trees were not so thick. She could just see the white gate-posts as she passed between them and came out on to the road.

Up to this moment she had not thought of where she was going. Away from Holt—away from Eustace and Aunt Helena—as far away as possible But now that she had come out upon the road, she had at least to decide whether she would turn to the right or to the left. If she turned to the right, she would pass Waterlow; and if she turned to the left, she would come, after seven miles, to Renton.

She stood in the road and thought about going to Timothy. Timothy was her friend, and he was kind. But he was Aunt Helena's brother. When she went to him before, he had taken her back to Holt. If she went to him now, and he said she must go back to Holt, she would be back in the cage again; and this time she would never, never get out any more. Her heart sank. Why hadn't Timothy come near her all day? He had taken her back to Holt and he had left her; and he hadn't come back. It wasn't any use going to Timothy.

She began to walk in the direction of Waterlow, and when she had gone a dozen steps, she told herself that she wasn't going to Waterlow, she was going to London. It wasn't her fault if she had to pass Timothy's house to get there. She began to wonder how long it would be before they found out that she was gone. It would take her three quarters of an hour to get as far as Waterlow. Even if she walked all night, she couldn't get to London. And she wasn't sure that she wanted to go to London. She thought of going to Marjory. But suppose Aunt Ida said that she must go back. No, she couldn't go to London. She would take the road that turned off just beyond Waterlow, because it went down into deep woods where she could hide. She thought she could walk as far as the woods. Then she could climb into a tree, and when she was rested she could walk on again. She had three pounds in her purse, and she could go for quite a long time without food.

When she came to the old stone pillars that marked the entrance to Waterlow, she stopped. The house drew her. The panelled room that looked upon the garden and the river drew her. In her thought it was lighted, and the garden was not so dark but that you could see the flowers. It was very dark here between the pillars, and she was tired already, though she had only come three miles.

She took a step in the direction of the house, and then checked, turned, and ran out between the pillars and along the lonely road. She was frightened because she wanted so much to run down the drive and tap at Timothy's window. She had to run away quickly to stop herself doing it. She ran on and on and stopped, panting, when her breath was gone.

It was whilst she was standing in the road with her suit-case at her feet, trying to get her breath and to stop feeling afraid, that she saw two bright starry lights far off where the road curved up over the hill. She stared at them, saw them disappear amongst the trees, and then shine out again. She began to hear the thrumming sound of a car coming nearer and nearer. The lights began to rush towards her, and the beam that they cast on the road slid before them, making black shadows in front of every pebble.

Valentine ran into the middle of the road and held up both her hands. The beam came rushing on. It touched her, enveloped her in a white blinding glare, and seemed to pierce her through and through. There was a grinding sound. The car came to a standstill, and a furious voice called out, "What the devil are you playing at?"

Valentine ran forward past the lights and caught at the side of the car. There was a man at the wheel. She blinked at him because she was still dazzled by the glare, and said,

"I'm so sorry."

Mr. Sloan had had a fright. Carew had told him he wasn't fit to drive the car, and he had told Carew to go to Jericho. And then to have a girl popping up out of the middle of the road! It made you wonder whether you were seeing things. He repeated his first remark in slightly unsteady tones:

"What the devil are you playing at?"

"I want a lift," said Valentine firmly and added as an afterthought, "if it wouldn't be too much trouble."

Old Mrs. Podbury always said, "If it wouldn't be too much trouble," when Aunt Helena offered her a lift. The proper answer was "Oh, no, not at all." Valentine waited for the proper answer, and hoped that it would come quickly, because she wanted to fetch her suit-case from the side of the road, and get into the car and be whirled away from Holt at as many miles an hour as possible.

The proper answer didn't come. Instead, Mr. Sloan switched on his dash-light and looked at her. He saw a very pretty girl with parted lips and appealing eyes, and all of a sudden his mood changed.

"Hop in!" he said, and extended a helping hand.

"Oh, but I've got a suit-case."

"Righto!" said Mr. Sloan.

Valentine disappeared into the dark. Mr. Sloan stared at the place where she had been. He was muzzy, but he wasn't binged. He couldn't have imagined her—not a girl as pretty as that. Carew was a fool. If he hadn't insisted on driving, he wouldn't have met this pretty girl. Carew was a fool.

Valentine came running back, and in a moment she was kneeling on the seat pushing her suit-case into the back of the car. Then, with a quick turn, she slipped down beside him and said,

"Please go on."

Mr. Sloan wasn't sorry to move again. He was all right as long as he kept going. He didn't care what Carew said, he was perfectly all right as long as he kept going. But he did feel a bit muzzy when he stopped. He stepped on the accelerator, and the car leapt forward with a bound. The dark trees on either side rushed past them and were gone. The long brilliant beam showed the empty road shut in by walls of night. Valentine watched the needle of the speedometer run up to fifty, and then creep on.

Mr. Sloan broke the silence with great suddenness. His voice was vague. He took his right hand off the wheel and wagged a finger at her reprovingly.

"And what I say is this—and don't lemme have to tell you again—d'you hear?"

"What mustn't I do?" said Valentine, astonished.

"Don't lemme have to tell you again. That's what I said. Popping up out of the middle of the road when I was doin' sixty. And lucky for you I wasn't doin'—more, 'relse—I mightn't have been able"—he wagged a finger impressively—"to stop."

Valentine thought him a very odd young man. She said, "You stopped beautifully. Which of those things do you pull to stop? How do you do it?"

"Like thish!" said Mr. Sloan.

He thrust at the brake-pedal with his foot and braced himself against the back of the seat. The car checked, skidded, and slid sideways in a sickening half-circle with a screech of protest from the brakes and the rasp of a locked rear wheel. Valentine was thrown violently against Mr. Sloan's left arm, wrenching the wheel over. His foot slipped from the brake-pedal. The car straightened up and shot forward. The needle once more began to approach fifty.

Valentine disengaged herself from Mr. Sloan and sat up.

"Thash what comes of trying to stop in a hurry," he said with a good deal of mournful reproach in his voice.

Valentine got as far as possible into the corner. They passed Holt like a flash, and the trees were over them. If she had wished to go fast, she certainly had her wish.

They began to go faster still. The wind which they made went by them with a zip. The black, unseen landscape was full of shadows that streamed past like rushing water. Valentine did not know how long it was before the pace slackened.

Mr. Sloan resumed his homily:

"And what I say is thish—don't be in a hurry."

"But I am in a hurry."

"'Sa bad thing. You—take it from me. I say—I haven't met you before, have I?"

"No."

"Couldn't forget such a pretty girl if I had. I say, you needn't—sit so far away."

Valentine would have sat farther away if it had been possible.

The pace dropped to a slow fifteen. Mr. Sloan began to sing in a manner rather reminiscent of his brakes:

"There ain't no sense sitting upon a fence,
All by yourself in the moonlight—"

He stopped with a giggle. "Isn't any moon, but whash a marrer with the dark?" He burst once more into song:

"There ain't no thrill by the water-mill,
All by yourself in the moonlight.
There ain't no fun, sitting beneath the trees,
Giving yourself a hug, giving yourself a squeeze.
Love's a farce, sitting on the grass,
All by yourself in the moonlight."

He took a hand off the wheel and stretched it out towards Valentine. "Come along and give us a kiss!"

Valentine turned the handle of the door.

"I don't kiss people that I don't know."

Mr. Sloan caught her by the arm.

"Must pay your fare!" he said. "Travelling without ticket shtrickly prohibited." He laughed, still holding her. "Thash a good word! If you can say—prohibited—you can say anything. Shall tell Carew that."

The car was describing an extremely erratic course. Valentine opened the door, struck hard at Mr. Sloan's hand, and twisted free. She got out on to the running-board and jumped for the grass at the side of the road. She fell sprawling, but she wasn't hurt. As she picked herself up, the car came to a standstill a dozen yards ahead. She scrambled down into a shallow ditch, climbed the bank on the other side, and half pushed her way, half climbed through the hedge at the top of it. She could hear Mr. Sloan calling her:

"I say—where are you? I say—"

His feet came stumbling back along the road.

"Never was so inshulted in my life! Girl running away! Inshulting! Thash the word—inshulting! Dash difficult word to say."

He was about to get into the car when he remembered the torch in the near pocket. He took it out and amused himself by throwing the beam hither and thither. On the left hand side of the road there was a ditch, and a hedge, and a wood. If that girl thought he was going ploughing about in a beastly wood looking for her, she was damn well mistaken. On the other side there was a rickety paling, one of those strung-out affairs; and water—quite a large sheet of water. The light dazzled on it. No—and he wasn't going to swim to look for her either. She could just stay where she was and stew in her own juice.

He went to put back the torch, and caught sight of Valentine's suit-case. Immediately red wrath flamed up in him. She'd run away and leave her beastly luggage, would she? He wasn't an hotel—no, he was dashed if he was an hotel. He'd show her. He took the suit-case by the handle and hove it over the paling into the water. It landed with a splash among the reeds a dozen feet away, and sank in the mud. The beam of the torch showed just a corner sticking up.

Mr. Sloan nodded approvingly and got into his car and drove away.

Valentine, crouched down on the other side of the hedge, heard him go past muttering. Then she stood up, and wondered where she was. The ground sloped up from the hedge, and it was very rough and uneven; there were bushes and tangly things that caught her ankles and pricked them. Suddenly she ran into a tree. It was so dark—thick, blanketing darkness. Things touched you, and you couldn't see them. There was no difference between the trunk of the tree, whose bark rasped your hand, and the damp, black air on either side of it.

By one such tree Valentine halted. It had a branch that ran out from the trunk on a level with her shoulder. She climbed on to the branch, and found there was another close to it, but a little higher. These two branches and the trunk made a safe enough seat. She sat on the lower branch and leaned back into the angle between the upper one and the trunk. Just before she shut her eyes she saw a beam of light go sliding down the road below her. It slipped away and disappeared. The throbbing of the engine died away in the distance. Mr. Sloan and his car were gone.

Valentine slept in her tree with her shoulders against a thick branch, and her head leaning against the trunk, the little red hat between her and the rough bark.

She slept, and she dreamt about the island. It was a new dream. She saw the island very far away, like a black speck at the end of a long bright beam which traversed a dark and tossing sea. On either side of the beam the waves came up with high silver crests, to fall splashing and thunderous. But the beam made a straight gold path, and Valentine moved along it dry-shod and not afraid. She went sliding over the gold faster and faster, and the island rushed to meet her. And then, all at once, when she came near the island, the golden path came to an end, and a great black wave caught her up and reared itself higher and higher until it overtopped the height of the cliff. Valentine hung on the crest of it and looked down on the palm-trees and the pool. And someone was calling her: "Valentine—Valentine—Valentine!" And then the dream changed and she saw Timothy looking at her. And he said, "Valentine!" Then she woke up.

Just at first she didn't know where she was, and she nearly fell. Then she remembered, and sat up and stretched herself. It was still quite dark, and the wood was very still. Nothing stirred, because nothing was awake except Valentine. She shifted her position, and dozed again. This time she did not dream; but she woke suddenly with a start, because she heard Timothy say, "Valentine!" But when she looked about her, there was only a lonely greyness everywhere. The night was thinning away. Faint ghostly shapes of tree and bush showed in the waning dusk. Halsey Mere lay like a clouded mirror under the brightening sky. It would be dawn soon.

Valentine thought how hungry she was, and wondered when she would be able to get something to eat. She was stiff, and a little cold; and all her clothes seemed to have got into the wrong places. She sat leaning against the trunk of the tree, and watched the sun come slowly up out of the mists beyond the lake.

## Chapter Thirty-Five

MRS. RYVEN SPENT the morning at the telephone. From the moment she knew that Valentine had taken a suit-case with her, her courage and presence of mind returned. "Girls who are going to do something dreadful"—she used no plainer words than that—"do not pack and take away a suit-case." The frightful visions of Valentine broken and crumpled under her own window, or sinking down like Ophelia into muddy waters and tangling weeds, gave place to the resentment which anyone might feel against a girl who had behaved so improperly, so ungratefully. Valentine, running away with a suit-case and leaving Eustace to be the laughingstock of the county, made no demands on Helena's compunction. A sharp gust of anger swept her mind clear.

She went in search of Laura Ryven, and found her in comfortable undress. Mrs. James Ryven never got up to breakfast. She considered the morning as a waste and empty space of time in which you couldn't play bridge—unless, of course, you were on a voyage.

She looked across her breakfast tray at Helena with a lively curiosity.

"My dear Helena, what on earth has happened? Agnes says—"

Helena frowned. Her manner indicated that she did not expect her housemaid's remarks to be retailed to her. She said in a repressive tone,

"I am afraid that the wedding will have to be put off."

"Put off?" said Mrs. James with raised eyebrows. "Helena—for goodness' sake—has she run away, or hasn't she?"

"Valentine has left Holt."

"She has run away. Do you know where she's gone to?"

Helena left that unanswered.

"It is all exceedingly painful."

"Must be. But, my dear, I could have told you she didn't care two straws for Eustace. Never saw a girl look so wretched in my life."

"I think that is rather exaggerated, Valentine appeared to wish for the marriage. But yesterday—" She hesitated. Laura would have to know. Everyone would have to know.

"My dear—what?" Mrs. James called everyone "my dear."

"Yesterday we had news." She found it difficult to choose the right words.

"News?"

"Very important news. Valentine is not Maurice's daughter. Edward Bowden left a statement, which has only just reached us. I haven't time to go into it all, but there seems to be no doubt of the facts this time."

"She's not Valentine Ryven, after all? My dear—how outrageous!"

Helena shook her head.

"She didn't know, of course."

"My dear, how *awkward*!"

"She wished to break off the engagement." (Yes, that was the line to take.) "But, naturally, Eustace wouldn't hear of it, and this morning we found that the foolish child had run away."

"Without a word?"

"She left this note—you can see it if you like."

Mrs. James took it eagerly.

"'M—" she said. "Short and sweet. Only wanted to give the money back. Not very flattering to Eustace. But then, of course, he isn't in love with her either—is he?" She gave the letter back. "Well, Helena, I'm sorry for all the upset—but I must say I don't think she was the wife for Eustace, and when this has all blown over you'll thank heaven she let him off. Who is she, by the way?"

"We don't know. She was born on the ship."

Helena went downstairs and began the difficult business of putting off some hundreds of wedding guests. By the time she had told her story half a dozen times, it came with an ease which surprised her. She telephoned to all the people who really counted. Most of them responded with friendly concern. Valentine receded.

When Timothy came in at half-past twelve with an abrupt "Any news?" she really was, just for the moment, at a loss. She put up a hand, and finished what she was saying into the telephone:

"Yes, of course—one does feel that. It's terrible for him now. But, as you say—"

"Helena! My God! What's happened?"

She shook her head impatiently and continued speaking:

"Yes, indeed—as you say, one lives to be thankful. Good-bye."

She hung up the receiver and turned.

"What is it, Timothy?"

"Is there news? What were you saying? What's terrible?"

Helena raised her eyebrows.

"There's no news. I was alluding to Eustace's position."

Timothy recovered himself. The last three hours had brought him to a state where a chance word could shake him as he had never been shaken in his life. He looked at Helena in astonishment. This morning she had appeared to be on the edge of a break-down; now she wore the pleasantly capable air of the woman who feels that emergencies are provided in order that she may display her command of them. She held a list of guests, and was ticking off those who had been dealt with. A "W" indicated a wire; the letter "T" a telephone call.

She said "Where have you been?" rather absently, and put a T against the name of Lady Mary Weare.

"I've been up and down the roads, and through the villages. No one's seen her. I've tried all the stations too. She's either quite near by, or she's got away in a car. Ida hasn't rung up again, I suppose?"

"Yes—just now. She wanted to know if she should come down, and I said certainly not."

"If—*when* I find her—I shall take her to Ida," said Timothy abruptly.

Helena turned round from the telephone.

"*You* will take her!"

"Yes."

"We ate very glad of your help, of course. But you are rather, shall I say, assuming a responsibility which I don't think really belongs to you."

"Doesn't it?" He gave a short laugh. "I think it belongs to me as much as to anyone else. You see, you're not her aunt any more, and Eustace isn't her *fiancé*. But I'm still her friend. That's where I come in."

"Friend?" said Mrs. Ryven with a peculiar intonation.

"Friend means a good deal," said Timothy. "It means just exactly what Valentine wants it to mean."

He went to the door and came back. "I don't want to quarrel, Helena. We've got to live pretty close to each other here, and it'll save a lot of trouble if you realize that I'm Valentine's friend. Now we won't talk about that any more. Where's Eustace?"

"He's gone up to town. He had an idea she might go to Mrs. Bell."

"Who's she?"

"One of the Community workers. She used to take Valentine round with her."

Timothy shook his head.

"She'd keep clear of anything to do with Eustace."

"Eustace thought she might go there." Helena's tone was stiff. "There, or to Katherine Hill."

"Who's Katherine Hill?"

"She used to be Eustace's secretary. Valentine took an odd fancy to her."

"Ring her up," said Timothy.

As they waited for the call to come through, he spoke again, forcing his voice:

"If she isn't there—we shall have to go to the police, Helena."

The telephone bell cut across Mrs. Ryven's protest. Timothy stretched out his hand for the receiver.

"I'll take it. Hullo! Is that Miss Hill—Miss Katherine Hill?"

"This is Mr. Elderthal's office," said a voice. "Do you want to speak to Miss Hill?"

"I want to speak to Miss Katherine Hill."

There was a little click, and a deep voice said "Hullo!"

"I want to speak to Miss Katherine Hill."

Katherine Hill said, "Who is it?" She held the receiver in a steady hand. She had not slept at all the night before. Her face was colourless, her eyes like desolate water. She had been engaged upon an intricate scheme of tent compensation, to which she had brought as much lucid thought and careful accuracy as if there were no such thing as quenched love and broken hope. She said, "Who is it?" and heard Timothy say,

"My name's Timothy Brand. You don't know me. I'm Mrs. Ryven's brother. I'm ringing up to ask whether you've seen or heard anything of Valentine?"

Katherine looked at the opposite wall. There was an almanac there; it hung a little crooked. The date stared back at her, very black—the sixth of September—Eustace's wedding day. What should she know about Valentine Ryven?

She said, "It's her wedding day," and heard Timothy say in an urgent voice,

"No—the marriage is broken off."

Katherine did not say anything. She couldn't. She looked at that black six on the wall, and saw it rush towards her and then recede until it was a tiny point in a white, wet mist. The damp of the mist was on her brow.

Timothy said, "Hullo! Are you there?"

Katherine said, "Yes." She wondered if he heard her. His voice was very insistent.

"Have you seen Valentine, or heard from her? Do you know where she is?"

Katherine said, "No."

"We thought she might go to you. She's gone off. We're very anxious. If she comes to you, will you ring me up and tell her I'm coming to her. Tell her Timothy's coming. Tell her there's nothing to be frightened about—no one's going to make her marry Eustace. Will you tell her that? And will you please take down my number?"

Katherine took it down mechanically. Then she repeated it, and said in the same breath,

"Where is Eustace?"

"He's gone up to town to look for her. We don't even know if she's got any money. He'll probably come and see you. You'll ring up at once if you hear anything—won't you?"

Katherine heard someone come into the room. She hung up the receiver and turned, to see Eustace standing just inside the door.

## Chapter Thirty-Six

VALENTINE WALKED ALONG the road on very weary feet. The day had lasted for hours and hours and hours, and it was a long time since she had had anything to eat. There had been blackberries on a common, and a cottage where the woman had made her some tea and cut bread and butter when she found that Valentine could pay for it. But that was a long time ago.

She thought she must be in a very lonely part of the country. The wood where she had slept rose to an open stretch of heath. That was where she had found the blackberries. But there were no houses on it, and she had walked for miles without seeing anyone. When she came to a road, it seemed to go on and on without getting anywhere. She had no idea where she was. But she knew where she wanted to be; she wanted to be at Waterlow with Timothy. If she hadn't been too frightened to think properly, she would never have run away from Timothy, because he was her best friend, and he would have helped her and have told her what to do. He wouldn't have made her marry Eustace. A best friend wouldn't make you marry someone if you were most dreadfully frightened about it.

She did not walk all the time. She had got used to wearing shoes and stockings, but she had never got used to walking long distances. After a mile or two she had to sit down and rest. You don't get on very fast like that. The grey day slipped into a grey dusk, and the dark came on.

She was limping when she came out on a tarred high road with cars passing on it. If it had not been for Mr. Sloan, she might have stopped one then; but some of the ignorant courage had gone out of her. She was hungry, and foot-sore, and homesick for Waterlow.

The road was very long and dark.

Timothy came home in the late evening. He had no news, and there was no message waiting for him. He rang up Helena. She had no news either.

"Eustace is sure she hasn't gone to London—I've just been talking to him. He's staying up. I wish you'd waited a little longer before going to the police. People will say—"

"Why should we care what they say? They can say anything they like as long as we find her."

Helena's voice became colder. Valentine had behaved disgracefully. All this publicity. The police. And Timothy in the most intractable mood. She said,

"You reminded me this morning that we had no authority over Valentine. What can you do if you do find her?"

"What she wants to do," said Timothy, and rang off.

He rang up the County police. No news. "But we'll ring you up, sir, if anything comes through."

He had some food, and spent half an hour trying to read the paper, with so much success that he could not even have told what the headlines were. He had done all that he could do. It was intolerable that there was no more to be done. He would have gone out again if it were not that he might miss a call.

He began to walk up and down the panelled room. Only forty-eight hours before she had been there. In heaven's name, why had he let her go? He could touch her chair. He could see her sitting in it, with her head thrown back and her hands lying in the lap of her dark dress. Why had he let her go? She had looked at him with a most piteous appeal, and he had taken her back to Holt and kept away from her all day. Where was she? Where had she gone? Why, they didn't even know if she had any money. And she was such a child, such a blessed innocent child.

He went to the long windows and looked out. A dark, cloudy night, warm and heavy with rain to come. Not a breath moved. The lightest air made a stir among the willows all along the stream. But there was no air stirring to-night. The willows were still, and the stream was still. The light from the yellow lamp threw a beam upon the nagged path and its border of cobblestones; it showed an autumn bloom or two on the old yellow rose that covered this side of the house. The roses hung down and touched the posts of the door. They looked pale in the yellow light. All the rest of the garden was hidden.

Timothy stood listening, and heard the silence.

When the telephone bell rang, he started. He had been keyed up for the sound—expecting it; but when it came, it made him jump. The bell sounded unnaturally loud.

He took off the receiver and said "Hullo!"

A man's voice said hoarsely, "Hullo!"

"Who's there?"

The hoarse voice said "Hullo!" again.

"Who's there?"

"Hullo! County police speaking."

"Yes—what is it?"

Someone coughed at the other end of the line, and inquired deliberately:

"Is that Mr. Brand?"

"Speaking. What is it?"

"Well, Mr. Brand—Inspector Wennock speaking—with regard to the young lady that's disappeared—" He paused and coughed again.

"Yes. Go on! What is it?"

"With regard to Miss Valentine Ryven—the fact is, something's been found."

Timothy's hand closed hard on the receiver.

"What's been found?"

"The suit-case, sir. Initials V. R.—brushes with same initials inside."

"Where did you find it?"

"In Halsey Mere, sir, sticking in the mud at the edge. It gets very deep further in."

Timothy became quite rigid. He heard his own voice like the voice of a stranger. It sounded loud and angry.

"How could it have got there?"

The inspector coughed again.

"We'll drag the lake to-morrow, sir. We can't do anything more to-night, but I thought I'd just let you know. Good-night, sir."

Timothy hung up the receiver. The telephone was a fixture on the wall beside the door which led into the hall. He had his back to the long open window. He hung up the receiver, and stood there unable to move, unable to lift himself under the crushing horror of his fear for Valentine. The deep, lonely lake with its shelving edges—a grey lake—very deep. Valentine—all alone—frightened—running away—nowhere to go—he had let her go.

He just stood there, thoughts all round him like wolves, ready to rush in and tear—frightful thoughts coming nearer, closing in. He couldn't keep them back—any longer. A horrible cold fear was paralysing him.

The sound came then—a very little sound. You wouldn't hear a sound like that unless everything was as still as death. Timothy shuddered violently away from the word.

The sound came again—the sound of something moving—softly. It came from behind him. Someone had moved on the flagged path. Someone had sighed—if a breath that barely stirs the outer edge of silence can be called a sigh.

Timothy turned round with a very great effort. He did not know what he was going to see. If there should be nothing except the dark, and the pale roses falling against the doorpost—If there should be—something—unknown—

He saw Valentine standing on the threshold. Her hair was tossed and damp, her face all white, her eyes wide and darkly blue, her lips parted to draw that sighing breath. Her coat hung open over the dark red dress. She held her hat in one hand, the other touched the jamb. She looked at Timothy, and said his name almost inaudibly.

"Timothy—"

And in an instant Timothy came awake. The nightmare was gone—the agony of fear, the horrible desolation. He came awake, and was himself; and he remembered that he mustn't frighten her.

He came to her, and she let her hat drop on the floor and caught at his arm.

"Timothy—I've come back."

Timothy picked her up and put her into his big shabby chair, a comfortable man's chair. She lay back in it and sighed deeply.

"Oh, Timothy—my feet!"

Timothy went down on his knees and took her shoes off. She curled her toes up like a baby and sighed again.

"I do—hate—shoes!"

"Val, I'm going to get you some milk. You won't run away again?"

Her eyes were closed, but her lips parted in an enchanting smile. It was very nearly too much for him. He went quickly, found his housekeeper with coffee just made, and came back with a breakfast-cupful that was nearly all milk.

When Valentine had drunk it she sat up.

"Lovely!"

"When did you have anything to eat?"

"A most dreadfully long time ago."

"What will you have?"

*"Lots,"* said Valentine.

Timothy burst from the room to tell Mrs. Sanders that Miss Valentine was starving, and what about it?

"Lor' now!" said Mrs. Sanders. "What a come off of it! You don't say!"

Timothy didn't wait to say anything. When Valentine was under his eyes, he could believe she was safe. But the minute she was out of sight, he remembered the bad dream. It simply didn't bear remembering.

She looked anxiously at him as he came in.

"You won't send me back?"

"No. Val, where have you been?"

"I don't know." She pushed back her hair. "A long way. A man took me in a car. I didn't like him—he tried to kiss me. Aunt Helena says men always try to kiss you. But you don't, Timothy."

Timothy was hard put to it.

"I wouldn't ever kiss you if you didn't want me to, Val."

Valentine looked up at him with an air of interest.

"I couldn't tell you if I wanted you to."

"Perhaps I should know."

"How?"

"Val, what happened to you? You haven't told me."

"He tried to kiss me, so I got out of the car—it wasn't going very fast. He stopped and tried to find me, but I hid in a wood."

"Was it by a lake?"

"Yes, it was."

"They found your suit-case—in the water."

"Why do you say it like that? Did you think I was in the water too?"

Timothy shook his head.

Mrs. Sanders began to come and go. She looked curiously at Miss Valentine, "with her hair that rumpled, and no shoes, and two great 'oles in her stockings fit to put your 'and through."

Valentine made a very good supper. She had a most happy feeling that everything was all right.

When Mrs. Sanders had gone, Timothy said,

"Val, are you very tired?"

"Not now."

"Because I want to take you to Ida."

"I want to stay here with you."

"You can't, my dear. I'll come with you."

"And stay?"

"If you want me to. I must go and get the car. Mrs. Sanders can ring everybody up when we've gone."

When he came back, she had two questions to ask:

"They won't want to make me marry Eustace now?"

"No, Val."

"Oh—Need I put on my shoes? I don't want to."

Timothy laughed unsteadily.

"You'd better take them with you. But you needn't wear them—I've got a rug to roll you up in."

As the car began to move, Valentine said,

"I did want to stay here."

There was a long silence before Timothy answered,

"You can always come back, you know."

They turned out of the gate and began to slide along, dream-fashion, just Timothy and Valentine in a darkness that shut them in and shut everyone else out. It wasn't a frightening darkness any more. It was like a soft wall all round them, keeping them safe.

Valentine said "Lovely!" under her breath. It was like flowing along on a river of light. It was like her dream. She remembered that she hadn't told Timothy about her dream. She said,

"Timothy—"

"What is it?"

"I didn't tell you why I came back."

"No."

"It was because I heard you calling me."

Timothy was silent. She was close against his shoulder. She had come back because she had heard him calling her.

"It was in a dream," said Valentine in a soft little voice. "It was my dream about the island. And someone kept on calling, only I didn't know who it was—I always woke up. But last night, in the wood, I knew that it was you, so I came back—only it was such a long way."

There was another silence.

Timothy's hand left the wheel; his arm went round Valentine. These things happened without his meaning them to happen. They just happened.

Valentine thought how nice and strong his arm was, and how safe. It made her feel quite, quite sure that she wasn't going to be made to marry Eustace. She waited a little, and then she said,

"Did you call me?"

"Yes, Val."

"Why did you call me?"

"Do you want me to tell you that?"

"Yes."

"I don't think I'd better."

"But I want you to."

"Don't you know?"

"Did you want me? Was that why you called?"

Timothy said, "I wanted you."

"Why?"

Timothy said, "For always, Val."

They went on sliding along the golden beam. The darkness was very kind and safe. Timothy's arm was very safe. After a while Valentine came closer. She said,

"I'm frightened about being married, Timothy."

Timothy said, "I won't frighten you, Val. You're not frightened of me, are you?"

"No."

Timothy was very safe and kind. He was her best friend. She loved him very much. That was why she had come back. She loved him very much indeed. She wouldn't ever be frightened of him, because she loved him.

She said in a very little voice,

"Timothy—"

"Val?"

"Timothy—would you like—to kiss me?"

Timothy stopped the car.

THE END

Made in the USA
Lexington, KY
23 June 2017